RED HERRING

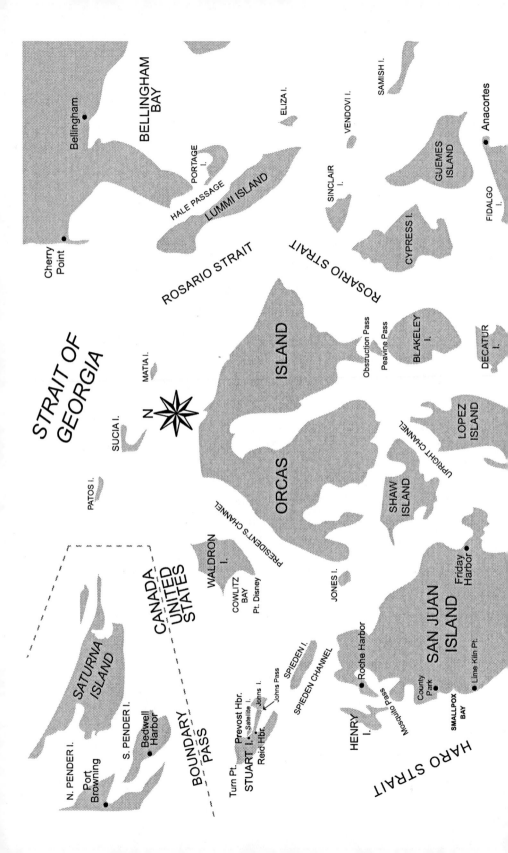

RED HERRING

CLYDE W. FORD

MYSTIC VOYAGER BOOKS

This is a work of fiction. Names, characters, places, and incidents either are the product of the author's imagination or are used fictitiously, and any resemblance to actual persons, living or dead, business establishments, institutions, events, or locales is entirely coincidental.

Nautical chart of story locations not for navigational use.

RED HERRING

www.mysticvoyagerbooks.com

Ford, Clyde W., date
Red Herring / Clyde W. Ford

ISBN: 1-58961-344-9

PRINTED IN THE UNITED STATES OF AMERICA

10 9 8 7 6 5 4 3 2

TO CHARA:
Every day a new journey in love.

RED HERRING

Prologue

K atherine Sullivan enjoyed pulling the afternoon duty shift, especially on a clear, late summer day like this, when she could watch the sunset over the Strait of Georgia while heading back to Station Bellingham with her crew. She turned away from the view out the window and rested a hand on her helmsman's shoulder.

"Mr. Crenshaw, it's getting dark. Keep her down below fifteen knots. With the extreme high tides we've had these last few days, we don't want to find a deadhead on our way back to the barn."

"Yes, Ma'am."

Even at this speed, the rigid pontoons of the aluminum coast guard patrol boat slapped through the water. Robert James, sitting next to Terry Crenshaw, had his eyes glued to the radar screen. Paul Larson stood beside Katherine, behind the others. Larson, a big guy, seemed permanently stooped inside the tiny, cramped cabin. He backed away from the rear door as Katherine reached to slide it open. She grabbed a pair of sound-protective earmuffs and walked out on deck. She took in a deep breath of salt air. On the horizon, a band of apricot and rose separated dark green water from dark blue sky, backlighting the jagged peaks of the Canadian Gulf Islands and the mountains running the length of huge Vancouver Island. House lights flickered on throughout the islands. Katherine looked northwest, up the vast expanse of the Inside Passage. Someday, she promised herself, she'd step onto her own boat, point it in that direction, and head into a sunset like this.

The rear door screeched as it slid open. Larson held a cupped hand to his face, fingers out, indicating a call for her. Katherine slipped off her earmuffs.

"Lieutenant, Group Seattle for you." Larson's voice barely reached over the howl of the outboard engines.

Katherine stepped inside. She pointed to a button on the VHF radio. Larson jabbed it with his thumb. An overhead speaker hissed.

"Lieutenant Sullivan here."

A voice crackled through. "Lieutenant, Vessel Traffic System radar's been tracking a target moving at eight knots, heading east along Boundary Pass, about to cross the Strait. We'd like contact, and confirmation of its destination."

"Roger that," Katherine said. She let her finger up from the microphone's red button and patted James on the shoulder. "Find that target."

The green glow of the radar screen threw eerie shadows across James's face. He tapped on the screen and nodded his head.

Katherine pressed the microphone's button again. "Seattle, we have your target."

"Lieutenant, request that you proceed at maximum speed to intercept."

"Mr. Crenshaw," Katherine said. She watched Crenshaw thrust two red levers as far forward as they'd go. The engines whined and the boat lurched ahead, jerking her backward. She grabbed the helm seat and held on.

"Looks like the signature of a recreational vessel," James blurted out. He picked up a clear plastic ruler and laid it over the screen.

"Lieutenant," James whispered. "This target's on a course straight for the refinery docks."

Katherine grimaced, then pulled the mike to her. "Seattle, we show the target heading for the refinery docks at Cherry Point."

She exchanged anxious glances with her crew.

"Roger that, Lieutenant, MIFCPAC's been notified. Be advised, the 660-foot oil tanker *Star of Juneau* is docked at Cherry Point, taking on a full load."

"Seattle, we're estimating our intercept of the target vessel in"—Katherine looked at James; he flashed an open hand twice—"ten minutes."

"Roger that, Lieutenant."

Katherine hung up the microphone. "Everyone, keep an eye out for running lights. Larson, use the night-vision glasses."

The patrol boat now skipped over the water, pounding hard into each small wave it encountered, rocking from side to side as it did. On their right, the domed storage tanks of the refinery shimmered under orange lights, tall smokestacks belched rust-colored clouds into the night sky. Katherine scanned the darkness settling outside, her heartbeat rising to meet the pounding rhythm of her boat.

"Larson, do you have a visual yet?"

"No, Ma'am."

"James?"

"Target's less than two miles off, Ma'am. We're closing." James's deep, resonant voice reminded Katherine of a radio announcer.

Larson burst out, "There." He pointed. "Coupla degrees off the starboard bow."

Katherine whipped around, grasped Larson's arm, then held her hand out. He lowered the binoculars into her hand. The hazy outline of a small boat jumped from the murky, yellow-green background Katherine saw through the night-vision binoculars. She handed the glasses back to Larson, then she snatched the radio's microphone from its holder.

"Seattle, we have visual contact with the target, which appears to be a recreational trawler running without lights."

"Copy that, Eighteen. Please advise when you have intercepted."

"James," Katherine said. "Try to contact that boat on VHF."

"Yes, Ma'am." James grabbed another microphone. "Trawler heading east across the Strait of Georgia, this is the United States Coast Guard patrol boat *Eighteen* approaching from your starboard beam."

A tense silence permeated the cabin. No answer came. James called again. Still, no response.

"Crenshaw, hit the blueberry and swing around so we come at this turkey from his forward starboard quarter."

A blue light pulsed into the night. Katherine reached for a microphone, then punched a switch marked "PA." She waited until they were fifty yards off the trawler, which came at them without stopping. "This is the coast guard patrol boat *Eighteen*. Skipper, please cut your engines and bring your vessel to a stop."

James yelled, "Still coming."

Katherine's heart pumped harder. "Crenshaw, swing around and come up alongside. Larson, hit the searchlight."

Suddenly a shaft of light stabbed into the darkness, illuminating the white hull of a boat, gleaming off its windows and polished wood.

"James. How far are we from the Cherry Point pier?"

"A little over four miles."

"ETA?"

"Matching the trawler speed at eight knots...about a half hour, Ma'am."

Katherine picked up a microphone. "Seattle, patrol boat *Eighteen*. Intercepted target does not respond to repeated hails. Target vessel make is...," she looked at James.

"Grand Banks 36," he said.

"Grand Banks 36," Katherine said. "Registration number is...," she motioned with her hand to Larson, who was busy staring out the window and scribbling on a slip of paper, which he handed to her. "Whiskey. November. Four. Fiver. Four. Eight. Juliet. Bravo. Vessel's name is the *Gaia Goddess.*"

"Good copy, Eighteen. Running that registration now."

"Crenshaw, can you get us close enough so we can take a peek in the window?"

"Yes, Ma'am."

The patrol boat thumped in the water beside the Grand Banks. Larson stepped on deck and painted the windows with a handheld searchlight. He stepped back inside.

"Nothing, Lieutenant. I didn't see signs of anyone at the helm."

"Damn," Katherine said. "We might have a skipper lying unconscious on the floor."

"Lieutenant, with no one at the helm that boat must be running on autopilot," James said.

"Eighteen, this is Group Seattle. Lieutenant, target vessel *Gaia Goddess* is registered to a Thomas Atherton from Bellingham, Washington."

"Seattle," Katherine said. "Target vessel appears to be on autopilot headed toward the refinery at Cherry Point. ETA is approximately thirty minutes."

"Copy that, Eighteen. MIFCPAC has a team standing by."

James looked up from the radar screen, his eyes wide. "They put a Marine Safety and Security Team on standby?"

Katherine ignored him. "Crenshaw," she said. "If we snuggle up to this boat, could we push it off course? Maybe head it out into the middle of the Strait?"

"Might buy us some time," Crenshaw said.

"Twenty-five minutes to the refinery," James said.

Crenshaw turned into the Grand Banks. He threw the throttles forward and back, easing up to the hull, gently tapping it. The moment he did, he gunned the engines, which groaned under the strain. A shrill whining sound floated above the noise of the outboards. Larson cocked his head toward the sound.

James called out, "It's on autopilot for sure. My guess is, GPS too. Hear that sound? It's the rudder trying to steer the boat. It'll fight us, whatever we do, and keep seeking its original course."

"Bring us up alongside, Mr. Crenshaw," Katherine said. "Larson, think you can get aboard that boat?"

"Yes, Ma'am."

"Lieutenant, twenty-two minutes," James said.

Katherine watched Crenshaw nudge up to the Grand Banks's hull again. Larson stretched an arm out toward the handrails, but the boats bobbed apart just beyond his reach. He stuck his head back into the cabin, breathing hard.

"Crenshaw, get me closer to the stern," Larson said.

"Mr. Larson. First sign of a problem, you pull back. Is that understood?" Katherine said.

The strapping kid smiled. "Yes, Ma'am."

"Lieutenant, twenty minutes to impact." James's voice rose.

Katherine watched Larson walk along the narrow side deck of their patrol boat. A gust of wind hit them, whipping their boat from side to side. Larson stretched toward a railing on the Grand Banks just as another gust swirled, ripping his cap from his head. He reached for it, but the wind momentarily pinned it against a window of the patrol boat before whistling it away into the darkness. A gap of ten feet loomed between the two boats.

"Kiss that boat softly," Katherine said.

Crenshaw brought the nose of the patrol boat into the right rear side of the Grand Banks. Larson let go of the railing and stretched toward the Grand Banks' gunwales, when another blast of wind hit, pushing the two boats apart. This time, Larson leapt from the patrol boat, lunged for a railing on the Grand Banks, and held on with his feet dangling just above the water while the two boats drifted apart. He swung up onto the rear deck and looked back at the patrol boat, giving them a thumbs-up and a big smile.

"Eighteen minutes, Lieutenant," James said.

Katherine's uniform clung to her skin, moist and clammy. She picked up a walkie-talkie.

"Larson, do you copy?"

"Roger that, Lieutenant."

"Get into that cabin and find the skipper," Katherine said.

Larson pulled open a door at the front of the cabin and disappeared inside. A long silence followed, before a light went on in the Grand Banks and Larson appeared at the helm. "Nothing, Lieutenant. Nothing…no sign of the owner…Lieutenant, the gearshift and throttle are engaged. GPS is on. An indicator light on the autopilot says 'NAV.' Wait…"

Another long silence set in.

"Larson?" Katherine said.

No answer.

"Mr. Larson."

Suddenly, "Shit…shit…Lieutenant, we've got a problem."

Katherine swallowed hard. "Talk to me, Larson."

"Mound of clay-like substance…on the galley counter… wired to a hand-held GPS…and a note…" Larson's words exploded between short breaths. "THIS IS A MESSAGE FOR ANYONE WHO WOULD DARE TO BUILD A PIPELINE ACROSS THE STRAIT OF GEORGIA AND DESTROY THIS FRAGILE ECOSYSTEM. BUILD AT YOUR OWN RISK. THE OCEAN LIBERATION FRONT."

Katherine dropped the walkie-talkie and ripped a microphone from its holder. Then she took a deep breath, clenched her free hand and put on a calm, professional voice. "Seattle, Eighteen. We have a man aboard the target vessel. He reports possible explosives wired to a GPS, and a note from a group calling itself the Ocean Liberation Front."

Silence followed.

"Seattle, do you copy?"

More silence.

"Standby, Eighteen."

7

"Fifteen minutes, Lieutenant."

Ahead, the hulk of the *Star of Juneau* grew ominously larger with each passing moment, its decks lit like a small town.

"Larson, be prepared to ditch. We'll pick you up. Is that understood?"

"Yes, Ma'am."

James looked up from the console. Crenshaw turned back from the helm. Katherine felt their eyes on her.

"Eighteen, Seattle. You are advised not to touch any of the target vessel's controls. Repeat. Do not touch the target vessel's controls. A Marine Safety and Security Team's in the air to your location. Your orders are to scuttle the target vessel while underway. I say again. Scuttle the target vessel and then proceed at maximum speed to a safe distance. The refinery has been notified. An evac is underway."

"Larson," Katherine said. "Group wants us to scuttle that vessel."

"Standing by for instructions, Lieutenant."

"Any of you rocket jockeys know a Grand Banks?" Katherine asked.

"Engine room is under the cabin sole," James said.

"Mr. James, I guess that makes you the on-scene expert." She handed him the walkie-talkie.

James didn't lift his head from the radar screen. "Larson, on the floor you should find some latches that pull up a section and open a way into the engine room."

"That you, Jamesie?"

"Roger that."

Larson grunted. "Access panel removed."

"Careful around the alternator belt," James said. "Look for the raw water intake. That's what we're going to cut."

"Raw water intake? Talk me to it, Jamesie."

James turned his cap backwards, closed his eyes. "Look for a fitting that goes through the hull. Maybe a valve and a large hose coming out of the fitting."

"Looking."

James's eyes popped open. He leaned into the radar screen, then let go of the transmit button.

"Lieutenant, we have about ten minutes. Even if Larson cuts the raw water lines it'll take longer than that for the boat to sink."

"Suggestion, Mr. James?"

"Group said not to touch the controls. What if we tricked the autopilot into thinking it *was* steering the boat?"

"Talk fast."

"Cut the hydraulic lines to the rudder but leave the electrical connections intact. Then Crenshaw can push the boat around and it won't be able to fight him."

"Jamesie," Larson said. "Found that raw water intake."

Katherine snatched the walkie-talkie. "Mr. Larson, do not cut that line." She lifted her finger from the button. "Mr. James, can you talk him through this?"

James sucked in a breath. "Uh huh."

"Do it." She shoved the walkie-talkie back at him.

"Larson, get the hell out of that hole and go outside to the rear deck. There's another access panel on the deck. Pull it up. And get a flashlight in there."

"Roger that, Jamesie."

Katherine could see the huge hawsers holding the *Star of Juneau* to the dock, and the turn screws perched atop an endless maze of pipes. "Mr. Crenshaw, bring us close to the Grand Banks, ready to push it back out into the Strait," she said.

"Jamesie, I'm looking down into another hole."

"Find the hydraulic lines that connect to the ram."

"What the hell's a ram?"

"Umm...big cylinder connected to the rudder post...has an arm that moves in and out."

Larson was silent.

"Four minutes left," James said.

"Got the ram, Jamesie."

"Now find the hydraulic lines and cut them. Don't mess with any electrical wires."

Larson went silent again.

"Get us close, Crenshaw," Katherine said. Ten, nine, eight, seven—Katherine counted the numbers next to the white stripes that showed how far down the tanker sat in the water.

"Damn, I can't see them," Larson said, his voice high, strained.

"Feel them, Larson. Feel them," James said. "Run your hand along the ram until you feel the hydraulic lines."

More silence.

"Two minutes," James said.

"Got 'em, Jamesie."

James yelled, "Cut 'em. Cut 'em."

"Stand by, Mr. Crenshaw," Katherine said.

"They're cut. They're cut."

"Now, Mr. Crenshaw. Now!"

"Hang on, Larson," James said.

Crenshaw rammed the Grand Banks, the sharp crack knocking Katherine to the floor. He spun the wheel hard over left and gunned the engines. Katherine pulled herself up in time to watch the bow of the *Star of Juneau* and the orange and green lights onshore twirl past the windshield. Crenshaw headed them into the darkness of the Strait, nudging the Grand Banks as they went. Katherine pulled herself up, grabbed James's shoulder and squeezed. He looked up at her and smiled.

"Seattle, Eighteen," Katherine said. "We did not scuttle the target vessel. Repeat. Did not scuttle target vessel. Instead, we left all controls intact and cut the hydraulic lines to the rudder arm." She squinted at James. He pursed his lips, nodded his head, and gave her a thumbs-up. "We're heading the target vessel out to sea using our boat."

"Copy that, Eighteen. Ma'am, ask that you remain on-scene until the MSST arrives."

hat you see is not what you get—nor is it what you hear. That pretty well sums up Johann Sebastian Bach for me. Forget his easily hummed, beautiful melodies and intricate, endless successions of notes and chords. Try to play Bach on a guitar, and you risk your fingers becoming tied in knots as they race up and down the frets. I sat on the rear deck of the *Noble Lady,* cradling my guitar, my fingers trying to avoid the perils of a transcription of the first Bach cello suite. I hadn't practiced seriously in years, and I'm not sure what motivated me to start again after all this time. But then, relearning the guitar was only one part of my life that I was starting over now.

I struggled through the piece until a tricky fingering up the neck placed higher notes on low strings, and lower notes on high strings. My fingers tripped over each other, right hand confusing left hand, then vice versa, until my playing ground to a halt. I backed up to the beginning and started over, but when I reached that measure, my fingers lost their way again, forcing me to start from the top. I don't know how many times I did this. Practicing

Bach reminded me of Sisyphus, condemned forever to roll a boulder up a hill only to have it roll down again upon nearing the top. I sighed. I couldn't get there on my own. I needed help, and I knew that. Still, I kept trying.

"Prelude from the first suite?"

A muffled female voice halted my fingers at the bottom of Sisyphus's hill. A whiff of subtle floral fragrance drifted my way, which meant the wind blew out of the north. When I lifted my head, I saw a woman standing on the dock, clad in dark brown pants and a matching short dark brown jacket with an olive blouse. The clear plastic enclosure surrounding the rear deck distorted the rest of her the way water distorts a reflected image.

I called through the plastic. "I'm surprised you recognized it. Do you play?"

"I used to," she said.

I laughed. "I used to, also."

"Cello," she said. "Once, in high school, many years ago. But I love Bach. To the ear so simple, to the musician so complex." She stepped back and eyed the *Noble Lady*, then reached out and ran her hand along the varnished teak cap rail. "Willard 36 Aft Pilothouse, huh? Not many of these around."

"Only five in the whole world."

"What is she a '67, '68?"

"'69."

"You put a lot of work into her."

"I did."

"She's a real beauty. Great lines. Nice rounded stern. Stout. Seaworthy. A Bill Garden design, right?" She had the hint of a New York accent.

"Uh huh. But she's not for sale."

The woman shook her head. "I'm not interested in buying her."

"Are you a broker?" I asked.

"No."

"A boater?"

"Used to be."

I laughed. "There's no such thing as a 'used to be' boater."

She laughed too. "You're right. I still have an eye for them."

"That you do," I said. "There aren't many people who would know this boat."

"I like old classics."

"Are you just out walking the docks?" I asked.

"No," she said.

"Looking for a new boat?"

She sighed. "No." She walked toward the front of my boat and I lost sight of her until she sauntered back. "This is the *Noble Lady*?"

"It is."

"And you are Charles Noble?"

"I am."

"Then I'm looking for you."

"It sounds serious."

"Permission to come aboard?"

"Permission granted." I set my guitar in its case and closed the lid. But before I had the chance to help her, she'd unzipped the plastic flap of the enclosure, reached in and unlatched the entryway gate. This woman knew her way around boats.

"Janet Paulsen," she said, stretching out her hand.

I'm about six feet tall, and the top of Janet's head reached my nose, which made her five feet eight or nine. She appeared to be a woman in her early- to middle-thirties with eyes the color of her olive blouse and dark hair the color of her jacket. She had a large silver pendant, tooled with a northwest Indian design, dangling from a chain around her neck.

Her half-smile sputtered out, like a candle unable to hold a flame.

"How can I help you, Ma'am?"

"Janet, please. Ma'am makes me sound so old."

"Sorry. It's on old habit. Twenty years in the Coast Guard'll warp your speech."

"You're an investigator, and I need your help finding someone," she said.

"My help?"

"Yes."

I chuckled. "Let's see. I've only been out of the Coast Guard for four months. Only been here in this marina for two. And I just got my investigator's license last week. I'd say you do a pretty damn good job of finding people on your own."

She looked away. "Seriously," she said. "This is Bellingham. It's a small town. I've lived here for fifteen years. You know, word gets around. When I asked, word got back that if anyone could help, it would be you."

"And that word came from whom?"

"Around."

"This Around is pretty clever."

"Do you always joke?" she asked.

"Are you always evasive?" I asked.

"No," she said. "I'm worried."

"About what?"

"Whom. I'm worried about Thomas."

"And that's whom you want my help finding?"

"Yes. He's my ex-husband."

I shook my head and threw up my hands. "I don't do domestic work. Marine investigations. Consultations on maritime safety and security. That's what I did in the Coast Guard. That's what I'm good at. That's the business I'm trying to start on my own now."

She winced. "But you are a private eye?"

"No, Ma'am."

Janet flinched. "I thought you—"

"Not a private eye. A 'fish-eye' maybe. Someone who sees the world a little differently from the rest."

She rolled her eyes and shook her head.

"Thomas's boat was found out there." She pointed out to sea. "Only he wasn't aboard."

"Did you talk with the Coast Guard?"

"I did, when they came to visit me. And I talked with the FBI, Customs and Border Protection, the ATF, and God knows how many others. I've had men in dark suits driving late-model unmarked cars visiting my home regularly for the last two weeks. I may be single, but believe me they weren't dates."

"Do you always joke?" I asked.

"You're frustrating," she said.

"I've been told that before."

"Do you remember about two weeks ago, a boat was found headed toward the oil refinery at Cherry Point under auto-pilot?"

"A trawler, Grand Banks if I remember. CG found explosives aboard along with a note from an ecoterrorist group?"

"Yes. That boat belonged to Thomas Atherton."

I pointed to her. "Your ex?"

"Yes."

"I see. Maybe you should step into my office," I said.

"Thank you," she said.

I opened the door to the boat and we walked in. Janet took a seat at the table across from my galley. I moved my breakfast dishes from the table to the sink. She looked around.

"Nice," she said. "New headliners and wall covering. New galley equipment." She ran her fingers over the seat. "New upholstery. You must live aboard."

"It's the only waterfront property I could afford."

"Once, before we were divorced—actually, I think it was before we were married—Thomas and I talked about living aboard."

"You like boats," I said. "You'd probably make a good liveaboard. Most people need terra firma under their feet."

"Boats're like people," she said. "Each has a different personality, character. They interact with their owners, and both the boat and the people are changed as a result. At least that's the way it was with the *Goddess*, our Grand Banks."

"The one found heading for the refinery?"

"Uh huh." She shrugged her shoulders. "It was all Thomas wanted from our divorce."

"What was?"

"The *Goddess*," she said. "He gave me everything else. Now the authorities think he used the *Goddess* as part of a bomb plot to stop the construction of a pipeline across Georgia Strait."

"A man who loves his boat wouldn't want to use it as a slow-moving torpedo."

"He didn't."

"And that's why you're here?"

"Uh huh. Will you take the case?"

"I don't know. Why's his ex-wife interested in finding him for anything other than alimony or child support? Do you think he faked his disappearance?"

She let her head flop back and took a deep breath. Her eye-lids trembled as though she fought back tears. "No. Thomas and I were friends, even after our divorce. He was a passionate man. He believed deeply in his work. But he wouldn't go this far. He's not a terrorist."

"And what kind of work did he do?"

She sniffled, and looked away. "Thomas was a professor of marine biology and environmental science at the university." Her voice wavered.

"Let me guess. He didn't like the idea of a pipeline across the Strait?"

"He'd already done a preliminary study showing the harm the construction of a pipeline would cause to the marine eco-system near Cherry Point. And he'd nearly completed a major environmental impact statement when he disappeared."

Sunlight illuminated the window, projecting a pattern of dark and light stripes through the galley blinds and onto the surface of the table.

"What did the suits say?"

"Suits?"

"The guys in the unmarked cars with the charming personalities."

"They were all looking for Thomas." She shook her head. "They wanted to connect him to the OLF. But—"

"Ocean Liberation Front?"

"Yes. Apparently, the group signed the note found on the *Goddess*. They often cite Thomas's research findings to support their call for direct action to protect the marine environment."

"Like setting fires. Blowing things up. Destroying research facilities."

"They're passionate young people."

"When I was young, I sought a different outlet for my passion."

Janet smiled weakly and nodded her head. "Anyway, everyone who's spoken to me seems convinced that Thomas was working with the OLF. None of them wanted to hear what I thought."

"Occupational hazard in the military," I said. "Chain of command breeds a culture of followers, not independent thinkers. What do you think?"

"That Thomas was kidnapped and right now he's bound and gagged, sitting in some wretched hell hole."

"And who'd do that? The OLF? It doesn't make sense. I thought they liked what he found…unless…his last study didn't reach the conclusions they needed."

Janet threw up her hands. "I don't know," she said. "That's why I came to you. I need you to find out where he is, to prove he's not a terrorist, and to bring him home. Will you do that?"

"I still don't know. Tell me more about the coast guard team that visited you."

She dropped her head and sighed. "Three men. Two from Seattle. One from Oakland. Seemed a long way to come just to talk about Thomas."

"Two from the Thirteenth DIO. The third probably from MIFCPAC."

She winced and shook her head. "I hate acronyms."

"Sorry. DIO stands for District Intelligence Office. MIFCPAC, for the Marine Intelligence Fusion Center of the Pacific, formed after 9/11 to coordinate maritime intelligence and threat assessment for the Pacific region."

"That's what they said too. Something about this being a threat scenario they'd predicated as likely to happen. Terrorists using a small boat guided by autopilot to strike a target."

"Bullshit."

Janet flinched.

"Sorry," I said. "But I wrote the original maritime threat assessment for Puget Sound and the Inside Passage. The likelihood of a terrorist attack by small boat is extremely low."

She threw up her hands. "Low or not, I don't really care." Her voice rose. "Either way, Thomas isn't a terrorist. I want him found and brought back safely."

I looked out the window. Up here, a north wind is as deceptive as a Bach cello suite. It brings clear, stunning weather, with dramatic mountain views, but it usually carries with it a wicked cold. "Tell you what I'll do," I said. "I'll visit the local coast guard station and see what they have on this. I think I still have a few friends left in the Guard."

Janet's eyes brightened. "Does that mean you'll take the case?"

"No. It means I'll see what the CG has to say."

"For a fee, of course. What's your fee structure?"

I laughed. "I don't even have business cards yet, let alone a fee structure."

"I own the Seaview Art Gallery in Fairhaven," Janet said. "We specialize in Northwest Indian art. I opened it a year ago. I ran a small gift shop before that. The gallery's not out of the red yet. I'm not well off, but I did get the house after the divorce and I'll take a second out on it if I need to."

"Whoa." I pushed my palms toward her. "Let me talk to the CG first. Consider it a prelude. If it seems like there's a case beyond that, then we'll talk terms."

"Thank you," she said. "You're as kind as I'd heard."

"From whom?"

"Around," she said.

"Around's not only clever but also flattering."

She pulled a business card from her purse and set it down on the table. She rose to leave. I picked up her card.

"I'll call you later today," I said. I studied the card with its image of an orca in red and black next to the gallery name.

Janet stepped off the boat and onto the concrete dock. I followed her as she walked away. I couldn't help but notice that the *Noble Lady* wasn't the only one with a nicely rounded stern. Before Janet reached the front of the boat, she spun around. I think she caught me observing her stern. Heck, that's what an investigator's supposed to do—observe. Anyway, she smiled politely and walked back toward me.

"Mr. Noble," she said.

"Charlie," I said.

"There's one other thing." She blinked her eyes. Her voice sounded unsure. "I grew up in New York City. I got my love of art riding the subway to high school and watching all the different people around me—Hassidic Jews with curled locks, Puerto Rican women with flamboyant makeup, young African American men strutting in outrageous fashions, you name it. I miss that diversity in this small town." She smiled again, and the light remained on in her face. "It's very comforting to have a black man to turn to for help."

"Why's that?" I asked.

She took a deep breath. "For a number of reasons," she said. "But mainly because I imagine you've experienced prejudice in your life, and perhaps, unlike those men in suits, you won't prejudge Thomas."

"Perhaps," I said.

C oast Guard Station Bellingham looked like a Spanish villa set behind wrought iron gates. The main buildings, with adobe-like white walls and red shingle roofs, gleamed in the bright sunlight. A walkway connected the complex inside the gate to a tan metal shed that sat over the water, its red roof protecting several boats.

An unmanned security kiosk guarded the entrance. I pushed a button underneath a speaker on the side of the kiosk. Static crackled, then a voice: "Coast Guard Station Bellingham, Seaman Miller. State your business, please."

"Commander Charles Noble, retired, to see the station CO."

"Sir, is the station CO expecting you?"

"No, son, he's not."

"Sir, would you please wait until I check with him."

"I will."

So I waited. It looked like two forty-seven-foot motor life-boats moored in the shed. I liked the forty-sevens. If they overturned, they'd self-right in less than eight seconds. I dreamed of the day when I'd take the *Noble Lady* for some serious offshore cruising—Hawaii? The South Pacific? Who knows?—with a few modifications she could make it. Before my wife's death, we'd talked about doing a circumnavigation. Life is so short. I wish we'd just pulled the plugs on our careers and shoved off.

I looked over at the forty-seven-foot MLBs again. The *Noble Lady* had stabilizers to dampen her roll, but I could only imagine piloting a boat able to self-right in less than eight seconds. I'd take on the southern oceans—Cape Horn, here I come; Cape of Good Hope too. The mast and superstructure next to the MLBs appeared to belong to a Grand Banks. Probably Atherton's.

Seaman Miller's voice brought me back from my fantasies of circling the globe. "Sir, the CO is currently occupied, but he's assigned Lieutenant Katherine Sullivan to assist you. Buzzing you in, Sir. Would you please report directly to the duty desk."

Inside the station, the white walls and nondescript dark carpet helped to create as drab and sterile an atmosphere as any other coast guard station I'd been in. The American and U.S. Coast Guard flags flanking the duty officer's desk at least provided a touch of color. I signed in and clipped a plastic badge marked "Visitor" to my shirt pocket.

When I turned around, a woman almost my height, dressed in work blues, walked smartly up to the duty desk. Her dark complexion, high cheekbones, and blue eyes gave her an exotic look. From nearly two decades in the Coast Guard, I knew that work clothes hid the subtler details of a woman's figure. Still, it was apparent that the lieutenant had—how would my mother say it?—a little meat on her bones. I smiled to myself. Whoever decided that men liked really skinny women hadn't consulted me. My late wife Sharon was tall. And like the lieutenant, she was full but not overflowing in all the right places. Frankly, I liked women that way.

The lieutenant gave me a crisp salute. "Commander Noble, Lieutenant Katherine Sullivan. Pleased to meet you."

She shook my hand, then stared as though she knew me.

"Lieutenant, have we met before?"

"This way, Sir," she said. She pointed down a hallway. "Third door on the left's a conference room that we can use." She spoke as we walked. "Sir, five years ago you lectured on maritime safety and security to our junior class at the academy. I believe you'd just finished a major review of the subject for the ICC."

"Ah, yes," I said. "In the days when I worked at the Intelligence Coordination Center. Pre-9/11. It seems like ages ago. The Coast Guard was a different place then."

We entered a conference room with a whiteboard at one end, flags on either side, photographs of the president and the Coast Guard commandant above the whiteboard, and pictures of ships on the walls. The lieutenant took a seat at the end of a long conference table that dominated the room. I sat in a chair at right angles to her. She sat ramrod straight, but her blue eyes scampered over me, the way my fingers scampered over the frets of my guitar. One of her legs twitched.

"Sir, if I may say so, your lecture left a long-lasting impression with me."

"Lieutenant, that was a long time ago."

"Yes, Sir, but what you said that day, that the assessment of maritime safety and security should not be based on fear, but on reason and integrity. How, when fear is let into that assessment, reason and integrity are sacrificed. How we need to understand the way our adversaries see us. Why our actions may provoke them to attack us. How reason is more powerful than force. Commander, those ideas never left me."

A surprising surge of warmth flowed through my body. "I'm impressed, Lieutenant. It sounds like you took good notes."

"Sir, you said all those things well before 9/11. Post-9/11, they ring even more true for me. You were the first senior officer to suggest that the military was more than just an instrument of brute force."

"Intelligence people tend to have a more nuanced view of the world, Lieutenant."

"Yes, Sir. That's one reason I followed the Commander's service career after that talk. I thought the intelligence branch of the Coast Guard might be a place for me."

"I'm flattered, Lieutenant."

"Sir, I was assigned to Station Bellingham last year. I believed you worked for MIFCPAC, with responsibilities for Puget Sound and the inland waters to Alaska."

I laughed. "Lieutenant, my assessment is that you've already got the instincts for intelligence."

"Thank you, Sir. But I was saddened to learn the Commander had retired from the Guard. I had hoped to work with you while on assignment here."

"Lieutenant, under the terms of my separation from the Guard, I'm not able to talk about those matters."

"I understand, Sir. Particularly when classified information may be involved."

"Lieutenant, you could assist me right now, though. I'm here as a civilian investigating the incident off Cherry Point two weeks ago."

Sullivan's face lit up. "Sir, I was the officer-in-charge on the patrol boat that intercepted that Grand Banks."

I guess I still did have friends in the Guard. Sullivan leaned forward. Her leg stopped jerking. Her blue eyes sparkled as she recounted the story in great detail. When she finished, I found myself wanting to ask her a totally unrelated question: "Lieutenant, how far down does your hair fall when its not stuffed into a bun under your cap?" But instead I said, "It sounds like you and your team did an exceptional job."

"Thank you, Sir. I've recommended them for a Meritorious Team Award."

"Lieutenant, were explosives actually found aboard?"

"We stayed with the vessel until the MSST arrived. We did not conduct a thorough investigation of the vessel, the Safety and Security Team did. District has kept all information about their investigation tight, Sir. The answer is, I don't really know."

"How about the state of the radar, GPS, the electronics other than the autopilot when Seaman...?"

"Larson, Sir. Seaman Larson boarded the target vessel. Other than the autopilot and GPS being on, he did not report on the state of the electronics."

"So you don't know where the target vessel originated, or when the autopilot was engaged?"

"I'm sorry, Sir, I don't. But I'm sure the MSST does. Perhaps you can check with them."

"Fuel. Oil. Engine temperature. Engine hours. RPMs. Did your team record any of that?"

She sucked her teeth. "No, Sir."

"Personal effects of Mr. Atherton. Any found aboard?"

Sullivan shook her head. "I don't seem to be of much help. Same answer, Sir. I don't know."

"Is that the Grand Banks docked out back?"

"Yes, Sir, but it's off limits to all station personnel. Maybe I could—"

The knock on the conference room door turned us both around in our chairs. Miller, the on-duty seaman, stuck his head into the room.

"Ma'am, the CO needs a word with you."

Sullivan turned back to me. "Commander, I'll be right back."

She reminded me of another young lieutenant who once served in the Coast Guard with optimism and hope. I looked at the far wall above the whiteboard. On one side of the president's picture was the commandant of the Coast Guard, on the other side, Rear Admiral Vincent Ritchie, Commanding Officer of District Thirteen, headquartered in Seattle. Ritchie's dark eyes stared from his craggy face.

I'd traveled the length of the Inside Passage, from Seattle to Alaska, visiting communities, talking to law enforcement and the military, studying possible targets and measures taken to protect them. I was convinced that a terrorist attack by small boat was highly unlikely, and that we were better off putting our resources into monitoring and inspecting cargo containers from overseas, most of which entered this country uninspected. I said as much in my report, only Ritchie didn't want to hear it. It meant less money for toys, like fast patrol boats outfitted with heavy weaponry.

How had Captain Townsend, my CO, put it after I turned in my report? "I don't give a damn about reason or integrity. What I give a damn about is the chain of command, which right now is chowing down on my six. (Think of standing in the middle of a clock face with your nose pointing at twelve, and you'll easily come to a conclusion about what relevant part of your anatomy is at six)."

My CO continued. "Vin wants it to read another way, and you've got two choices, Commander: Change your threat assessment report to give him what he wants, or change your threat assessment report to give him what he wants."

I didn't change my report.

The conference room door swung open abruptly and Sullivan walked in. Her face was red, the sparkle gone from her eyes. She stood at attention, but refused to make eye contact.

"Sir, I'm sorry but I'm under orders not to discuss any aspect of this incident with you further." The subtle quivering of her bottom lip belied her stoic demeanor. "The station CO has asked me to escort you from the station immediately. If you'll follow me, please, Sir."

The chain of command had just chowed down on a young woman's six.

I followed Sullivan down the hall, stopping at the duty desk to relinquish my visitor's badge. Sullivan stood at the door. When I walked past her, her body went rigid. I stopped and turned to face her. She remained at attention with her eyes focused somewhere faraway.

"Lieutenant," I said. "You'll be a fine officer with a good career in the Guard. Follow orders. Keep your head down. And hold on to your principles as best you can. Remember, the most important person you'll ever salute is the one you see in the mirror each day."

She opened the door for me, then stood outside. Her shoes clicked when she brought her feet together. She barked, "Yes, Sir." Then she raised her hand in a sharp, snappy salute, that she held as I walked away.

Halfway toward the main gate, I turned back. Sullivan still held her salute, so I returned it. She whipped her hand away from her face, pivoted and disappeared back into Station Bellingham.

I walked five minutes from the coast guard station to the marina. The north wind had picked up strength. Smoke lay down flat as it billowed from the stacks along the waterfront. Out in the bay, whitecaps frothed. Clattering halyards greeted me as I made my way down the metal lattice gangway at Gate Nine. I didn't miss stuffing anger and disbelief behind a uniform and a rigid stance, although I did feel sorry for young people like Katherine Sullivan who had many more years of stuffing ahead of them. The military will tell you it's the only way to ensure discipline among the ranks.

I'd heard about a group of Israeli soldiers and fighter pilots who refused to bomb civilian targets or fight in Palestinian areas. Maybe, like them, I'm naïve enough to believe you can salute your flag and your conscience too. I let myself imagine the slapping halyards now applauding in support of that belief.

I sat at the galley table on the *Noble Lady*, eyeing Janet Paulsen's card, twirling it through my fingers. I knew the smart thing was to call and tell her I hadn't made any headway with the Coast Guard, and I probably wouldn't make much headway finding her ex-husband. This is not the kind of work I'd envisioned myself doing, so the smart thing would be to bail out before I got in too deep. But the smart thing also would have been to alter that report. After all, Ritchie was just after a bigger budget to buy more hardware for the stations under his command. *Too intense. Focused to the point of obsession. Unable to compromise when called for.* You'd find those phrases in my service record.

Damn. I slammed Janet's card down on the table, like a poker player slapping down the last card of a winning full house. Western Washington University, where her ex worked, was on the way to her studio. I could at least drop by the Department of Environmental Studies before I told her, "No."

I left my car at the marina and rode my bicycle up to the college. No, I wasn't trying to fit in and show that I was a good environmentalist. But parking on campus was next to impossible, and, besides, I needed the exercise.

It's a real thigh-burner to pedal up Forest Street to the campus. The university occupies high ground in Bellingham with a commanding view of the San Juan Islands and up the Strait of Georgia, made only that much more spectacularly clear by the north wind blowing today.

I locked my bicycle in a rack in front of Huxley College, a rectangular brick building whose top floor looked like a long greenhouse with a huge solar panel resting on top. I located the Department of Environmental Studies on the fifth floor. I stepped into a bathroom first, splashed some water on my face, and gave myself time to catch my breath.

Then I found the departmental chairman's office and strolled in. His secretary introduced herself as Myra Willis, a slender woman with short-cut brown hair wearing a bright floral-pattern dress. She informed me that Dr. Richard Collingsworth had not yet returned from lunch. When I asked if I could wait for him, she tapped a few keys on her keyboard and frowned.

"Dr. Collingsworth has a very crowded schedule this afternoon." She squinted at the screen, then ran a finger across it. "Perhaps I could fit you in the day after tomorrow."

"I'm here about the disappearance of Thomas Atherton."

"Oh, I see." She looked over top her glasses. "One of them."

"One of whom?"

"FBI, DHS, ATF, MIF…blah, blah, blah. An alphabet soup of government departments with more letters than sense."

"No. I'm not one of them," I said.

She leaned back, squinted at me through her glasses, then craned her neck forward and looked me over again. "Sweatshirt, jeans, tennis shoes. I guess you're not. They all wore suits."

"And…" I said.

"And what?"

I smiled. "They were all white."

Myra finally laughed. "Hadn't thought about it, but now that you mention it, yes. Guess you're really not one of them."

"No. I'm a private investigator working for Janet Paulsen." I thought about what I'd said to Janet about being a fish-eye, not a private eye, and I had to bite my tongue to keep from laughing. Maybe I should put that on my business card, whenever I got around to making them up.

"Poor thing," Myra shook her head. "First a divorce, then this. She didn't deserve any of it, but he was so…so irresistible."

"Irresistible?"

"Yes."

"Did he have affairs?"

"Heavens, no." She rolled her eyes. "He was…" She rolled her hand as though coaxing the answer from the air. "I mean, Thomas was like a rock star. Electrifying as a teacher. Huge waiting lists for his classes. Students would cite him as their reason for coming to Huxley."

"Academic groupies?"

"Yes, some. Particularly among his grad students. They adored him. Lived and breathed his every word. But then, even I attended his lectures when I could." She took a deep breath and leaned back in her chair. "Just to feel his energy, his passion." She blushed. "Especially when he talked about protecting and saving the environment."

"Gives PhD a whole new meaning," I said.

Myra wrinkled her face.

"Pretty hot Dude."

She smiled mischievously. "Thomas got his students excited…about learning."

"Bet he did."

"It's so dreadful, what happened. Thomas's boat found with explosives on it. I pray that nothing serious happened to him. He's a good man."

"Good enough to be an ecoterrorist?"

She sucked in a big breath. "Thomas—"

Suddenly, the office door burst open and a blustery wind whipped into the room. Short, portly, and wearing a god-awful mismatch of a tweed jacket atop a red sweater with a blue button-down shirt and brown tie, he blew right past me. Myra lowered her head to her desk.

"Important messages, Myra?" His voice had a flourish to it that begged for acknowledgement of the many letters I'm sure came after his name.

His secretary handed him a wad of pink slips. He pivoted toward his office, then stopped to look me over. His glasses, hanging from a chain around his neck, moved forward and back with each breath. He shook his head dismissively before pivoting again and disappearing behind a door marked, "Richard Collingsworth, BA, MA, MS, PhD, Department Chair."

Myra scurried from behind her desk. She put up her hand. "He's got his first afternoon appointment in five minutes," she said. "But maybe I can squeeze you in." She knocked on Collingsworth's door, then stuck her head in.

"Dr. Collingsworth," she said. "There's a private investigator here to see you about Professor Atherton."

Collingsworth cleared his throat. "Haven't I granted enough interviews already? The man's like a dead poet, more famous when he's not here than when he is."

"He's working for—"

"Janet Paulsen," I said, pushing past Myra and through the partially open door.

Collingsworth's office looked like an antique shop. He sat behind a highly polished walnut Victorian desk. The Tiffany lamp atop his desk illuminated a butterfly in its stained glass shade. I took a seat in one of two high-back chairs with crushed velvet seat covers. Persian rugs covered the floor.

Collingsworth mumbled, "Impertinent ruffian." He cleared his throat again.

"You impertinent ruffian," I said.

He cocked his head. "What?"

"James Joyce, *The Dubliners*. The line began, '*You* impertinent ruffian.'"

"And you are…?"

"Noble," I said. "Charles Noble."

"Working for Janet Paulsen?"

"Yes."

With an arrogant backhand flip of his hand, Collingsworth dismissed Myra. "And you're here to inquire about the circumstances of Professor Atherton's disappearance?"

"Yes."

"Mr. Noble, I'm a very busy man. I haven't much time."

"I'll make it short. You can give me the Cliffs Notes version."

The whites showed beneath Collingsworth's eyes, which bulged ever so slightly from his clean-shaven face with its wine-red hue. I placed Collingsworth in his late fifties. His bald head glistened except around the edges, where a band of graying dark hair fringed it. From beneath bushy eyebrows, he eyed me with a gaze that I'm sure wilted many a young student.

"What was Thomas Atherton working on before his disappearance?"

"My God, man. That's your lead question? I don't have time, so let's get to the heart of things, shall we? Thomas was a

31

controversial figure. Well loved by students because of his…"
Collingsworth rolled his pudgy hand in midair. I recognized the
mannerism, which Myra had apparently adopted. "His charis-
matic persona," Collingsworth said.

"Which means the students loved him, but his colleagues
and superiors didn't," I said.

"Sounds like you know universities, Mr. Noble."

"Not really. I do know organizations with strict lines of
authority. Famous for vicious infighting over extremely small
stakes."

Collingsworth chuckled, sending his entire body jiggling as
he did. "You have a colorful way with words," he said. "But the
stakes here at Huxley aren't small. A lot rides on the research of
our faculty."

"Like the construction of a pipeline across the Strait of
Georgia?"

"And more. You see, some faculty questioned Thomas's dili-
gence and integrity as a research scientist."

"Meaning they thought he cooked his results?"

"A rather crude way of putting it. Let's say that some questioned whether his data supported the extravagant conclusions
and accusations that he made."

"He'd done one study that showed the construction of the
pipeline might harm the Strait's marine ecosystem."

Collingsworth waved me off. "A preliminary study."

"Doesn't matter much, huh?"

"What matters are herring."

"Herring?"

"Yes, herring. There's a large spawning ground right off the
docks of the refinery where Thomas's boat was found. Herring
are a critical link in the food chain, and Thomas had perfected a
bioassay, a—"

"Test that measures biological toxicity based on the concen-
tration of a given toxin."

Collingsworth's squint also reminded me of Myra's. "Are
you really a private investigator?"

I whipped out my wallet and flashed my license for the first time. I smiled, "Just got it in the mail last week."

"I'm sure many of our students wish they could get their degrees that easily."

"What did Atherton's latest results show?"

"He wouldn't say, but in the last several weeks he walked around campus with a huge grin, which some thought a smirk."

"Where's that data now?"

"Ah, finally the right question, Mr. Noble. And to your credit, I might add, arrived at more quickly than the others."

"Quick study," I said.

Collingsworth's voice dropped to almost a whisper. "Thomas's data is lost."

"Lost? It's got to be on a computer or a disk somewhere. The man couldn't have written his results on scraps of paper."

"You'd think, wouldn't you? But the FBI sent one of their computer whizzes to scour our computers. After a week, she found nothing."

"What about the bioassay test equipment and procedures?"

"Oh, the test equipment's still there. At our Shannon Point facility. But the data's not."

"Shannon Point?"

"Huxley maintains an extensive marine teaching and research facility on the water, close to the San Juan Islands ferry terminal. Thomas worked there with our graduate students."

"And the current status of the pipeline?"

He raised an eyebrow. "PDI, the Seattle company that's building it, is set to begin construction. But a last-minute legal challenge was filed about a month ago by a consortium of environmental groups."

"Shortly before Atherton's disappearance."

"Yes." Collingsworth cleared his throat another time.

"Let me guess. The legal challenge is based on the results of his Cherry Point herring findings. No herring data, no case."

Collingsworth pursed his lips and nodded slowly. "My, you are a quick study, aren't you?"

"Is anyone else trying to recreate his findings?"

"It's not that easy. The Cherry Point herring stock spawns between April and June. Thomas's results were based on last season's spawning activity, so it would be almost six months before any new samples could be collected."

"And, of course, pipeline construction is set to begin before the next spawning season."

"Yes."

Collingsworth's telephone rang. He picked it up, nodding his head several times before saying, "Okay," then hanging up. "Mr. Noble, school's been in session for just a few days and I have an afternoon full of student appointments."

I stood to leave, then turned around. "Two quick questions," I said. "What do you think happened to Thomas Atherton?"

Collingsworth cleared his throat, stared at the surface of his desk, then raised his head. "Thomas was given to strong passions. And I believe this time his passions swept him away."

"And the OLF?"

He grimaced. "Nothing more than a bunch of terrorists wrapping themselves in the mantle of environmental protection."

I scanned Collingsworth's name on his door as I left. An alphabet soup with more letters than sense, wasn't that what Myra said?

I'd intended to ride my bicycle to Janet Paulsen's gallery, but I decided to ride back to the marina instead, take a shower, and call her from the boat. At the top of the Gate Nine ramp, I stopped at the small set of mailboxes for us liveaboards and picked up my mail. I shuffled through the bills and junk mail until I came to a letter with a return address that read, in bold red, white, and blue, "Senator Mark J. Dutton," and under that, "Washington State," and under that, "Republican." I turned over the envelope and opened it.

"Dear Commander Noble (ret.), I received your letter regarding the circumstances of your departure from active duty in the United States Coast Guard. The charges you make alleging corruption in the Coast Guard in the assessment of terrorist threats and budgetary requests to meet those threats are, indeed, very troubling. However, I regret that I am unable to investigate these charges further. I also regret informing you that I am unable to intervene with the Department of Homeland Security, or the Commandant of the Coast Guard, in the matter of petitioning to have your service discharge upgraded from general to honorable. Thank you for alerting me to these matters. I will pass along your concerns to the appropriate governmental authorities. Sincerely, Mark J. Dutton."

I balled the letter and tossed it in a nearby trash bin, then I locked my bicycle in a rack. By the time I reached the bottom of the entryway ramp, a few things were obvious: My career as a whistle-blower didn't look very promising; my efforts to gain an honorable discharge after twenty years of honorable service didn't look very promising either; and I hadn't gotten much exercise, since the return route from campus was essentially a straight shot downhill.

What wasn't clear was whether I should take on Janet Paulsen as my first client, or suggest that she let the "alphabet soup" of federal agencies handle the case. And that wasn't the only riddle...

Pipeline construction's about to start. An environmental challenge arises based on a missing scientist's findings. If the findings or the man don't appear, there's no case, and construction begins. That was one possible answer to what happened to Thomas Atherton, but it didn't point to the Ocean Liberation Front.

Or: Pipeline construction's about to start. An environmental challenge arises based on a missing scientist's findings. Those findings didn't turn out the way the environmentalists wanted. Environmentalists switch to plan B—guerilla action. That was another answer, which did point to the OLF.

And those were just two possible answers to the riddle of Atherton's disappearance.

I don't like living with unanswered questions. *Determined.* Isn't that what one commanding officer wrote? *Unable to let things go.* That's what my wife Sharon used to say.

It was only two thirty. I made a turkey sandwich and wolfed it down. Then I placed a call to a man named Frederico Oller. I got his answering service. I left my name and number and told him that the owner of a local music store had given me his name as a classical guitar instructor. Afterward, I headed back up to the parking lot. The refinery was too far away by bike this late in the afternoon, so I decided to drive. If pipeline construction was about to begin, there had to be a contractor's site somewhere near the refinery. I'd nose around and maybe ask some questions. I made a mental note to call Janet Paulsen when I returned.

Seven or eight years ago, I almost marched into my CO's office at the Intelligence Coordination Center in DC, demanding an answer to why my recommendations for beefed-up inspection of cargo containers before they left foreign ports had not made it into his report. Sharon stopped me on my way out the door. She marched me back into our living room, sat me down in an easy chair, and told me to take a few deep breaths.

"Let it go, Lieutenant Commander," Sharon said. "Like oil in water, truth has a way of floating to the surface for everyone to see."

I remember saluting her. And Sharon was right. A week later, my CO's CO asked about foreign cargo container inspection at a departmental meeting. When I fired off a list of recommendations, he asked for my report directly, bypassing my immediate CO, who glowered at me from across a table. God, I wish Sharon was still here to read me the riot act about letting things go.

After exiting the freeway, I crawled behind an endless line of trucks heading for the refinery. It looked like a military convoy moving equipment for a pending invasion. To add to the setting, the main refinery stack belched a mushroom cloud of white smoke into the sky. One quarter of a mile before the refinery's gate, the trucks swung left, but a sign along the road read, "Pipeline Development, Inc. Site Office, next left."

I took that turn and followed a rough-hewn road through a dense stand of cedar and fir trees, which ended in a clearing with an expansive view of Georgia Strait and the San Juan Islands. The sun, beginning its descent, cast the islands in dusky blue shadows set atop darker blue water, and against a lighter blue sky. A large white trailer stood at the far edge of the clearing.

Yellow earth-moving equipment littered the grounds. Pairs of men in orange hard hats carried long black pipes perched atop their shoulders. I pulled up to the trailer. When I stepped from my car, a sweet smell of cedar laced with salt air greeted me.

"PDI," read the green letters on the side of the trailer.

I walked toward the trailer, where cigarette smoke swirled around a group of men talking and laughing. Almost at the trailer's steps, a gravely voice barked, "Hey, buddy."

I spun around. The man speaking held a coffee cup in his heavily callused hand. The lines traversing his weathered face reminded me of plaster cracks. He looked to be in his sixties.

"You here for a job, we ain't hiring."

"'Sides, fucking environmentalists 'bout to have us all outta work anyway," another voice said.

"I'm here looking for the on-site supervisor," I said.

"That'd be me," the man who first spoke said.

He nodded toward the trailer. "Ain't no one in there. We're all out here taking a break. Whaddya want?"

"I came to ask about Thomas Atherton."

"Who?"

"The guy whose boat was found heading toward the refinery pier about two weeks ago."

The supervisor's body stiffened. "You one of them?"

"One of whom?"

"Tree-hugging sonofabitches."

The laughter and talking stopped. Everyone stared my way. "No."

"FBI, DHS, ATF, all them goddamn agencies already been here. So whoddya work for?"

"Party that wants to know what happened to Mr. Atherton."

"What happened to him?" He pointed his coffee cup at me. "I'll tell you what happened to him. Sonofabitch couldn't stop the pipeline any other way so he used his boat to try to blow up the refinery."

"Maybe someone was afraid his latest research showed the construction of the pipeline would harm the Strait."

"Yeah, well it ain't no sweat off my back if he is lost. He's the one that'd let a tiny goddamn fish hold up a $300 million job?"

"Apparently that one goddamn fish is a crucial link in the food chain."

"And this one goddamn pipeline is a crucial link in the chain that puts food on the plates of these foremen." He pointed to the men standing near him. "The men who work for 'em, and all their families."

"Crucial enough so someone would see to it that Atherton went missing? Maybe use the boat thing as a cover-up?"

"Why, you sonofabitch. You accusing one of us of a crime?"

"Just asking what you know."

"I know this, buddy." He jabbed the coffee cup at me. "It's time for you to leave." He turned to the other men. "Some of you boys want to escort this man to his car? Maybe have him deliver a message to the environmentalists for us: Don't mess with our jobs." He took a sip of coffee.

Five men stepped forward. A big man in the middle tossed his cigarette butt to the ground, then crushed it beneath his foot.

I pointed a finger at them. "Don't," I said.

The men froze in their tracks. I heard a grunt. Then like a bullet exploding from a pistol, the big man lowered his shoulder and barreled toward me. I guess he was trying to catch me in the stomach, but he came at me from too far off. No sooner had I sidestepped him and pushed him away than two more men headed for me with their fists. I'm not a brawler. I'm the guy who walks away from barroom fights. I don't like people or nations that unnecessarily resort to violence. And I do like playing classical guitar, which means I'm obsessive about the safety of my hands. But I'm also a realist, with military training in close-quarter combat.

I dropped into a slight crouch, put one foot ahead of the other, and raised both hands under my chin, fingers curled into loosely held fists. I took a deep breath and eyed the men coming at me. The first man threw a right, which I blocked, then I swept his leg out from under him with a kick and he plummeted to the ground. But the second man caught me with a glancing blow off the side of my head, and I staggered backward. That's when the big man tried to catch me in a bear hug from behind. I let my elbow fly into his solar plexus, and I heard him gasp for a breath.

The second man came at me swinging his right hand. I parried with my left, stepped in close, then spun him around rapidly, locking his neck between my forearms. The big man came at me again. I tightened my choke hold and arched back, lifting the second man off the ground. His face turned beet red.

"Call 'em off," I said to the supervisor.

He sipped coffee, watching like an emperor gazing down on gladiators fighting. All of the men froze, turning their eyes toward the supervisor, who looked on without expression. I ratcheted my choke hold tighter. The man under my grip coughed. His arms flailed.

"Call 'em off," I said.

The supervisor nodded subtly off to one side, and the other men dispersed. I let go of my choke hold and the man doubled over, grabbing, rubbing his neck.

"Maybe next time I won't call 'em off," the supervisor said.

"Maybe next time I won't stop with a choke hold." I backed toward my car.

"Message's still the same," he said. "You tell them goddamn environmentalists stay out of our way, or else."

"Sorry," I said. "But I'm not a messenger boy."

The supervisor glared, then resumed sipping his coffee.

I opened the car door, slipped behind the wheel, and pulled away from the trailer. I took a back road home, which wound around the edge of Bellingham Bay. Across the rippled water, Mount Baker stood watch over the city, its snowcapped summit bronzed by the setting sun.

When I turned into the marina parking lot, I drove past two dark gray cars with government plates. Both pulled out to trail close behind me. I swung into a parking space facing the boats.

Before I could get out, the other cars angled to a stop behind my car. The front doors of each vehicle swung open. Four men in suits rushed out and circled my car. One knocked on the window, which I rolled down.

"Afternoon, officer," I said. "Did I exceed the parking lot's speed limit?"

A lantern-jawed man with a blue shadow over his face glared at me, then gestured for me to get out. We were both the same height.

"Turn around. Place your hands on the roof of the car."

He frisked me quickly.

"You Charles Noble?" he asked.

"I am. And you are?" I turned back around.

"Special Agent Stafford."

He had a steely gaze.

"Special to whom, Agent Stafford?"

"None of your damn business."

"That a new department under Homeland Security?"

Behind closed lips, his jaw muscles flexed. "Listen, wise guy. You—"

"No. You listen. You stop me for no reason. Frisk me. Then tell me you're a special agent but you won't say with whom. You never flash a badge or an ID card. What's the next step? You arrest me as an enemy combatant and strip me of my rights?"

My body exploded with a searing blast of pain that knocked my breath from me. I looked down to see Stafford's hand buried into my gut. My knees buckled. I doubled over and oozed down the side of the car. Stafford stiff-armed me with his massive hand and kept me from sinking further.

"The next step is I tell you that this investigation is under federal jurisdiction. You're out of your league, Noble. Interfere and you'll be arrested."

He pulled his hand away abruptly, and I sank to the ground.

When I looked up, a man with silver hair and a mole on his right cheek reached down with his hand. He pulled me up.

"Fred Crowley," he said.

"Let's see, you must be the Good Special Agent, and he's the Bad Special Agent?" I nodded toward Stafford.

Crowley chuckled low. "Look, Noble, we've been on the heels of the OLF for almost a year now, ever since they bombed that laboratory in Oregon. With this latest bomb threat, we think we're close. We just don't want an amateur messing up a lot of hard work."

"So you send out the goon squad? How professional."

"Look, you worked intelligence. You know the drill. We haven't infiltrated the OLF. So, we don't know how many members they've got. We don't even know for sure the identity of anyone in the group. Atherton's our first break. The OLF doesn't give us much to go on. Just an anonymous e-mail communiqué now and then claiming responsibility for some action they took."

"And did they take responsibility for the attempted bombing of the refinery?"

Crowley laughed. "I'm not at liberty to divulge that." He grabbed me by the arm and pulled me closer. "I hear that you were a good intelligence officer who crossed the line and disobeyed a superior's command. Cost you your career. That's too bad. Look, like Stafford said, you don't know what you're up against here. Crossing the line and interfering with our investigation might cost you a lot more than your career this time."

Crowley let go of me. He grabbed the door handle of his car and yanked the door open. He jumped into the back seat. Car doors slammed shut and engines revved. The vehicles backed up, turned quickly, then sped away.

I massaged my tender abs. Apparently, I'd managed to aggravate a number of people already. Not bad for my first day on a job I still wasn't sure I should take.

F rederico Oller had left a message for me yesterday, in a voice that sounded formal and close to a whisper. He pronounced the double "l's" in his last name as a "y," and said he had time for a lesson tomorrow morning at eleven. I phoned him back, got his answering service again, and said I'd take it.

Afterward, I pulled out my guitar to practice—warm-up exercises, scales, then the Bach Prelude. Just before I reached the section of the prelude where my fingers usually gridlocked, the cell phone rang. Janet Paulsen sounded bright and cheery.

"Thanks for leaving a message on the gallery's voice-mail last night," she said. "After I picked it up this morning, I realized I didn't give you my home number. Here, take it."

She didn't leave me much choice, so I scribbled down her number on the back of a receipt, which I duct-taped to a metal porthole in the galley.

"I guess we need to talk," Janet said.

"Yes." My stomach growled. "Have you had breakfast?"

"Actually I haven't. I came into the gallery early this morning to prepare for an opening of northwest Indian art on Saturday."

"Like to join me?" I asked.

"Love to. Where?" she asked.

"Old Town Café."

"That's my favorite breakfast spot. I'll be there in ten minutes."

Nestled in the midst of a block of renovated nineteenth-century buildings, the Old Town Café hearkens back to the 60s. From the unpretentious, down-to-earth décor and the word "organic" sprinkled liberally throughout the menu, one can still easily imagine the days when the restaurant catered to Bellingham's "Peace and Love" generation. But today aging hippies, businessmen and women in suits, and ex–Coast Guard officers rub shoulders there because the food's inexpensive, damn good, and they serve breakfast until three in the afternoon. Best of all, it's only a ten-minute walk from the marina.

I got to the café before Janet and grabbed a wooden booth by the large picture window. Across from me, a black guy in a Greek fisherman's hat and heavy woolen sweater marked up the pages of what looked like a book manuscript with a red pen. In between his animated strokes, he took long, reflective sips of coffee. His lips moved as though he was talking to himself. I'd seen him in here before. I'd heard that one of the liveaboards on Gate Six was an African American author. Perhaps that was him.

He must have felt my stare. He looked up from his work and nodded to me. I nodded back. There aren't many black guys into boating, especially liveaboards. I'd have to introduce myself to him soon.

Janet arrived, wearing black pants and a tan sweater. A different pendant dangled from her neck. This one made of silver and copper. She slid into the booth, facing me, and grabbed a menu. A waiter I'd gotten to know named Sean came over with place settings.

"A or B?" he said to me.

"A."

"Sunny-side up?"

"Yep."

"Organic eggs?"

"Twist my arm." I nodded.

He smiled, then eyed Janet. She raised her head. "Order of hotcakes and a side of sausage."

"Organic maple syrup?" the waiter asked.

"Uh huh."

Sean left and Janet turned to me. "I'm impressed. You must come here often."

"Couple of times a week."

"'A'? So what did you get?"

"Two eggs sunny-side up, split order of black beans, and home-fried potatoes with sourdough toast."

Janet smiled. "Okay, what's B?"

"What you ordered."

"At least you've got good taste." She placed her folded hands on the table and stared at me eagerly. "So, you will take the case?"

"I'm not sure I should."

Her shoulders slumped. "What do you mean, not sure you should?"

"There're obviously a lot of people interested in finding Thomas. I worked as an intelligence officer for years, but I don't have any formal training in this type of investigation. I'm just starting out; just starting over. If you want to find Thomas, maybe you should hire someone with experience, who's been at this kind of thing for a while."

Janet slapped the table, rattling the silverware. A young student across from us looked up from her books.

"No," she said, shaking her head. "No. I want you." She pointed. "In part because you're so damned honest it's painful, but it also makes me trust you more. Most people starting out would jump at any business that came their way." She squinted slightly. "Are you afraid of failing? Afraid you won't find Thomas?"

45

"Maybe…mostly, I feel out of my element. I can ask questions and try to make sense of answers, but I feel like someone threw me onto the set of *The Rockford Files* and told me to act the part of Jim Rockford."

Janet smiled and pointed at me. "That 70s detective series with James Garner, right?"

"Uh huh."

"I love him. I saw the made-for-TV movies, and caught some of the reruns. He's great in that role."

She waved me off. "Hell, you'll do fine. You've already got a leg up. You suffer from the same warped sense of humor as Rockford does. Now we need to talk about your fees."

She smiled, and it melted my resolve. I guess I also suffered from Jim Rockford's inability to turn down a case. "What if you pay me whatever you think my services were worth, after I've found Thomas, or given up."

"Heavens." She let out a short, high-pitched laugh. "You won't stay in business long that way. Trust me, I'm a businesswoman. I expect to pay for the services I need."

"And I'm just starting in business on my own. Let's call it a Grand Opening Special. A guarantee of a satisfied first customer and lots of great referrals."

"You're very different," she said. "I haven't met many men like you, which is both refreshing and frightening."

"Refreshing?"

"Because money doesn't appear to motivate you, unlike most people."

"Frightening?"

"Because money doesn't appear to motivate you, which makes me wonder what does."

I smiled. "I spent twenty years in the military, working hard with no other reward than a CO's salute and the personal knowledge of a job well done."

She nodded. "Honor and duty. How appropriate."

"Appropriate?"

"Or should I say how noble?"

"Imagine what I'd be doing if my last name was Knave."

She let out a carefree laugh. "Might be fun to imagine."

Sean arrived with our breakfast plates, which he set down before us. While Janet glided a dome of butter across her hotcakes, I performed my sunny-side up ritual: break one yolk with my fork, then sop the running yellow with a point of toasted sourdough before it reaches the home fries. Janet ate hotcakes the way my father did, meticulously cutting them into strips and only then pouring syrup over them. I chomped down on the end of the egg-soaked toast.

"AWOL." She stared at the strip of hotcake dangling in midair from the tip of her fork. "Isn't that what you military people call it? You have such a wonderful way of putting things, stripping away emotions by turning everything into an acronym. "AWOL." She pushed the hotcake into her mouth, then mumbled, "Could have been Thomas's middle name."

I jammed the heel of my hand into the bottom of a ketchup bottle positioned so that a few red blobs dropped strategically over the mound of golden home fries. Then I stabbed a potato with my fork and crunched it in my mouth. Ahh. Done just the way I liked it: crispy outside, soft inside. I waited until I had swallowed.

"Thomas went missing a lot?"

Janet grimaced. "Disappeared? No. I mean he was so wrapped up in his work he was missing from the rest of his life…our life."

"Think it's genetic?"

She nodded. "Uh huh. Even when men don't work, they still manage to avoid being present in family life. I did my Master's thesis on gender roles in aboriginal societies around the world. Take the South Pacific, for example, where long ago in some societies women did much of the work while men sat around twiddling their"—she chuckled—"well, mostly their thumbs. And when they got bored twiddling they'd organize a war with a nearby tribe. The fighting would go on until the first man was killed. Then they'd stop and go back home to twiddle until the next war."

"So that's where the 'sudden death playoff' came from?" I took my turn at chuckling. "There's not much that's changed today, except that wars don't stop after the first death."

"My point, exactly," she said.

My toast ran out too quickly, which meant I had to switch to sopping egg yolk with home-fries. Several minutes passed in silence while we ate. Janet finished her breakfast before me.

"Where will you begin looking for Thomas?" she asked.

I popped the last "ketchup and egg yolk" fry into my mouth. "I already started."

I hit the high points of my first day on the job for Janet—the Coast Guard, Collingsworth, the PDI construction workers, and the unidentified special agents.

She shook her head slowly. "It's not only honor and duty. You're very determined, and I bet you have a problem with authority. You don't like to be told 'No,' do you?"

"You sound like a former CO. The problem I have with authority is who wields it and how."

"Funny." She cocked her head and smiled. A few strands of hair partially covered one eye. "You remind me of Thomas. Sense of honor and duty. Determined. Distrusts authority. They're qualities I liked about him. But they also seemed to get him into trouble."

"What kind of trouble?"

"On campus mostly. The students loved Thomas. They'd camp out overnight to register for his classes. But many of the faculty disliked his popularity. Thomas was an assistant professor. He was up for tenure this year. The last time we talked he said he saw storm clouds gathering to deny it to him. Collingsworth was his chief nemesis."

"Why Collingsworth?"

"Because around the world, when people speak of Huxley's Department of Environmental Studies they almost always mention Thomas in the same breath. He's more well-known than Collingsworth, though Collingsworth has been at the university many years longer than Thomas."

"Jealousy?"

"Yes."

Sean gracefully gathered our dishes, then deftly slid the black guest-check folder between us. I reached for it. So did Janet. We held each onto an end as I have often seen a pair of gulls hold a crab between them in their beaks.

"Our agreement was that I pay based on satisfaction after the fact." She stared hard. "I'm very satisfied with breakfast, so I'll get it."

She jerked the guest-check folder from of my hand. I wanted to salute her and say sarcastically "Yes, Ma'am." But she already knew my problem with authority, so I settled for a kinder, gentler, "Thank you."

Her eyes softened. She pulled a credit card from her purse, slipped it into a folder pocket, then motioned to Sean, who walked over and plucked the folder from her raised hand.

"What will you do next?" Janet asked.

"Drive down to the university's facility at Shannon Point once we leave here. I want to talk to Thomas's colleagues and maybe some of his graduate students."

"Yes," she mused. "Thomas's grad students."

Sean must have sensed the delicacy of our conversation. He stepped back slightly as he patted the folder on the table, then nudged it in front of Janet.

"That'd be Melissa," Janet said, hissing the name.

"Colleague or grad student?"

She studied the bill, then reached for the pen, which she dangled in midair. It appeared she was computing the tip. Janet pressed the pen hard onto the receipt and scrawled her name. Then she raised her head, cutting her eyes at me. "Grad student," she said, "That's whom he enjoyed being with most."

"Melissa?"

"His grad students. They're his family. Mostly women. He's like...like a man with many wives."

"Does he have affairs with them?"

"No. At least none that I ever discovered. Not that any of them would refuse Thomas. I saw it in their eyes whenever he and I were around them. They wished that I would disappear so they could have him all to themselves."

"And once you got divorced, they did."

She shook her head. "I don't think Thomas ever slept with any of his students. Though I wouldn't put it past them to try to seduce him. Especially Melissa. They're his Muses, his intellectual courtesans." Janet looked down again and sighed. "I'm not interested in bugs and critters. They are. So he gets from them something I could never give him." She raised her head. "Were you ever married?"

"My wife died of cancer five years ago."

She sighed, and I thought I saw tears forming at the corners of her eyes. "God, life is so sad sometimes." Janet stood up abruptly. "I'm ready to leave," she said.

I waved to Sean as we walked out the door. Outside, Janet and I turned in different directions, but I stopped and pivoted around. "Does this Melissa have a last name?"

"Buchanan," Janet said. "Melissa Buchanan, but everyone calls her Bucky."

On this sunny day, Chuckanut Drive was the scenic route to take south. Minutes outside of Bellingham, the drive went past Chuckanut Bay, a huge aquatic amphitheater with tiny Dot Island in its center. Receding in the distance beyond the bay, the dusky blue-green humps of islands, stacked one atop the other, broke the surface of the water like the backs of leviathans surfacing to breathe.

The drive twisted and turned its way south with hard rock on one side. On the other side, the curtain of trees occasionally parted to reveal breath-taking views of the labyrinth of land-on-water known as the San Juan Islands.

Like Sirens beckoning Jason from his *Argonaut*, these islands seduced me when I first meandered through them with the Coast Guard, more than a decade ago. I'd been reassigned from the high-speed drug interdiction boats zooming out of Miami to the lazy buoy tenders creeping through these islands north of Seattle.

To some, in those days before 9/11, my orders seemed like banishment to the "Gulag Archipelago," out of the mainstream of the action. And it seemed that way to me at first.

Then, not long after I learned to kayak, I saw a gray whale turn on its side and swim toward me with its huge searching eye sliding just inches below the water's surface, then slipping under my small boat. And one day, while on a work detail repairing the old Turn Point Lighthouse on Stuart Island, we stopped to watch a pod of orcas cavort in a tide rip beneath us. Two years later, when a promotion took me to the Intelligence Coordination Center in Washington, D.C., memories of these islands served as a balm for the blood sports of politics and power there.

Suddenly, Chuckanut Drive dropped down from the mountains and into marshy flats, truncating the expansive view. Outside of downtown Anacortes and close to the San Juan Island ferry terminal, the quiet, tree-lined road I drove along looked every bit like it would end at a posh waterside estate, but instead it took me to Huxley College's marine science facility at Shannon Point.

Long planks of cedar faced the main building, which had no windows on the side where cars parked. I got out and took a gravel path around to the water. The other side of the building had lots of glass. I kneeled in the sand and rocks for an eye-level view, peering out at the passages between the islands that looked like doorways into a watery mystery world. Behind me a door opened.

"It's a beautiful view of the islands," the female voice said.

Still kneeling, I twisted to see a petite young woman walking my way. Her short, flaming red hair stood out against the dark green boughs around her. Freckles covered her face. She wore Birkenstocks and blue jeans, with a white T-shirt and no bra, which gave her a mischievous, tomboy look. She kneeled beside me.

"When you're here so much, you begin to take it all for granted," she said, pointing out toward the islands. "But if we don't protect it, it will be lost to us someday." She spun around. "Are you a visiting professor?"

"No."

"A grad student?"

"No."

She screwed up her face, which bunched her freckles together. "Undergrad?"

I laughed. "I just drove down from Bellingham."

"For the view?"

"To find someone who works here."

"Who's that?"

"A grad student named Melissa Buchanan."

She laughed. "You came looking for Bucky, eh?"

"Do you know where she is?"

"Maybe. It depends on who you are."

"Charlie Noble."

She laughed. "Like, you're kidding, right?"

"No."

"Someone named you for the galley stovepipe?"

"My dad, Vincent Noble. He cooked aboard a merchant vessel, where he said Charlie Noble was his best friend. He told me that during the 1850s a captain in the British navy insisted that the galley smokestack be cleaned and polished every day to reduce the fire hazard. Eventually, the smokestack itself became known by this captain's name. And periodically, cooks on old wooden ships fired a pistol up the smokestack to clean out the soot and tar. A practice they called "shooting Charlie Noble." I don't think my dad ever shot his Charlie Noble, but I'm sure he kept it clean. I'm impressed—it's only boating traditionalists who usually recognize the name."

"Makes me feel a lot better about mine."

"Which is?"

"Bucky Buchanan." She thrust her hand toward me. "Like my dad nicknamed me after a football player, but I'd prefer to think of Buckminster Fuller, eh?"

"Canadian, eh?"

"Hard to hide, eh?"

We both laughed. The sun hit the rippled surface of the water, creating a blinding point of light from which thousands of sparkles radiated. I closed my eyes and turned toward Bucky. She put her hand up to her eyes.

"You want to step into my office?" she said, nodding over her shoulder.

She stood up and walked over to a huge driftwood log lying at the interface of sand and grass, then sat down and nestled her back into it. I joined her. A large cedar branch hung down above us, providing shade and a sweet, piquant aroma that hinted of cherry. She flashed her blue-gray eyes at me.

"Tall man like you," she said. "Like, I'm tempted to call you 'Stovepipe.'"

"Resist the temptation," I said. "That was my nickname on the academy football team."

Her eyes narrowed. "What academy?"

"Coast Guard."

"You're with the Coast Guard?"

"Was."

Her face softened.

"So, what are you here to see me about, Mr. Noble?"

"Charlie, please. I'm here about Thomas Atherton."

She bore into me with her stare, said nothing, then turned away. A moment later, her body heaved and she started to cry. Finally she turned around and wiped away tears.

"He isn't only my teacher, he's my mentor, my friend. Now they claim he's turned into a terrorist who sent a boat loaded with explosives heading toward the oil refinery." She put a hand to her chest. "That's not the Thomas Atherton I know. Thomas is a gentle soul. He wouldn't do anything like that. He's concerned about the environment, concerned about people, opposed to violence. He lives for his research, his work, his teaching. He—"

I touched Bucky's shoulder softly. She sniffled, but stopped talking. It was all a bit much and brought to mind a picture of a famous redheaded stage and screen diva of my parents' generation, Tallulah Bankhead, known for emotional outbursts—most often contrived.

"Has the FBI been to see you?" I asked.

She nodded her head. "And the Department of Homeland Security, Alcohol, Tobacco and Firearms, Coast Guard, and I don't know how many others. I told them all the same thing. That Thomas was a gentle man. That he wouldn't do a thing like that. That—"

"Whoa." I touched her shoulder again, stopping her before she launched into her shtick. "I'm sure he was."

She sniffed back tears. "So who are you with?" she asked.

"I'm working for Janet Paulsen."

Bucky swallowed hard. Her eyes narrowed.

"Oh. Like, what's she want?"

How quickly emotions change.

"Presumably the exact same thing that you do, to find Thomas."

"Like, I wouldn't make the presumption that Janet and I want anything the same."

"How's that?"

"She never left Thomas alone, even after their divorce."

"I thought they were friends."

"Some friends," Bucky said. "It's more like she stalked him. She'd come down to the lab just to bring him lunch. Then hang around for the afternoon, getting in everyone's way. She wasn't a scientist. She didn't understand the importance of Thomas's work. His vision. What he was trying to do. Not like those of us who worked closely with him every day."

"How many grad students worked under Thomas?"

"Five. We're a small, close-knit group."

I pulled out a pad and pencil from my pocket. "Names?"

"The only other grad student around right now is Matthew Voltmann. Theresa and Keila are at the University of Florida working on a project in the Everglades. And Ute Mueller took this semester off to return home to Germany."

I scribbled down one name. "Is Matthew around today?"

"No," Bucky said. "It's his first year as a grad student. He's teaching a class on campus."

"When I spoke with Richard Collingsworth, he said that Thomas was involved in a project to measure the health of the herring population off Cherry Point."

"As though he cared."

"As though who cared?"

"Collingsworth. He hated Thomas, like much of the faculty. Thomas is brash, I'll admit that. He doesn't suffer fools easily. And our department is top-heavy with them."

"Tell me about the results of Thomas's bioassay of the Cherry Point herring."

Bucky brightened. "You're really an investigator?"

I held up two fingers. "For two whole weeks."

"And you know what a bioassay is?"

"Ever hear of a cab driver with a PhD?"

She smiled. "Job market's tough, eh?"

"No 'Golden Parachute' when you get laid off from the military. Tell me about the results of the bioassay."

She took a deep breath. "*Clupea harengus pallasi*," she said.

"English, please."

"That's their Latin name. Pacific herring. DNA analysis proved that the Cherry Point population was a distinct subgroup. The bioassay is a long process. Each female deposits twenty to forty thousand eggs that adhere to eelgrass, kelp, even rocks or a jetty. We wait until low tide, then cut the grass and carefully harvest the eggs, which we place into a number of experimental holding containers. Some of the eggs we do nothing with. We use them—"

"As experimental controls."

Bucky squinted. "Like, if you already know this stuff, why ask me?"

"Hey, I don't know anything about herring. I worked at a coast guard center that prepared for terrorist threats. We used equipment that sampled air and water for the presence of biotoxins that terrorists might use."

"And now you're a private investigator? If you know so much, why'd they let you go."

"Maybe that's why they let me go. Look, could we get back to the herring?"

"Yeah. Sure. Where was I?"

"After you separate out the experimental and control eggs…"

"Yes, like, after we separate the egg samples into experimental and control groups, we begin introducing suspected biotoxins into the water the experimental eggs are maintained in. We stage the introduction over the development of the herring from egg to larva because one developmental stage may be more susceptible than another to the effects of the biotoxins."

"What biotoxins did Thomas test for?"

"P-A-H." Bucky smiled, cocked her head, widened her blue eyes, and waited.

I said nothing.

"Got ya, eh? Polycyclic Aromatic Hydrocarbons. You want to hear all the gory details?"

"Could I get the Cliffs Notes version?"

"Principally TCB and Pyrene. TCB, trichlorobenzene, is a solvent with lots of uses—degreasing, lubricating, heat transfer. Pyrene is a by-product of combustion, an effluent from industrial smokestacks."

"The kind of chemicals you'd find coming out of refinery smokestacks like those at Cherry Point."

"Uh huh. Highly carcinogenic biotoxins that find their way into the ocean with extremely severe effects on marine life."

"Is that what Thomas's experiments showed?"

"The preliminary data showed effects on all stages of herring development, with undersized and deformed fish, some incapable of biological reproduction. But the data was incomplete. All the results had not been analyzed before…well, before—"

"Thomas went missing, and his Grand Banks 36 loaded with explosives nearly drove itself into a refinery's docks."

Bucky turned her head away and looked out to the islands. "Yes. Before he went missing."

"What happened to the data?"

"Thomas was obsessive about his experimental data. He knew what he was doing was controversial, so he logged data onto a separate computer, not connected to any internal or external network. Like, he didn't want anyone to hack into it."

"I find it hard to believe that he logged all the data himself. That's grunt work. It's what grad students exist for."

"Thanks. But only Thomas had the passwords. When we entered data for him, he logged us on and logged us off."

"So what happened to his computer? His disks?"

"The computer and the disks are here, but, like, the data isn't. Like, the FBI took everything, but apparently they couldn't find any evidence of Thomas's data either."

"Did he take it with him?"

"I suppose he could have."

"Is there any chance that the results of the bioassay could have turned out differently from what you expected?"

"We're scientists, Mr. Noble. There's always a chance that we'll disprove our own hypothesis. And with this bioassay, any number of other factors could have been at work to explain the dramatic decline in herring stocks in the last decade. Natural variation. A problem with the herring food source. Improper experimental methods on our part. Yes, the final results could have shown just the opposite of what most of us believe."

"Which is?"

"That the refinery contributes significantly to the pollution of the Strait of Georgia, and building the pipeline would only make matters worse. Herring are like a canary in a mine. Only this mine is the food chain. Big fish eat herring and herring eat smaller marine life. If the herring aren't healthy it means something's toxic in the mine."

"What about the OLF?"

Bucky's body stiffened. "Like, I don't know much about them. You'll have to ask Matthew."

"The new kid?"

"Yeah, he's actually gotten communications from the OLF."

"What kind of communications?"

"You know, like, after a direct action a mysterious e-mail shows up in his in-box announcing what they've done and why."

"Anybody trace the e-mail back to its source?"

Bucky threw up her hands. "Like, that techno stuff is beyond me. Matthew's the ecogeek."

"Ecogeek?"

"Hey, it's the current term of art."

"Thanks," I said. "You've been really helpful."

"Like, it's a lot more fun talking to you than those uptight government guys. They don't know half as much about biology as you do. Like, you could tell 'em anything, eh?"

"And I bet you did."

She gave me that mischievous tomboy smile. I got up to leave, but Bucky stayed seated, staring out toward the islands. I'd only walked a few feet when she called out.

"Mr. Noble, did you ask Janet, like, why she left with Thomas on the boat the night he went missing?"

"She did?"

"Kinda makes you wonder, eh?"

Like, I needed to ask Janet why.

D riving back from Anacortes, I had every intention of paying Janet Paulsen a visit at her gallery. But when I came to the turn-off for the back route into Bellingham, a voice inside told me to keep going straight. And when I got to the freeway entrance, that same voice said to go south to Seattle. So I slipped in a CD of guitarist Andrés Segovia, cranked up the volume, and relaxed back into my seat. Segovia's fingers danced over the strings while, outside, the dramatic snowcapped peaks of the Cascade Mountains danced by. Damn. How could he play the Bach Prelude so fast?

If I was ever going to find Thomas Atherton, I had to know what happened on the water between the time he left port and the time the Coast Guard intercepted his boat. If this were a robbery at a convenience store or an ATM, it would be a simple matter of securing the videotapes from the surveillance cameras. While there are no videotapes to record what happens on the water, fortunately there is Puget Sound Vessel Traffic Service, located in the Coast Guard's Marine Safety Office building on the waterfront, just down the hill from the Pike Place Market in Seattle.

Segovia's music traveled south, too, from the German composer, Bach, to the Spaniard, Isaac Albeniz. I hummed a few bars of Albeniz's *Recuerdos del Alhambra* while the grand old maestro plucked it, imagining how nerve-wracking and exhilarating it would have been to sit in on one of Segovia's master classes.

I checked the dashboard clock. The VTS center stayed open twenty-four-seven, but I wanted to get there just before five, which meant I'd have about three hours to kill in Seattle. I smiled as Segovia trilled the notes of the *Recuerdos* smooth and fast while also playing its melodic line, blending the parts to sound like two guitarists hard at work instead of one. I'd have three whole hours to indulge in my favorite guilty pleasure. Way to go, Charlie, mixing work and fun.

I pulled into the parking lot of a marina at the south end of Lake Union, grabbed a local microbrew and turkey sandwich, then headed off to walk the docks and ogle boats—the kind of thing only "hard core" boat addicts do.

I bypassed the sleek, shiny boats at the head of the dock and walked toward the end, where the bow of an older, wooden boat caught my eye. Fifty feet away, I knew I was looking at a classic, a 1960s era Romsdal, built in Norway to withstand the toughest conditions of the North Atlantic. Her name was *Wanderer,* and she was double-ender, just like the *Noble Lady,* only twice her size.

I heard the dock timbers creak behind me and turned to see a broker named Jeff walking toward me, a smile on his face. Jeff was an older man, with weathered skin beneath his thin gray beard. He'd sailed to Tahiti and back with his family twenty years ago. We'd met like this many times.

"She's a real beaut, isn't she, Commander?" Jeff said, extending his hand.

We shook.

"Sixty-five-foot 1960 Romsdal," I said.

"Yep." He slapped his thigh, then pointed at me. "Damn. You've got an eye for the ladies. Go aboard. She's open. I know I don't need to show you around. I'm down on the docks checking on a fifty-five-foot 'gin palace' that we just sold."

I opened the boarding gate and entered the salon through a teak door on the starboard side. Nice. A tiled fireplace sat in one corner. Next to it, a bookcase and lounge chairs. The entire area was exquisitely done in teak. I hiked up the steep staircase into the pilothouse and sat at the helm. I wrapped my hand around the controls. A single engine. That's all she had, and that's all she needed.

I eased the throttle forward, imagining the throaty whine of the diesel beneath me as I headed out the Strait of Juan de Fuca and turned south for Mexico, on the first leg of a five-year circumnavigation. That had been our plan, until Sharon's illness changed things.

She was diagnosed with ovarian cancer when we were living in San Francisco. We wanted children and tried unsuccessfully for more than a year to get pregnant. A fertility clinic doctor discovered the cancer. We owned a twenty-four-foot sailboat at the time, which we sailed in San Francisco Bay. After a round of chemotherapy, Sharon's cancer went into remission.

To celebrate, that summer we decided to cruise British Columbia's Desolation Sound. We wanted to maximize our time, so we rented a powerboat, not one of those fast-moving, gas-guzzling speedsters, but a recreational trawler with a diesel engine. The forty-two-foot Krogen we picked up in Seattle moved only a few knots faster than our sailboat, and we had the comfort of a warm, dry inside helm.

I know some die-hard sailors look down their noses at motorized vessels, but Sharon and I fell in love with the idea of voyaging under power. That's when we hatched the plans for our great five-year getaway.

On the way north that summer, we stopped at Tribune Bay on Hornby Island in British Columbia. Sharon soaked up the sun on its mile-wide white sand beach. While there, we watched a Tibetan monk complete an intricate sand painting at the island's community center. It took him an entire week, and he said it would bless all life on the island. And when he finished, he carefully swept the sand into a container, then poured it into the bay to bless all life under the sea.

Not long after we returned home, Sharon's cancer returned as well. This time with vengeance. It spread fast. And despite all of the treatments doctors offered, Sharon and I knew they were clutching at straws. She faced death like she faced life—head-on. Though we didn't know how long we had together, we planned another cruise to Tribune Bay the following summer. She took bottles of chemo and strong pain medicine with her, which she insisted on injecting herself.

One evening, I sat on the rear deck of the Krogen, while Sharon finished her injections. The sun was setting over the mountains of Vancouver Island, coloring the cliffs surrounding the bay golden. The boat rocked gently. Sharon, her body weak and ravaged, crawled into my lap and said, "Hold me, Charles." And those were the last words she ever spoke. A year after her death, I returned to Tribune Bay alone and spread her ashes over the spot where the monk had blessed the waters.

I blinked tears from my eyes and shook my head. I brought myself back to *Wanderer* and resumed familiarizing myself with her helm instruments as though in two hours Sharon and I would be casting off for our round-the-world cruise.

When I finished with the pilothouse, I climbed down and started at the furthest forward berth, examining every inch of the boat, still saving the "holy place" for last. Finally, I entered the engine room through a hatch at the rear of a small office below decks. I stood agape in front of the cast-iron deity of the boat, a big yellow Caterpillar engine. By the time I walked back through the entryway door, Jeff was walking down the dock toward me.

"Four-thirty," he said. "Time to lock the gates. You ready to make an offer on her, Commander?" He pointed to *Wanderer*.

"I'm ready," I said. "But my bank account isn't."

A peaceful feeling settled over me as I walked back to my car. Sharon would have liked *Wanderer*. Her mother and father came from Louisiana. She spent her summers as a child along the Gulf, watching shrimpers ply the waters. She liked boats because they reminded her of those peaceful, playful times.

I don't know exactly what grabbed me about boats. Maybe I loved them because I grew up along the New Jersey shore, always looking out to the sea for my merchant marine father to come home. Or, maybe it's because a boat lets you reach a distant horizon, and beyond that an adventure into the unknown. I bought the *Noble Lady* not long after Sharon's death. People think I named her after me, but they're wrong. The noble lady was Sharon.

Fifteen minutes after leaving the marina, I walked into the VTS office. A young guard wearing a Department of Homeland Security patch stopped me.

"Business, Sir?"

"Commander Charles Noble, retired, here to see Louis Ng at VTS."

"One moment, Sir," the guard said. He lifted a phone and punched in a few numbers.

"Commander Charles Noble for Mr. Ng," he said. He nodded several times, then finally said, "Yes, Sir," before hanging up.

I emptied my pockets into a plastic tray and the young man waved me through a metal detector. On the other side, I picked up a visitor's tag, which I clipped to my shirt pocket. Stepping off the elevator at the top floor, I pushed through a set of glass doors with a coast guard emblem, and underneath that the words "Puget Sound Vessel Traffic System."

A man in a wheelchair, wearing a red vest and cowboy shirt, rolled up to meet me. He stuck out his hand.

"Commander, nice to see you. But I'm surprised. I heard you were...well, that you'd moved on to calmer waters."

I smiled. "Lou, it's nice to see you too."

"Now that you're a civvie like me, what can I do for you?"

I nodded down the hall. "Can we speak in your office?"

Louis smiled, then twirled the small joystick on his armrest, spinning himself around before shoving the paddle forward. The motor whined as he rolled down the long hallway. At the end of the hallway he made a sharp left, disappearing through an open door.

Louis Ng, a Vietnamese Viet Nam War veteran, had fought with the U.S. and was wounded in the war. He went on to become an air traffic controller. After Ronald Reagan broke the back of the air traffic controllers' union, Louis joined the Coast Guard as a civilian employee, where he worked his way up to manage the Puget Sound Vessel Traffic System.

By the time I turned into his office, Louis had a telephone to his ear, explaining to one of his controllers the intricacies of the new rules for coast guard boarding of foreign vessels entering United States waters. I closed the door behind me and took a seat. Behind Louis, the downtown Seattle waterfront glowed orange in the dying rays of the sun. He hung up the telephone and rested his elbows on his desk.

"Two weeks ago, the CG intercepted a trawler headed toward Cherry Point—"

"About eight-thirty at night," Louis said. "One of my controllers had been tracking it for an hour before he called in a request for a visual. It didn't respond to VHF hails. And when the CG boarded they found it on autopilot with explosives aboard."

"Obviously you know the vessel I'm talking about."

"Know it? Do you know how many requests I've had for the archived data of that night?"

"Lemme guess. FBI. ATF. DHS. CGI."

Louis laughed. "That's just the beginning. Agencies with acronyms I've never heard of before."

"Who thought Homeland Security would streamline things?"

"Not me," Louis said. "Anyway, what's your interest?"

"I'm trying to restart life as a private investigator, and the boat owner's ex-wife asked me to find him."

"You and everyone else are after that guy. And I bet you want to see the archived radar data for that night?"

"Right."

"And you know that showing it to you could cost me my job."

"Right."

"But you think you're my friend?"

"Right.

"And you're hoping that counts for something."

"Right again."

"Wrong," Louis said.

I sucked in a breath. Louis frowned, then lowered his head to his computer, typing furiously, moving the mouse around, clicking.

"Loi?" I called him by his real name. He used Louis or Lou, to make it easier on the rest of us.

He looked up from the keyboard. His wrinkled face softened and he laughed. "It counts for a lot. Pull a chair up. I'll show you what I've got."

I dragged my chair around to Louis's side of the desk. He already had a screen full of radar images.

"This is the package I've been sending out to the agencies. I can't let you have one, but I can let you look at it here with me. They're fifteen-minute intervals from six thirty that evening until nine." He clicked on the first image, enlarging the green-on-black window until it occupied his entire screen. "Nothing here. At least not our boat." He pointed to the top of the image. "That's a southbound tanker, about to make the turn at Saturna Island then head down Boundary Pass for Haro Strait and the Strait of Juan de Fuca."

He clicked through three more images, which showed essentially the same thing. "Here," he pointed to a bright green dot in the middle of the screen of the next image. "Our vessel's just uncovered from the radar shadow of Waldron Island, moving along Boundary Pass headed for the Strait of Georgia." He clicked through several more images that showed the green dot moving toward Cherry Point, then another green dot moving rapidly up Hale Passage to intercept it. "And that's the show." He held up his hands.

"There's not much that's interesting there," I said.

"No," Louis said. "Why?"

He looked at me like a schoolteacher challenging his class.

"'Cause it's where the vessel came from that's important. We all know where it was headed."

He whipped his index finger at me. "Right."

"So call CVTS and see if the Canadians have a record of it, before our system picked it up."

Louis grimaced. "That's exactly what I would have done," he said. "But that's what's so strange. Day after all this broke and every agency in the federal government was clamoring for radar recordings, I got a visit from the 'Old Man'—"

"Ritchie? Here?"

"Uh huh. Sitting in the same chair you are. And he told me point blank that I was not to make contact with CVTS or Canadian Customs on behalf of any government agency, including any branches of the Coast Guard."

"And so you didn't."

"Who'd dare disobey an order from Vin Ritchie?"

I raised my hand.

"And look where it got you."

Louis hit a key and, without speaking, pointed to the screen. He put his finger to his lips, and with the other hand clicked through several radar images. The Canadian VTS images had a red, maple leaf icon in the upper right hand corner; the American images, a U.S. flag in the bottom left-hand corner. Louis clicked through them slowly again. I checked the timestamps. He had us traveling backward in time, and the green dot of Atherton's boat on the American images matched perfectly with a green dot picked up by Canadian radar.

Then he scrolled further back in the Canadian images, pointing to the upper portion of the screen where another green dot came across the screen from the Canadian Gulf Islands until it intercepted Thomas Atherton's green dot, then fifteen minutes later it traveled back from where it came. Louis smiled, then clicked in a corner of his screen and it went blank.

"Have you had dinner, Commander?" he said.

"No, I haven't."

"Do you want to grab a bite along the pier?"

"Love to."

◎   ◎   ◎

LOUIS AND I SAT at a table with a commanding waterfront view. Two lighted ferryboats crisscrossed each other's path.

"Ferryboat captain for a day," I said. "That'd be my dream."

Louis looked at me, then out at the ferries. "Walk-on passenger," he said. "That'd be mine."

I nodded. "Mine for you too."

I ordered crab cakes. Louis ordered baked halibut.

"Minh Thi was very happy to receive your birthday card. She misses the days when you came to visit us regularly."

I loved being with Louis out of the office. When he relaxed and dropped that monotone, all-American vessel controller's voice, you heard his native land permeate his words, which rolled off his tongue with a mellifluous, hypnotic ring as though a Buddhist monk tapped lightly on a prayer bell to coax each word out.

"It has been a long time. Too long. I'm closer now, starting to settle in. I will drive down to see you and Minh Thi."

"And it's good for you in Bellingham?"

"It's different. A slower pace. Not like the hectic days when we first met."

Louis chuckled. "Those first few weeks after 9/11. My God, more meetings scheduled than hours in the day to have them."

"Everyone worried about the next threat," I said.

"And not from al Qaeda," Louis said. "But from a redrawn organizational chart of Homeland Security that carved out portions of their turf for someone else."

The waiter set down a basket of steaming warm bread next to a plate of olive oil and balsamic vinegar encircled by a thin layer of coarse salt crystals. I reached for a slice of bread.

"Right. And there you and I were, championing a "go slow" approach based on reason and assessment. People looked at us like we were from Mars."

Louis grabbed some bread as well.

"A black man and a paraplegic Vietnamese man, both working for the Coast Guard. We might as well have been from Mars."

We laughed, then sopped oil and vinegar with our bread.

"Looks like you're on your first case," Louis said. "That's exciting. Will it work out for you?"

"The case?"

"No, being an investigator."

I shrugged. "I don't know. It's not what I thought I'd be doing at this point in my life. I'm not sure it's what I should be doing. But I need the work."

Louis's gentle nod and serene smile recalled a benediction. "When I was a boy in Viet Nam, a Buddhist monk named Bichu was a frequent dinner guest at our house. He never tired of saying, 'Only when you surrender to change, do you become steady.'"

The waiter set down our plates. I thought about the monk's saying while Louis started into his baked halibut. "Bichu sounds like a wise man," I said, before starting into my crab cakes.

Midway through his dinner, Louis set his fork down. "What'd you make of those Canadian radar recordings?" he asked.

"Boat left Canada," I said. "Then made the short crossing over Boundary Pass to the American side, where it intercepted

Atherton's boat. Then it returned to Canada. Looked like it came from Bedwell Harbor on South Pender Island."

"You're good," Louis said. "And Canadian customs had no record of it leaving or re-entering their waters."

"You called?" I asked.

"Not exactly. I had someone who worked for me call."

"Ah hah. Plausible deniability in case Ritchie found out." Louis winked.

"What size boat would you make that out to be?" I asked.

"Small but fast. I measured its speed. Not that anyone asked me to. Twenty knots."

"Now if I only had a connection to NSA."

"Why?"

"For a satellite image of the passengers on that small boat."

"Do you have any ideas?"

"It could be an ecoterrorist group."

"The Ocean Liberation Front?" Louis asked.

I nodded. "You're all over this. Maybe we should trade places. I'll do VTS, you'll be a private investigator."

"Trade places?" Louis shook his head and gave me a gentle smile. "I don't think you'd like being confined to a wheelchair."

"Sorry," I said. "Why do you think the Old Man forbade you from disseminating the Canadian data in the first place?"

"He said it was a matter of national security."

"When Ritchie takes a dump he claims it's a matter of national security. My guess is that he's already seen the Canadian radar data, but he doesn't want his rivals to see it. CGI. FBI. ATF. DHS. The glory goes to whoever captures those responsible for that bomb-rigged Grand Banks. And Ritchie does not like it when the glory goes to someone else."

I sank into the plush couch, staring out the massive picture window at a view of Bellingham Bay framed by two tall cedar trees at the end of a gently sloping, deep green, manicured lawn. Fresh red roses were arranged in a white porcelain vase atop the dark wood of a baby grand piano across the room from me. A subtle sweet floral scent wafted through the air. I rested a hand on my guitar case. A door opened somewhere down the hallway and footsteps shuffled over the carpet toward me.

"Ah, Mr. Noble," Frederico Oller said, "It's a pleasure to meet you, and to welcome you to my daughter's lovely home."

Oller extended a hand to me. He was short and thin. His olive-colored skin glowed, sagging ever so slightly around his jowls. I put him in his mid-seventies, or even older. He wore a dark suit, and a white shirt with a narrow tie.

"Thank you," I said, shaking his hand and feeling the muscles beneath the soft flesh of his palms.

"Please," he gestured toward the staircase. "My daughter is kind enough to give me a studio downstairs. While she teaches at the university, I teach here."

His dark eyes twinkled. I picked up my guitar case and followed the scent of his cologne, which trailed behind him as we descended the staircase. He opened the door to a small room where a large floor-to-ceiling window looked out on a grove of fir trees whose cones littered the ground. An old, framed photograph of a young Mr. Oller playing (yes, playing) with a young Andrés Segovia hung on the wall, amidst a collection of certificates, diplomas, and awards, most in Spanish. Two chairs, two music stands, and two footstools occupied the center of the small room. I didn't see Mr. Oller's guitar or case.

"Please, sit," he said.

I did, and I opened my guitar case. He pointed to my guitar with an open hand and said, "Please, play."

I pulled out my guitar, plucking each string, then tuning it. Everything about this man was formal, yet cordial. I had the sense of being transported several decades back in time, and a continent away. I could have easily imagined myself not in Bellingham, but in some small villa along the Costa Brava in Spain.

I played what I still could play moderately well. *Lagrima*, a Bach boureé, a piece by Villa-Lobos. As long as I didn't try too hard, my fingers seemed to have a memory of their own and I made it through each work. Mr. Oller cocked his head slightly, watching my fingers, listening, it seemed, with his entire body. After I finished my small repertoire, I set my guitar across my lap. He shook his head. I looked up at the picture of him with Segovia and braced for the bad news.

"No," he said. "Play. Not what you know, but what you are least sure of."

So I picked up my guitar again and started into the Prelude from the first Bach cello suite. Mr. Oller's face lit up, and when I stumbled at the passage that gave me fits, he smiled even more. I backed up to start again, but he rested his hand gently on my knee.

"Thank you," he said. "Now I understand why you are here." He squinted at me. "Your heart yearns." He touched his chest.

"Your hands are ready." He held up his hands. "But your head is unsure whether you can do this. So we have to practice here." He tapped his head. "As well as here." He held up his hands. "So your head allows your hands to express what is in your heart."

He stood up and went to a closet, where he rummaged around and emerged with a tattered, yellow piece of music. He set an old copy of the Prelude on my music stand, pointed to the first three measures, and said, "Please, play only these. And when you are finished, play them over again."

Mr. Oller didn't say much. While I played, he touched my shoulders to relax them, asked me to breathe deeply, to focus on my posture, to be aware of my arms, my legs, and my feet. Then, he rested his hand on my knee. I stopped playing, and he said, "Thank you. We can have another lesson next week, at the same time."

I placed my guitar in its case and reached into my pocket for my wallet, but Mr. Oller waved me off. "No," he said. "Please, you cannot pay for the first lesson, but you can pay next week for whatever benefits this lesson has brought. That way, you will always be paying for what you have gained, and not for my time."

He escorted me upstairs and to the front door. The whole lesson had consisted of only three measures, but I learned more than I had in the last six months of practicing on my own. And I left feeling that I'd received not only a lesson in music, but also a gracious lesson in life.

◎   ◎   ◎

BACK AT THE *Noble Lady*, I called Janet on my cell phone.

"Do you have time for lunch today?" I asked.

She sounded surprised. "So soon? Is this for business or pleasure?"

"For lunch," I said. "I've got more questions about Thomas."

"Oh," she said. "I see your investigation is proceeding. I'll have to take a rain check on lunch. I'm too busy right now, but how about a walk later?"

"I could use the exercise. When? Where?"

"I can get away from the gallery and meet you at three. As to where, it depends on what shape you're in."

"Excellent."

She laughed. "Then I'll meet you at the Cedar and Pine Lakes trailhead at three."

Janet gave me directions to the trailhead, which I wrote on a slip of paper and duct-taped next to her telephone number on the porthole. I made a smoothie for lunch, then headed off to the university to find Matthew Voltmann. I checked in with Myra in Richard Collingsworth's office, who informed me that Matthew was teaching an undergraduate class in marine invertebrate biology. As I turned to leave, Collingsworth stuck his head out from his office.

He sneered. "You again? What now?"

Myra chimed in a cheery voice, "He's here to see Matthew Voltmann."

I wished she hadn't.

Collingsworth's face reddened. He stepped out of the office and pointed a finger at me. "You listen to me, Mr....Mr. Nobel."

"Noble," I said.

"You leave our students alone. Do you understand? If I hear that you're harassing them, I'll have security arrest you the next time you set foot on this campus."

I didn't respond, instead I slipped out of the office and left him standing there in the middle of his snit. I'm sure Collingsworth didn't play the guitar, but he still could use a lesson or two in graciousness from Frederico Oller.

The door on the first floor of the Huxley College building opened with a loud clunk. I found myself in a windowless lecture hall shaped like a small amphitheater that sloped down to where Matthew Voltmann stood in front of his class. He looked up and threw a sideways glance my way. About fifty students occupied the front rows. Several students also turned around and scowled but most stared in rapt attention at the young man in blue jeans, with a long, dark ponytail, lecturing to them. I slipped into a seat in the last row, which reminded me of watching a basketball game from the nosebleed section.

Matthew Voltmann stood in front of a long blackboard. In big letters on the middle section he'd written the words, "The Sex Life of Amphipods." Ah hah. Perhaps that's why the students were so attentive.

"Now let's look at the slides," he said.

Magically, a screen dropped down, the lights dimmed and a picture of two critters that looked like translucent shrimp appeared. One was twice the size of the other. The large one wrapped the smaller one in its finely serrated appendages, so together they looked like a small "c" nestled inside a big one.

"This is a slide of two amphipods mating," Matthew said. "They're tiny. The male, the larger one on this slide, is only two millimeters long, less than a tenth of an inch. The female, one-millimeter. When a male matures sexually, his eyes bulge from his antennae, his chemoreceptors swell, and he swims around looking for females."

It sounded to me like a pretty fair description of teenage boys.

"The male then grasps a female between his legs, and they swim around entwined for several days until she molts, exposing her genital duct into which he deposits his sperm."

Suddenly, the lights flashed on. Matthew raised his voice. "There are billions and billions of these critters." The b's exploded from his mouth. "The reproductive cycle follows the growth cycle of their nutrients, mainly phytoplankton. At any one time, a number of different amphipod species are probably mating at different ocean depths. In other words, sex is going on in the ocean billions and billions of times every moment. Think about that the next time you go swimming."

Or boating. Okay, now Matthew had me listening with rapt attention too. He went on to talk about phytoplankton, tiny one-celled organisms like algae that produce up to 50 percent of the oxygen we breathe. Then he flung his arm out and pointed to a wall, I guess since there weren't any windows.

"Our orcas are impressive," he said. "But without the salmon, we wouldn't have orcas. And without the herring we wouldn't have salmon. And without the amphipods we wouldn't have herring. And without the phytoplankton we wouldn't have amphipods. So next time you see an orca or have a baked salmon dinner, say a prayer for these lowly little critters, the amphipods and the phytoplankton they feed on, because they *are* the basis of life in the oceans and on this planet. And if we don't protect our oceans, tiny microscopic life will falter, and with it the rest of life."

He slapped his hands together in front of his chest, and held them there in what looked like an Eastern prayer gesture.

"Don't forget, a summary of the reading assignment is due two classes from now." His hand somersaulted twice in the air. "I guess that's it for today."

The class applauded, and I found myself joining in. Atherton wasn't the only one at Huxley who gave a great performance in front of a class. It escaped me why Bucky referred to him as an "ecogeek." I waited until the lecture hall emptied, then I skipped down the steps toward the front. Matthew had dreamy dark eyes and a single dimple above his chin. I'd estimate three-quarters of the class were female. There could be other reasons he held them in rapt attention as well.

"Auditing?" he asked.

"No. But you sure make something as arcane as the sex life of amphipods sound more interesting than the sex life of Britney Spears."

He chuckled, then sized me up with a quick glance. "Oh, you're here about Thomas aren't you? Mr....Pride?"

"Noble," I said. "I see my good name travels quickly."

"Bucky told me she met you at the lab yesterday." He stuffed a file folder full of notes into his backpack. "She said you're working for Janet."

"I am."

"How convenient."

"For whom?"

"Her."

"How so?"

"Hiring you draws suspicion away from her."

"You think she had something to do with Thomas Atherton's disappearance?"

"She did leave on the boat with him. She returned but he didn't. You don't need a PhD or even a Master's to figure that she had something to do with it."

He was about to sling his backpack onto his shoulder, when I asked, "Have you got a minute?"

"Not much longer," he said. "I'm a grad student. I need to spend most of the morning squinting into a microscope at copepods."

"What?"

"Horny little critters. Cousins to these amphipods."

"Horny?"

Matthew smiled. He laid his backpack on a front row seat. "Not like that." He slid his curled index fingers up along the sides of his head. "Like this."

"What's the Ocean Liberation Front? And why do they contact you?"

He shook his head slowly. "The Ocean Liberation Front is a spin-off of the Earth Liberation Front."

"The group that bombs SUV dealerships, sets fire to luxury homes, damages genetically engineered crops, and otherwise destroys property in the name of protecting the earth?"

"They call it 'direct action.'"

"Most people call it terrorism."

"Only, one person's terrorist is another person's hero."

"So the Ocean Liberation Front takes direct action against targets they consider to be damaging the marine environment?"

"Yes," Matthew said. "Like factories that pollute. Ships that dump sewage. Boats that overfish."

"Or companies that build undersea pipelines?"

"Perhaps. Like I told the FBI, ATF, DHS, etc., etc. The OLF never contacted me after Thomas's boat was discovered."

"Doesn't mean they didn't do it."

"Of course. But it doesn't mean they did."

"How do they make contact? And why you?"

"I'll go to retrieve my e-mail messages and find an anonymous one from the OLF, claiming responsibility for a direct action."

"But an e-mail message is pretty easily traced."

Matthew shook his head. "Sure. And I tried to. I'm good. The FBI's good. But so is the OLF. All of their messages are routed through a random string of anonymous proxy servers. It's like trying to track down the origin of a speck of dust that landed on your desk. It can't be done. Why they chose me? I don't know."

"Maybe someone heard you lecture about the sex life of amphipods and got excited."

"Maybe." He reached for his backpack.

"What about Thomas Atherton's data on the herring bio-assay? It's missing?"

"It went missing every night," Matthew said.

"What do you mean?"

"Thomas stored it on a special CD that he took home with him each night. I think he slept with that disk under his pillow so it wouldn't leave his side."

"He must have made a backup copy."

"I'm sure he did, but he didn't tell any of us grunts about it."

"You think he took the disk with him when he left on the boat?"

"I don't know."

"And the final results of the bioassays?"

"He kept those pretty close too. The prelims looked positive for industrial pollutant contamination. Maybe enough to support a shutdown of pipeline construction."

Matthew swung his ponytail out of the way, then hoisted his backpack over one shoulder. He started up the steps and I followed behind him.

"Was Thomas Atherton opposed to the pipeline?"

Matthew stopped and spun around. "Opposed to the pipeline?" He sounded as though I'd asked an insane question. "In 1973, Cherry Point had 15,000 tons of herring. This year, only 1,600 tons. That's a 90 percent decline. At that rate, they'll disappear soon, with ramifications up and down the food chain."

I glanced back at the blackboard. "Phytoplankton to amphipods to herring to salmon to orca," I said.

"That's just the beginning. Of course Thomas was opposed to the pipeline."

"Enough to blow it up?"

"The pipeline needs to be stopped." Matthew's voice rose.

"By any means necessary?" I asked.

When I looked into his eyes, the passion seemed to have turned to fire.

"It needs to be stopped. Now, Mr. Noble, my critters are calling me."

He shouldered his way out the lecture hall door.

Good cop, bad cop. Threaten with one hand, hold out an olive branch of reason with the other. Were Thomas Atherton and Matthew Voltmann the equivalent of environmental good cops, while the OLF were the bad ones? All still working on the same team?

Over the marina, the sky had turned a moody gray. Flags and windsocks on the masts and stays of sailboats stood at attention pointing northeast, which meant the wind had changed direction and now blew from the southwest, ushering in a front. I slipped out of my jeans and tennis shoes and into my black jogging outfit: pants, polypro shirt, running shoes. I also pulled a lightweight rain jacket from my locker.

I hopped into my car and wove my way through town to get to the Cedar and Pine Lakes trailhead, nestled in a valley at the base of the mountain range flanking the southern border of Bellingham. At the head of the parking lot, Janet stretched in front of a gray hybrid vehicle that must have pleased Atherton and his environmental groupies. I stopped next to her and checked out her attire. She'd dressed for serious hiking: heavy boots, trail pants, and a water bottle hanging from her fanny pack. I got out and joined her to the sounds of a babbling brook. Above us, a layer of fog settled in the higher branches of the trees.

I bent forward and touched my toes. "I thought we were going for a walk, not an ascent of Mount Everest."

She smiled mischievously. "You said you were in excellent shape, and this is a walk for people in excellent shape."

I leaned against the front of her car, grabbed an ankle, then pulled my legs alternately up behind me to stretch my quads. Janet stretched her legs so wide, she almost sank into a split. Then she stretched her arms over her head and bent sideways.

"Ready?" she asked.

"Almost," I said.

She walked around the gravel lot while I finished stretching, then we walked over to the trailhead, marked by a huge concrete block with the trail painted on it. It didn't look too bad: switchbacks in the beginning, then a straight section that split, one trail going from there to either of two lakes. But a few feet beyond the trailhead, the incline shot straight up, and I bet we hadn't gone more than fifty yards when I turned around and looked down on our cars a hundred feet below us.

"Hell of an elevation gain," I said.

"Steepest in the county. Mountain climbers use it to train."

I hadn't dressed for the occasion. I was already breathing hard by the time we rounded the first switchback, and while the second didn't look all that far away, I had to raise my head pretty high to see it.

"You sounded like you needed to talk," Janet said.

"I do. Did you go out on the boat with Thomas the night he disappeared?"

Janet didn't say anything, but she did pick up her pace. My thighs burned even more just watching her glide up the trail. She waited for me at the next switchback, bent over at her waist, hands propped on her legs. She breathed hard, vapor from her mouth mixing with the thickening fog.

"Where'd you hear that from?"

"From Melissa Buchanan—"

"The little bitch, she—"

"Also Matthew Voltmann."

"Thomas's dwarves."

"Did you leave with Thomas?"

She sucked in a breath, then started off again. "Yes. I did go out with Thomas."

I forced myself to catch up with her, grabbed her by the shoulder and held her back from walking. I slid around in front of her, leaning backward up the incline. "Why the hell'd you hire me, if you went out with him that night? Did you help him set the boat on autopilot, then escape to Canada?"

She shook free of my grip. "Canada? What the hell are you talking about?"

"I'm talking about I don't like being set up, and that's what seems to be happening here. I think you must already know where he is and you hired me to divert attention from you."

"Well, then I guess congratulations are in order, for you've solved your first case and it only took you twenty-four hours. You can turn around and go home now."

"I will unless you tell me the truth about that night."

Her eyes had tears. "I hired you to find Thomas," she said. "And you're wasting your time with me based on what his goddamn grad students said."

I shook my head, turned around and started down the hill. I didn't look back. What a relief it was to walk down. I neared the lower switchback, when I heard Janet call out.

"Wait, I'll tell you."

Damn. That meant I'd have to slog uphill again. When I got back to Janet, I was breathing hard. I looked for a place to sit, but nothing seemed inviting.

"There's a flat part just around the next switchback," she said. "We can sit there."

I had to will my legs to take each step, but we finally climbed to a flat part of the trail and found a fallen log to sit on.

Janet stared at the ground, picked up a stick, and began tracing random patterns in the dirt. "Thomas was very agitated that day. Something big was up with his herring study, but he wouldn't tell me anything other than he needed to attend a meeting without others knowing. He asked for my help, and I agreed. So, late in the afternoon, we went down to the dock together, just like we used to when we'd go out on a trip. Thomas was tight-lipped. He wouldn't say where we were going or why."

"And you let him get away with that?"

She tapped a rhythm on the log with the stick. "Look, by agreeing to help him, I agreed to his terms. We left the marina, but not very long after the breakwater he stopped the boat, lowered the dinghy and asked me to take it back in, then to have dinner alone at one of the marina restaurants. If anyone saw me, I was to say that I felt sick and decided not to go with him. And if they asked about Thomas without his dinghy, I was to say that he had a kayak aboard."

"That's a strange request."

She flexed the stick between both hands. "Damn strange. But Thomas was nothing if not eccentric. He said he was trying to make it seem as though he and I were going out on an ordinary cruise. Maybe he thought someone was watching him. Maybe he wanted to escape from his grad students. Who knows? Anyway, I did as he asked. I motored in with the dinghy, pulled it up to a dock, and had dinner alone at the Marina Restaurant. After I ate, I brought the dinghy back to the empty slip. We often left it at the marina when we went out with our kayaks, so it wouldn't have looked strange." A few tears rolled off her cheeks. "The next morning I read that his boat was found heading for the refinery without him aboard."

"Didn't the FBI and the police question you?"

"Yes. I just didn't tell them the whole truth. I told them I went down to the boat with Thomas, but that I decided not to go out."

"And when they checked with the restaurant and your credit card company, they found your alibi held up."

She went back to tracing patterns in the dirt. "Yes."

"Did you run into Bucky or Matthew that night?"

"No."

"Then how'd they know that you left with Thomas?"

She snapped the stick in two, flinging both halves into the brush. "You should have asked them that before you asked me."

"You can be sure I'll ask them now. Is your dinghy still in the slip?"

"No. The Coast Guard towed it away as evidence. It's with the *Gaia Goddess* at their dock. That's the truth. That's what happened. That's why I got in touch with you. Thomas cruised off to a meeting from which he never returned."

"Did he ever spend time in Canada?"

"We cruised in the Gulf Islands, if that's what you mean."

"Did he have friends there? People he knew or visited?"

"He went over to Vancouver Island several times to speak to the Friends of Georgia Strait, a group that's leading the opposition to the pipeline from the Canadian side."

"Are they like the OLF? They'll blow up things if they don't get their way?"

"I don't know much about FOGS, but I've never heard of them committing violent acts. What makes you think that Thomas went to Canada?"

"It's the closest location to where VTS radar first picked up his boat." I didn't think it wise to say anything yet about the boat Canadian radar picked up intercepting his Grand Banks.

"What I don't understand is why Thomas would run. He had too much to lose back here—his job, his students, his friends. He was passionate and impulsive, but not like this."

"Assuming he ran," I said.

Janet snapped her head around. "What are you saying?"

"I don't know. In fact, the more I dig into this case, the more I don't know." I stood up and brushed bark from my pants. I pointed to the trail. "How far along are we?"

"About halfway to the halfway point."

"Hmmm. Does it stay flat from here?"

"Right." Janet laughed half-heartedly. With her arm, she gestured around the nearby area. "This is just a tease that makes you think the worst is over."

"Let's make it to the halfway point, and see about going on from there," I said.

She offered me her hand, and I pulled her up from the log. "Once I start up this trail I never stop," she said. "It's far too tempting to turn around and head back down. I'm worried. You think Thomas might have fled to Canada?"

"I don't know, but it's something I intend to find out."

Not long after we started walking again, the trail rose up and around a switchback, then it took off steeply. Two switchbacks later, we walked along the side of a cascading stream until we swung around the next switchback, which had me on my toes to make the steep grade.

"This is the push before the halfway point," Janet said. "We can rest there."

"Tell that to my knees and legs again," I said. "They don't believe you."

Orange cedar needles littered the trail before us, and a spicy sweet smell filled the air. I leaned forward into the steep grade, which seemed to make walking easier. And just when I thought I couldn't take another step, the trail crested, then settled out. A small tuft of fog hung over a sign high up on a Douglas fir that read, "Cedar Lake, 1.0 mi. Pine Lake, 1.2 mi." The arrow pointed left. I stumbled toward a cut log with a smooth surface worn on top, which looked like it had served as a resting stop for many other weary hikers. Janet didn't appear too winded.

"Do you do this trail often?" My words snuck out between breaths.

"Three times a week. If I don't I get out of shape like that." She snapped her fingers. "And I have to work my way up to this from the baby trails again."

Janet handed me her water bottle. I took a swig.

"Do you have any idea what that meeting was about? Or who it was with?" I asked.

"No, I don't. Maybe he was meeting with the OLF?"

"And they decided to send a boat to bomb Cherry Point? Loading a boat with explosives then setting it on autopilot heading for a target could make for an inexpensive, poor man's 'smart torpedo.' But a lot could also go wrong: Autopilot steering. Vessel speed. What did your Grand Banks do, eight knots? Damn slow torpedo. GPS acquisition. Other vessels in the way? The fact that, using GPS alone, you could not reliably hit targets other than those permanently onshore."

"But you're saying it could be done?"

"Sure, and Coast Guard Intelligence has gamed the scenario. In fact it's one of Vin Ritchie's personal obsessions."

"Who's he?"

"The district commander for this region. I'm sure he has nightmares of a flotilla of GBs loaded with explosives, heading for us under autopilot on different courses to hit different targets. On a scale of one to ten, ten being most likely, I'd rate an attack by a trawler under autopilot at two or less. He'd rate it at nine or ten, which is why he's still the district CO, and I'm in civvies struggling up this hill."

"I don't follow you."

Without going into detail, I told Janet how my disagreement with the Admiral cost me my career.

She touched my arm softly. "I'm sorry," she said.

"I'm trying to look on the bright side. Being squeezed out forced me to determine what I wanted to do after the Coast Guard, and act on my plans."

"Being a private investigator?" She sounded incredulous.

"No, circumnavigating the world. Being a private investigator for several years is just a means to an end."

She sighed. "Thomas and I talked about circumnavigating too. We—"

First came a chuff, then a small puff of air, then a dull thud between us. A few pieces of wood flew into the air. Instinctively, I fell backwards, wrapping my arm around Janet as I did and yanking her down behind the log.

"Someone just shot at us," I said.

Janet's eyes flashed wide. She gripped my arm but she said nothing.

I pushed Janet down into the dirt behind the log, and fell on top of her.

"Are you hit?" I asked.

She stared at me with glazed eyes and a chill ran through me. She shook her head rapidly as though she had a tremor.

"No," she said. "I don't think so."

I propped her against the log with her head down, then I joined her. Another muffled crack sounded through the woods. Janet sucked in a breath and her body stiffened. The bullet whizzed off the log, grazing the top, showering wood dust on us. I grasped Janet's leg.

"We can get out of this, but I need your help."

I patted my pockets. Damn. I'd left my cell phone on the boat.

"Do you have your cell phone?"

She looked into her fanny pack, then sighed. "No," she said. "It's in my car."

The gunman sent a volley of bullets over our heads. Some crashed into the log, vibrating it against my body. A few hit the trees and the ground behind us. Janet closed her eyes and her body trembled. Her faced looked ashen.

"What do you need me to do?" she asked. Her voice sounded feeble.

I twisted around, then peeked over the log in the direction of the shots. On the other side of the trail, a wide gully dropped down to the stream we'd walked along. A high, wooded ridge rose from the other side of the stream, providing a gunman with a likely perch. Around us, fog drifted through the trees, like a sea of ghosts floating through an uneasy stillness. Then another gunshot broke the silence of the woods, this one raining down leaves and a few branches from above our heads. I touched Janet's chin, gently turning her head to face me.

I pointed to my lips. "Tune out the gunfire and focus on the sound of my voice."

I pointed to my lips again. She nodded slowly.

"He's aiming too high. The fog's making it difficult for him to see, or maybe he's just trying to scare us."

"Well, I'm scared," Janet said.

I pointed ahead to a path that disappeared into the brush, away from the log and the gunfire. "Where does that lead?"

"Umm." Janet closed her eyes and bit her lips.

A bullet whistled through the air above us. She arched back into the log. I shook her gently, and she opened her eyes.

"My voice," I said, pointing to my lips. "Tell me where that path leads."

In a breathy voice, she said, "To a…to a bluff, a lookout point over the bay and the city."

"If we take it, can we cut back to the main trail?"

"I…I think so."

I gripped her shoulder. "Look, we can get out of here without getting hurt, but you have to follow my instructions, okay?"

She nodded.

"When I tell you, I want you to kiss the ground, keep your butt down, and crawl to that big tree over there." I pointed to a Douglas fir. "Do you understand?"

"Yes," she said.

I watched the wispy fog swirl through the woods. The gunman fired on us again, and the moment the volley ended, I pushed Janet from the log.

"Now. Kiss the ground. Butt down. Crawl to that tree. I'll be right behind you."

She hesitated. I pushed harder. Finally, she moved away from the log.

"Kiss the ground."

She dropped to her belly and slithered in the dirt. I waited until she made it to the tree. After she got there, she rose to her knees and looked at me with saucer eyes. Gunfire erupted again. I tamped the air furiously with my hand, and Janet dropped to the ground. When the next round of shots subsided, I dove to the earth and snaked my way toward her. Breathing hard, we both propped our backs against the tree, but it didn't provide us with enough cover, especially if the fog lifted and that gunman had a telescopic sight.

"We can't stay here now," I said. "We've got to keep moving. You've got to get us back down to the trail."

Janet closed her eyes and sucked in a breath. Then she hit the ground and crawled through cedar needles. I followed her. The gunman must have seen us moving. I looked toward the ridge, where a bright flash broke through the fog, then a hail of bullets whined by overhead.

"Just keep moving," I said.

Fifty yards into the woods, Janet turned right. "If we go any further, we'll put too many small hills between the trail and us," she said.

"Okay," I said. "I'm following you."

Up ahead a fallen cedar tree blocked our way, apparently snapped by high winds. We crawled through a tangle of sharp branches and needles, with the scent of cedar in the air. Around us, clear patches had opened in the fog. Suddenly, Janet stopped.

"It's a straight drop down to the trail," she said.

We'd come to the edge of a ridge. I crawled up to her and looked over and down to the trail—only thirty feet below us but too far to jump. Twenty yards away, another fallen cedar tree stretched its limbs out over the edge, with one large branch dangling down. It looked strong enough to hold our weight. I pointed to the branch.

"Let's swing down from that branch."

Janet led the way. But moving through leaves and downed branches must have telegraphed our location. The gunman opened fire, two shots whistling above us. Janet froze. I crawled up to her.

"He's shooting at sound," I said. "It makes a lousy target in the fog."

When she got to the branch, Janet hesitated again. I caught up to her and looked down at a twenty-foot drop, which still seemed formidable.

"The branch'll bend under your weight," I said. "We'll both climb out and that'll help it bend more."

We had to hurry because the fog had turned into a wispy smoke.

"You'll have to go upside down, hold on with your hands, wrap your legs around the branch and work your way out," I said.

Janet looked back at me.

"It's like the monkey bars when you were a kid," I said.

She didn't complain. She grabbed onto the branch, swung herself down and slowly shimmied forward. She'd made it a quarter of the way out when I swung beneath the branch, which groaned under our bodies. A sharp crack followed. I looked back to see the branch beginning to splinter. Then another crack, this one muffled and followed by the ping of a bullet ricocheting off rock. The tree limb cracked again, dropping us further toward the ground.

"Swing down and jump now," I said. "Tuck and roll when you hit."

Janet let go and landed like a paratrooper finishing off a jump. But the branch snapped back, jerking me upward, then down, cracking and splintering further. I held on as several more bullets whined through the air near me. Another sharp crack said the branch was about to give way. I swung down, letting myself fall, then rolling out of the way as the large limb thwacked the ground. I scrambled to my feet and shoved Janet ahead.

"Go. Go."

Shots peppered the ground near where the branch hit.

The ridge with the gunman paralleled the trail, and the further down the trail Janet and I ran the more the fog lifted. On the other side of the stream, I could hear the gunman moving through the brush, stalking us. Past the next switchback, I could see a shaft of sunlight stabbing through the trees. We'd be in the open once we got there. I called to Janet.

"Stop."

She pulled up at the switchback and looked back. I motioned her down to the ground, and a moment later joined her. We both breathed heavily. She pointed to the brush at the angle of the switchback. "There's an old, overgrown trail that enters this one from over there. It exits much further down, but it'd be out of the line of fire."

"Take it. And when you get to the parking lot call the police on your cell phone."

"By myself? What about you?"

"I don't like being shot at. I'm going find out who that is and why we're in his sights."

"But—"

"Go. Take the path," I said. "If I stay, I'll draw his attention away from you."

Across the gully, the sounds stopped. I pointed to the grassy area at the switchback, and whispered to Janet this time, "Go now. Move as quietly as you can."

I couldn't see a path. But Janet rose and, crouching, ran toward the brush. She looked back once, and I waved her on before she disappeared behind a curtain of green. Then I picked up a small branch and tossed it back up the trail, hoping to draw the gunman's fire there. It worked. The gunman fired a few shots toward the branch. I thought about running back up the trail, crossing over the stream, then coming up behind the gunman. Though it might drive him further along the ridge, where he'd have a better shot at Janet.

I crept back up the trail, found the same branch I'd just thrown, then tossed it from the spot I'd just left. Sure enough, the gunman fired through the fog at it. Then I scooped up one more branch and heaved it down the trail. But I didn't wait for the gunman's fire. I took off, barreling down my side of the ravine and throwing myself against the incline on the other, while the gunman fired at the spot where the branch had landed. I clawed my way to the top of the ridge and dove to the ground, I think before he realized what had happened. But he must have heard me, because several shots whizzed past me as I sank behind a tree trunk.

With the fog still providing some cover, I picked my way through the trees. I heard the gunman coming after me. I got to the other side of the ridge, which dropped off sharply to a tiny lake. I found a large stone, stripped off my jacket and shirt and bundled the stone in them. Then I hurled the stone and my clothes down the incline. I swung under the exposed root system of a nearby cedar.

With little space to stand, I wrapped my fingers around the tough, woody root stems and dug my feet into the eroding soil. Overhead, the gunman shuffled along the ridge. He stopped and fired several shots at my clothes, lying at the bottom near the lake.

"Shit," he said, before he resumed walking my way.

He paused directly above me, his body brushing against the trunk of the cedar tree. He breathed heavily, and under his breath I heard him mutter, "I got you now."

The gunman either knelt or lay down on the ground, because his breathing grew louder, closer to me. I forced myself to breathe as shallowly and quietly as I could. He must have been taking aim, perhaps scanning the area around the lake with his telescopic sight looking for me, because suddenly the rifle barrel came into view. In one quick motion, I let go of a root with one hand and lunged for the barrel, pulling it down, then swinging my other hand around and grabbing hold of it, tugging sharply. He grunted once before we tumbled down the side of the ridge, grappling for the rifle, which flew out of our hands.

We hit a log hard, and we both bounced to our feet, standing on uneven ground that slanted up from where we'd fallen. I dropped into a defensive stance, but so did the stocky man. He had thinning dark hair and intense eyes, which saw prey, not a human being, in front of him.

He turned slightly and kicked to the back of my leg, but the uneven ground threw him off-balance and he couldn't take me down. Instead, the kick sent him almost to his knees. I dove at him and we tumbled further downhill. I had hold of his legs, but he kicked one free and hooked it around my neck. He tried to crank me into a scissor hold with his legs, but I held on to his other leg. The gunman whipped his leg from around my neck, then drove his foot several times into my collarbone like a piston. My body ached, but I ducked low and one of his kicks missed, sending his leg out in space, allowing me to turn him over on his stomach, grab his arm behind him and mount him on his back.

He sent an elbow into my chest that had me gasping for air and reeling backward. Then he pounced on me and dug one knee into my chest, but before he could swing his other leg around to straddle me, I swung my arm up hard into his groin, then grabbed an arm and spun him over. He tried to crawl uphill to gain leverage. I kneed him hard in his tailbone and cranked his arm up his back. He grunted, and his neck turned beet red. I thought about choking him into submission, but I didn't want him unconscious.

I yelled, "Who sent you?"

"Fuck you."

"Not the right answer."

I ratcheted his arm even higher.

"Who do you work for?"

"Fuck you."

"You need to do better than that."

Unfortunately, he did. He swung his free arm over his head and smashed a large stone into my forehead. My head jerked back, and blood splattered over the man. I rolled to one side. The gunman sprang to his feet and dipped a hand into his back pocket, emerging with a small tactical knife.

I arched my back and tried to bounce up, but I was too woozy from the blow to my head. The gunman curled his lips into a smirk as he came at me.

Suddenly, a short, sharp crack, like a handclap, exploded from above. The gunman's eyes flashed wide open and blood gurgled over his bottom lip. The knife fell from his hand. I rolled out of the way as he crumpled to the ground. And when I looked up I saw nothing, but I heard footsteps moving rapidly away from the ridge.

B y the time I made it back down the trail, police cars and a SWAT team van filled the parking lot, red and blue lights flashing. I stumbled, aching and shirtless, toward my car. Two SWAT guys in full battle gear raced over to me, pointing the stubby barrels of automatic rifles at my head and ordering me to kneel and place my hands behind my head. I fell to my knees and interlaced my fingers atop my head. Then, one of the men jerked my hands behind my back.

"You stupid bastards," I said. "I'm the one who was shot at. The guy who did the shooting's up there." I motioned with my head up the mountain.

The SWAT guy cuffed me anyway, yanked me to my feet and frisked me. Then he pushed me toward the gathering of squad cars. A plainclothes detective came over, an older man about my height with gray showing beneath the edges of his cap. The SWAT guys stood behind him.

"Name?"

"Noble. Charles Noble."

He looked back to another squad car, where Janet sat on the back seat with her legs out of the open door, talking to an officer. Then he looked at me, while pointing toward Janet.

"You're...?"

"Yeah," I said. "I'm with her."

"What happened up there?" he asked.

"Take these goddamned cuffs off and maybe I'll tell you."

"Oh," he said. He motioned to the SWAT guys and they unlocked my cuffs without an apology.

"Remind me to return the favor," I said to them as they walked off toward their van. One man turned around and glared.

"What happened?" the detective asked again.

"First, tell me how she is?" I motioned to Janet.

"Shaken up," the detective said. "But she's not hurt."

I told him about the gunman, and the mysterious figure who shot him. He squinted as though finding it hard to believe.

"Who the hell are you?" he asked.

"A private investigator."

"Do you have a license?"

"It's in my car."

We walked over to my car and I reached under the wheel well for my keys, opening the passenger-side door, then popping the glove compartment open. I got out my wallet and handed my license to the detective. He walked quickly back to a squad car and handed the license to someone inside.

I went over to Janet. She gasped when she saw the gash on my forehead, and leaped from the squad car. "My God, you're hurt." She shook her head. "I'm sorry. I'm so sorry. Forget finding Thomas. It's not worth risking your life."

"It's probably not," I said.

We leaned against the police car and talked. The SWAT team eyed us as they milled around their all-black van.

The detective finally came back. "What the hell is a former coast guard commander doing working as a PI?"

"Long story."

"Damn." He squinted. "Name's Ben Conrad," he said. "My kid's in the Coast Guard. Think you can help the SWAT team find where that body was? Chief wants 'em to scour the area for the second shooter."

"With pleasure."

Conrad handed me my license, then led me over to the SWAT team van.

"Listen up," he said. "Commander Noble will instruct you where to find a body up this trail, and the probable direction a second shooter took."

I grinned at the two men who'd handcuffed me, then proceeded to tell the SWAT team approximately how far up the trail they'd find the arrow I'd fashioned from stones, pointing to where the gunman lay. The thought of them climbing that steep trail in all their gear was satisfaction enough for the rough handling they'd given me. After I finished, I turned to Conrad.

"Am I free to go?"

"Yeah. But I could use you to stop by the station tomorrow to complete an incident report."

"I'll do that. Do you need Janet any longer?"

"Nah, we already took a statement from her."

I strolled back toward the car.

"Commander."

I turned to see the Conrad still squinting.

"Sorry. Those SWAT guys don't always play by the rules."

"Racial profiling?"

"Probably. We don't see many black PIs up this way."

"You'd better get used to it."

"Hope you're not the kind of guy who attracts lots of dead bodies?" He smiled.

"I hope I'm not either."

Janet was now leaning against her car.

"We're free to go," I said.

"I need a bath, and a stiff drink," she said. "How about you?"

"A bath sounds great, but—"

"But you don't have one on your boat," she said. "You can come over and use mine."

I smiled. "I started to say…but I'll settle for a hot shower."

"Oh." Her face flushed, and she looked away.

"Do you want me to follow you home?" I asked.

"No. I think I can make it now. But I want to thank you for what you did up there." She nodded in the direction of the trail. "Talking me through my fears. You're good at what you do."

"I've only had my license for two weeks. It may be too early to know whether I'm good or not."

"I'm not talking about being a PI," she said. "You're good with people, and because of that you'd be good at any job you do."

I opened the door for Janet. Before she got in she gave me a big hug. Her body trembled softly. I slipped behind the wheel of my car, following Janet out of the parking lot. Conrad smiled and gave me a lazy two-fingered salute as I drove by.

FEAR STRIKES ME AFTER the fact. I remember a few years ago while coming home from a trip up the Inside Passage, I'd just passed Powell River, British Columbia and entered Malaspina Strait, when the weather suddenly changed from moderate southerlies to strong southwest gales. And Malaspina Strait, a narrow body of water that amplifies and funnels the wind, threw fifty-knot gusts and eight-foot seas at the *Noble Lady*'s nose. The bow rode up over each wave crest, then crashed down into the trough as I gripped the wheel. Midway down the Strait, my anchor broke loose from its chocks, slipped over the side and began pounding the hull. I couldn't let that go on for fear of it knocking a hole in the side of the boat.

So I put the *Noble Lady* on autopilot, slipped on my foul-weather gear, stepped out of the pilothouse, went belly-down on the deck, and slithered forward, one stanchion at a time. I finally reached the anchor and managed to secure it again. When I returned to the helm, I grabbed the wheel and wrestled the boat into the calm, protected waters of Pirate's Cove. But the moment after I'd anchored and shut down the engine, I fell onto the settee, my body trembling, and slept for fourteen hours.

I drove back to the marina from the Cedar and Pine Lakes trailhead and collapsed onto the settee, resting my head in my hands. My legs felt rubbery and insubstantial, as though the life force, drained from them, had not yet been renewed. It didn't help that the unmarked car still sat at the top of the Gate Nine ramp. It seemed the more I learned and the deeper I got into this case, the less I understood about why Thomas Atherton went missing. And now someone had tried to kill me, which made me only that much more determined to find out who and why.

I cleaned and bandaged the gash on my forehead. Then I threw some clothes into a duffle bag and headed up to the marina washroom for a long, hot shower. Afterward, I pulled a pizza from the freezer and popped the cork on a bottle of ten-year old rosé, the last from a case bought when Sharon and I traveled to Australia a decade ago. I promised myself I'd save this last bottle for a very special occasion. And being alive after today qualified.

The settee in the *Noble Lady's* large midships salon converted into a queen-sized berth. I slid the bottom of the settee forward, unfolded the mattress and arranged my sheets and blankets. Before I retired, I pulled my 9 mm Browning semi-automatic from a drawer, worked the action to make certain I'd chambered a round, then rested it on the floor next to my berth. I fully expected that I might need fourteen hours of sleep.

But not long after I'd fallen asleep, a knock on the back window startled me awake. I hurtled out of bed, grabbing my pistol as I rubbed my bleary eyes. I pushed the blinds back slightly with the nose of the Browning. Under the orange, sodium dock lamps, Janet Paulsen stood trembling in a long coat. I hid the Browning under a towel on the galley counter and stepped out onto the deck without stopping to think I only wore my boxers. I don't think she even noticed.

"I'm scared," she said. "I couldn't think of anyone else who'd understand, so I came here. I'm sorry if I'm a nuisance, but may I please come aboard?"

Once inside, I turned on the galley lights. Janet sat down. Tearstains lined her cheeks. I walked into the salon and found a robe. When I returned, I poured the last two glasses of rosé.

"It's for special occasions like being alive," I said, pushing one across the table toward her.

Her hand shook as she raised the glass to her lips.

"I was fine driving home," she said. "I got into the bath, and as my body relaxed the gravity of what could have happened to us this afternoon flooded into me and I started sobbing." Her chest heaved and tears rolled from her eyes. She pointed to herself. "And I haven't been able to stop since. I tried to sleep but I couldn't."

I slid into the seat beside Janet and put my arm around her. She rested her wineglass on the table and her head on my shoulder.

"You had a perfectly natural reaction to a sudden, overwhelming threat," I said.

"I felt safe with you, even in the face of danger," she said. "I need to feel that safety again." She sucked in a deep breath. "God, I'm so embarrassed to ask this…but can I stay here with you tonight?"

"Yes," I said. "But the quarters are cramped. You can have my bed. I'll crawl into the v-berth in the bow."

She squeezed me tighter.

"No," she said. "I know I'm asking a lot, but can you sleep with a woman without having sex?"

I pulled Janet closer.

"Yes," I said. "I can and I'd enjoy doing that."

We both stood and Janet slipped off her coat, revealing a short, pink, silk nightgown underneath. I tossed my robe onto the galley table and took her hand, leading her down the steps to my bed. We crawled beneath the covers and I spooned her. I'd be lying if I said that the generous curves of her body didn't feel wonderful against me. And I'd also be lying if I said that I didn't have a mild erection, which pulsed against her. Images of making love floated through my mind. But as we settled into sleep, another image took over: a little "c" nestled inside a big "C." Evolution, thank God, had not forsaken such essential moments as this. Perhaps we humans weren't really so far removed from Matthew's lowly amphipods after all.

I barely remember Janet leaving in the morning. And when I awoke I found a note on the pillow that read, "My heartfelt thanks." And under that a small envelope, from which I pulled out an invitation to an art opening at her gallery.

A t the Bellingham Police Department that morning, Ben
Conrad met me in a windowless conference room down
the hall from the receptionist. He wore a gray sweat suit
the color of his hair, with dark sweat stains bleeding from his
collar and under his arms.

"My tour doesn't start for an hour," he said. "But I come
in early to work out. Got to stay in shape to keep up with these
youngsters, you know. You look in pretty good shape too. Do
you work out?"

"I should. I just moved up here a few months ago and I
haven't gotten back into my routine."

"Listen, I knew you might drop by today, so I asked to be
alerted if I was here when you came in. Pretty strange with the
body the SWAT guys brought down."

"How so?"

Conrad grimaced. "Chief gets a call last night from some
high muck-a-muck in Washington. National Security. Terrorism.
This guy tells the chief, hands-off the corpse and the rifle. The

rifle was a high-powered job, the kind used by snipers and SWAT teams. No autopsy. No blood screen. No fingerprints. Nothing. A few hours later someone shows up from a local funeral home with instructions to transport the body to Seattle for a flight back east."

"You didn't get a name for the dead guy?"

"Nah. I'm sure you saw he didn't have any ID on him. Pisses me off. Ever since 9/11 some damn official screams 'National Security' then screws you behind your back. Take us. Homeland Security gives us more responsibilities since we're the largest force this close to the Canadian border. You think Washington would also give us more money? Hell, no."

"Any idea what department called the chief?"

"They didn't say. But the chief called the Department of Homeland Security with a case number this guy gave him, and DHS verified it was legit."

"So you've got nothing on him."

"Zip," Conrad said. "Do you know anything? Weren't you hired by that woman to find her husband? The guy whose boat was intercepted headed toward the refinery with a bomb aboard."

"Uh huh."

"So who do you think took a shot at you?"

"Someone who doesn't want me to find Atherton."

"And who shot the shooter?"

"Someone who wants me to find Atherton."

Conrad wrinkled his face. "Goddamn confusing."

"Uh huh. Be glad the feds took the case off your hands."

He shook his head. "Hell, I still don't like it when the feds barge into a community they know nothing about, yell 'terrorism,' then throw their weight around. The shooting'll be all over tomorrow's paper. We tried to keep it low-key, but that's impossible in this town. Some hot new female reporter at the *Herald* was all over the chief this morning. People use that trail. Now they'll be scared and we can't provide them with any answers. That's a form of terrorism if you ask me. Anything turns up, I'll call you. Maybe you'd be kind enough to do the same."

"I will."

I got up to leave.

"Say, Noble."

I turned around.

"I heard you're a liveaboard down at the marina. Whaddya got?"

"Thirty-six-foot Willard."

"Older model sedan?"

"No, an aft pilothouse."

He whistled low again. "No way. That's a rare classic. Got a '67 Grand Banks 36 Woodie, myself."

"That's a classic too."

"Let's talk boats sometime," Conrad said. "I want a tour of your Willard."

"You're on," I said. "And I want to see your GB."

I'M THE KIND OF guy for whom even the most trivial excuse is sufficient to get me to take the *Noble Lady* out for a cruise. And an on-scene inspection of the area where Atherton's boat may have rendezvoused with a vessel racing over from Canada seemed anything but trivial. So, when I got back to the *Noble Lady*, I checked the weather forecast: ten- to fifteen-knot southwest winds for the next several days. Perfect cruising weather. I stowed loose items lying around the boat and dumped my unwashed dishes in the sink.

Then I descended into the engine room and checked the *Noble Lady*'s vitals—oil, water, air, alternator belt. Everything checked out okay. I climbed up to the pilothouse, turned the ignition key and the *Noble Lady*'s engine fired right up. I let her warm for several minutes before sliding back the pilothouse door, stepping out onto the deck, then jumping off onto the dock.

I pulled the power cord from the shore power box, bundled it, and stowed it in a locker on the rear deck. Finally, I unraveled the lines tethering the *Noble Lady* to the dock and slowly pushed her back out of her slip. I hoisted myself up and under the handrails, onto the foredeck, then I stepped back into the pilothouse.

It doesn't matter how many times I've done it, I always get a thrill maneuvering the *Noble Lady* out of her berth. Unlike piloting in open waters, maneuvering into and out of a slip requires finesse that takes into account many factors simultaneously—wind, current, tight spaces, the boat's characteristics. It's a real test of boat handling skills.

And I'm a traditionalist. No bow or stern thrusters for me, to make it easy to push the boat sideways. With her rounded hull and huge, barn door rudder, a blast from the propeller and a deft hand on the wheel is all I need to turn the *Noble Lady* on a dime or put her wherever I want. I spun the wheel hard over to port, backed up and gave her a healthy shot of forward throttle, repeating the maneuver several times. Then we slipped down the fairway between rows of gleaming white boats and crawled out of the harbor. When I rounded the harbor breakwater I brought the throttle up and the *Noble Lady* purred.

Once I'm at the *Noble Lady*'s helm and we're cruising in open water, I try to find her "sweet spot." Somewhere between 1900 and 2000 rpm her deep, throaty, diesel whine gives rise to an even deeper pulse that moves through the entire boat at a rhythm close to my heartbeat. At that speed, I'm about as close as a man can get to his engine, and his boat.

I edged the throttle up to 2000 and Miss Perky, (she's my Perkins diesel engine) whined higher. The *Noble Lady* shot ahead from seven to seven and a half knots. I listened. Nothing. So I pulled back down to 1900. The *Noble Lady* slowed to...seven knots. I listened again. Close. I nudged Miss Perky up to 1975 and the *Noble Lady* screamed back up to...well, almost seven and a half knots. But I'd found the sweet spot.

I let out a sigh and pushed back in the helm seat. The gals and I were now content: Miss Perky in her groove; the *Noble Lady* chugging along at her cruising speed. And me? Well, I'm always more content on the water, where I can look back and gain perspective on the troubles of the land.

Occasionally, the VHF radio cackled with boaters hailing each other. I kept the pilothouse door open, allowing a gentle salt air breeze to swirl around me. Out the window to my left, the snowy dome of Mount Baker poked through a gap in the verdant hills surrounding the city. While in the distance directly ahead of me as I crossed the bay, the jagged, snowcapped peaks of the Olympic Mountains etched a cerulean sky.

At this speed, it would take me about three and a half hours to reach the point where Atherton's boat was intercepted by a high-speed vessel crossing over from Canada. I'd just made it about halfway across the bay when my radar picked up a high-speed vessel moving up from behind me.

I stuck my head out the pilothouse door and looked back. With its blue light flashing, the vessel appeared to rock back and forth, while careening toward me on a pedestal of white foam. I looked around. I was the only vessel on the water, which meant that coast guard patrol boat was out after me. I slowed the *Noble Lady* down and took her out of gear. She pirouetted slowly in the gentle wind.

The coast guard vessel, one of the new shiny aluminum patrol boats sitting on black pontoons, zoomed in close then stopped, throwing a wake that rocked the *Noble Lady*. A tall woman stepped from the cabin of the coast guard boat. She had a blue coast guard cap on, which shaded her face. I didn't recognize Katherine Sullivan until she looked up and called to me.

"Commander," she said. "Port of origin?"

Now, we both knew the answer, and we both knew the game.

"Bellingham," I said.

"Destination port?"

"Prevost Harbor, Stuart Island." It was the closest anchorage in American waters I could think of near the interception site.

"Have you ever been boarded by the Coast Guard?"

"Yes, Lieutenant, about three months ago."

"Permission to board and inspect this vessel again?"

"Yes, Lieutenant. Welcome aboard."

Sullivan ducked back into the cabin, where her three crewmen waited. The helmsman of her vessel must have been an inexperienced kid. With almost 500 horses of power behind him, he hadn't yet learned the meaning of "go slow." He came at the *Noble Lady*'s too quickly and rammed the boat. The flotation pontoons, built to withstand the impact of hard seas and even small arms fire, bounced harmlessly off the *Noble Lady*. Sullivan stepped out again, her face red.

"Sorry, Commander, we'll get it right this time."

"Why don't you let me throw you a line first?"

She ordered the helmsman to cut the engines. I tossed her a line from my bow, and then one from my stern, and together we pulled the boats to each other. She and a crew member secured their end of the lines, then they climbed aboard the *Noble Lady*. Meanwhile, the other two crewmen stood at the back of their boat casting steely-eyed glances at me, while resting their hands on their holstered semiautomatic pistols.

Sullivan first checked my registration and identification. Then she crawled around with the young seaman in tow. The kid couldn't have been more than twenty. They read from a list flashed to them on the screen of a handheld portable digital assistant, checking for things ranging from the obscure (like whether the valve on my septic holding tank was locked to prevent overboard discharge) to the obvious (like whether I had enough life vests for each person aboard, when I already had mine on).

They went from item to item on the list; and the young crewman offered me hollow compliments on how nice my boat was and how well I maintained it. Katherine winced. She knew that I knew he was only mindlessly mouthing the phrases he'd been fed in his coast guard class on vessel interdiction and inspection. Phrases meant to put a suspect at ease, so he might slip up and say something unintended but revealing.

Since 9/11, the Coast Guard stopped more vessels for such inspections, which was probably a good thing. What irked me was that I told Sullivan I'd been boarded three months ago and she never bothered to ask for the certificate of that boarding and inspection, nor did she have a crew member look it up on the Coast Guard's main computer system. She was determined to board the *Noble Lady*, and I didn't understand why.

We bobbed gently for almost an hour, while Sullivan completed her inspection. Evidently there was some problem looking up my name on the Coast Guard's central computer, which was tied-in to a massive database of criminals and terrorism suspects maintained by the Department of Homeland Security. The search software will flag you if your name is vaguely similar to a wanted suspect, or if you have the same birth date. A crewman on the patrol boat called up to Sullivan asking for my social security number. The young man with Sullivan turned to me. My patience had worn thin.

"No," I said. "I'm not required to give you that. I already showed you a driver's license. Tell them to use that."

He stiffened and put his hand on his pistol.

"Tell him to read the regs," I said to Sullivan.

She didn't make eye contact with me, but she did say, "Stand down, Mr. Crenshaw. Tell them that they've got all they need, and all they're going to get."

The crewman glowered at me, then stepped outside. Sullivan placed her handheld computer next to a small printer, which whirred as it spit out a receipt. She signed, I signed, and then she handed a copy to me.

"Thank you, Sir, for keeping your vessel up to coast guard standards. While this receipt won't prevent another boarding, it will show that you have been inspected."

"As long as the officer in charge asks to see it."

She patted the receipt on the chart table, then she and her crewman disembarked. He untied my lines and threw them to me. I caught the stern line, but he didn't make an effort to heave my bow line high enough. It fell into the water. He looked down at the line and then turned away. The coast guard vessel zoomed off, leaving me to pull a waterlogged line from the sea.

Once I had the lines secured on deck, I fired up Miss Perky, found her sweet spot again. I headed the *Noble Lady* across the bay, letting the aggravation of the coast guard inspection trail away in my wake.

Directly ahead, the sun dipped behind Lummi Island, casting the east side of the island in shadows. I neared Point Francis, the south tip of Portage Island, and once around the point I headed up Hale Passage, dodged a car ferry to Lummi Island, then angled across Rosario Strait, into the Strait of Georgia.

Normally, I would have jogged right across Rosario and into the San Juan Islands, but I wanted to cruise toward the refinery at Cherry Point, and then backtrack the course of Atherton's boat to see if I'd pick up anything else about what happened that night.

I pulled my binoculars from atop the instrument panel, and looked to see a huge tanker docked at Cherry Point. A plume of white smoke billowed skyward from the refinery's smoke stack, creating a small cloud and what looked like a tiny weather system over the plant. The tanker appeared ready to leave, because two large tractor tugs stood by waiting for it, and a small coast guard patrol vessel did "wheelies" on the water near the docks.

A half mile from Cherry Point, the patrol boat's radar must have picked me up, or maybe VTS radar did. The patrol boat stopped circling and sped my way, its blue light pulsing. So for the second time in less than two hours, I brought the *Noble Lady* out of gear and stepped out of the pilothouse to an eager coast guard officer. This young man wore aviator sunglasses.

He started by asking, "Port of origin, Sir?" And he continued with all the requisite questions and mindless small talk about my boat. Then he asked the clincher, "Have you ever been boarded by the Coast Guard?" I told him less than two hours ago and asked if he wanted to see my boarding certificate. He waved me off, then asked for permission to come aboard in order to do a vessel inspection.

Before I answered, I reached into the pilothouse, grabbed the inspection certificate, and shook it at him. "I was just inspected less than two hours ago," I said.

He stripped off his sunglasses and stared stonily. "My orders are to stop and board every vessel that comes within a one-mile perimeter of Cherry Point. Permission to board, Sir?"

I nodded.

I didn't help them dock alongside. I sat in the galley while this man and another seaman went through the *Noble Lady*, asking the same damn questions Sullivan's crew had asked. And when they'd finished, the officer in charge handed me my second boarding certificate of the day.

The coast guard boat sped back to the tanker. After starting the *Noble Lady*'s engine again, I turned left and headed out into the Strait of Georgia. I pounded the rim of the wooden steering wheel with the flat of my hand.

These two coast guard stops had an eerie ring of familiarity about them. When I worked drug interdiction for District Seven out of Miami, we played "bump and run" with the boats of known drug dealers. Every time certain boats left port, or we saw them on the water, we'd stop and board them, even if they'd just been stopped and boarded hours before. We weren't expecting to find drugs or anything illegal. The stops were intimidation, pure and simple. A message that said: Better you stay in port.

I slammed the steering wheel again. Then I realized I'd forgotten to find the sweet spot, so I fiddled with the throttle until I felt the *Noble Lady*'s pulse, and we both settled down. Out my starboard side window, a speck grew larger on the horizon of the Inside Passage. Probably a tanker or a tug towing a barge, heading this way.

I swung around Patos Island, a lone outpost among the San Juans, just this side of the Canadian border, and headed west along Boundary Pass. The sun sank low, and the barren side of Saturna Island, on the Canadian side of the Pass, glowed orange-gold. Further west, near where that boat crossed from Canada the night Atherton went missing, the windows of island homes flickered in the reflected light.

If Atherton hadn't taken that small craft into Canada, what else could he have done? It's not like he could have pulled in anywhere. Boundary Pass was a body of water with Canada on one side, the sparsely populated shores of Waldron Island on the other, and a wicked current running like a river between them. Besides, his boat hadn't stopped. VTS radar tracked him moving continuously.

I checked my GPS to see how fast I moved. The current already had me up over ten knots, and an hour later I was coming up on the area where Louis and I figured the vessel from Canada intercepted Atherton's boat. But I didn't see anything except the current churning the water into a half-dozen minuscule whirlpools.

Canada was the only possibility that made sense.

The dashboard clock read seven p.m. Bedwell Harbor was not more than four miles away, which meant I should be able to make the Canadian Customs dock just before eight. I switched to the Canadian Vessel Traffic Service channel before heading across Boundary Pass. Turn Point was just a little further west, and I'd been surprised more than once by a huge cargo ship whipping around the point.

The CVTS controller reported no traffic coming from that direction, but the speck on the horizon I'd seen while crossing the Strait had now become the *Bering Voyager,* a 700-foot oil tanker turning at the east end of Boundary Pass and heading my way. I made it across with plenty of time to spare and looked back at the huge red behemoth skulking in the twilight toward the open Pacific.

I tied up at the customs dock at Bedwell Harbor, but the office had already closed, so I called Canadian Customs on my cell phone. They gave me a clearance number, which I scribbled on a piece of paper then taped to my pilothouse window. I wasn't at the dock for more than a few minutes before I untied and cruised the short distance over to Beaumont Provincial Marine Park, where I anchored off Skull Island amidst a handful of boats.

After I shut down the *Noble Lady,* I lowered the dinghy by crane from the boat deck and putted over to the private marina that shared small Minstrel Cove with Canadian Customs. Large boats were moored in the marina, and the villas and condos of a chic resort community littered the hill behind the cove.

I tied the dinghy to the dock and walked up the long ramp to the Minstrel Cove restaurant. I found a seat at the bar. Most of the patrons looked "yachty," dressed in color-coordinated pastel outfits with soft-sided leather shoes. The bartender, a big, blonde guy in white shorts and a blue floral Hawaiian shirt came over.

"Whaddya have?"

"Stout on tap."

"Guinness okay?"

"Yeah. How about a menu too?"

He slid the menu my way, and shortly after that, a tall glass of dark beer with a head of foam. I ordered crab cakes, then slurped some foam.

When the bartender returned with my order I told him, "It's been a long time since I was here. Last time I came in it wasn't called Minstrel Cove, and it wasn't as...well—"

"Wasn't as fucking high-class?"

"Uh huh."

"Lot's changed on the island over the last few years, eh? Ever since that international corporation bought out the owners of the marina and began developing the hell outta the place."

"Betcha the locals don't hang out here."

"Hell, no," the bartender said. "They're not welcomed, and beside the drinks cost too much."

"It's not my kind of place, you know."

"Port Browning," the bartender said. "Islanders go there, outsiders come here."

The crab cakes came the way I liked them—made with real crab. I finished the Guinness and the cakes. When the bartender came over with my tab, I took a picture of Thomas Atherton from my pocket. I'd cut it out of the Bellingham paper.

"Ever seen this guy in here?"

The bartender pulled my hand closer, staring at Atherton's picture with his bloodshot eyes.

"Can't say I have, but then a lot of people come through here. You a cop?"

"No. An investigator, working for the guy's ex-wife."

The bartender let out a belly laugh. "Owes her alimony, eh?"

"He went out boating by himself and he disappeared."

The bartender winked. "Owes her alimony. Good plan, going missing. Maybe I should do the same thing."

I paid him, then left.

Port Browning is just around the corner from Bedwell Harbor, but it's too far to take a dinghy. So I hoisted the anchor, towed the dinghy behind the boat, and headed deeper into the harbor toward Pender Canal, a narrow, shallow cut that separates North and South Pender Islands.

In the dark, I went dead slow and turned the *Noble Lady*'s docking lights on so I wouldn't miss the buoys marking the only safe route through the canal. At the entrance to the Canal, my depth sounder plummeted, showing less than two feet of water under my keel. I gripped the wheel hard and kept on. I'd been through here several times with the tide even lower than it was now, and I'd never had a problem.

I slipped the *Noble Lady* between the huge upright timbers supporting the bridge over the canal, while cars rumbled overhead, and beyond them stars sparkled. Past Shark Cove, I turned left and it wasn't long before I was at Port Browning.

Not everything's in a name. Port Browning is not a port in the sense that New York or Los Angeles or Seattle are ports. It's a deep, wide cove with nice homes lining the sides, and a funky old marina with rickety wooden docks at its bitter end. The beach to one side of the marina is "steep to," its drop off so sharp that thirty yards from shore you're in thirty feet of water. I anchored close to shore, climbed into the dinghy and landed on the beach. Then I walked around to the Shark's Cove Bar, where the islanders hung out.

Jeans and boots were the style in the bar. I didn't see a pastel color or a soft-sided leather shoe. I grabbed a barstool. Liquor bottles perched unevenly on three tiers in front of a large mirror set off soft sparkles that reminded me of sunlight playing across the rippled surface of water. Behind me, pool balls clacked in the dim light, over the buzz of conversation. The scent of cheap perfume mixed with alcohol drifted my way. A moment later the bartender appeared.

"Whaddya have?" she asked.

"Guinness."

"American, eh?"

"Forgot my eh, eh?"

She smiled, and a network of fine lines raised at the corners of her mouth. She'd tied her sandy blonde hair into a frizzy bun at the back of her head. Her eyes were red. Her breasts nearly fell out of the white tank top she wore over her blue jeans. She pushed a dish of pretzels in front of me and winked.

"Be right back."

She turned to walk off. A tattoo of Neptune wearing a red crown and holding his trident dominated her back, undulating as she moved. Her tight blue jeans appeared painted onto her body. The scent of her cheap perfume and alcohol lingered.

"Angie's something, eh?"

A massive hand clapped my shoulder. I spun around on my stool to face a grizzled, older man. His fingers and palm had a thick layer of callous, and a spider web of cracks.

"She is," I said. "Do you fish?"

"Are you American?" he asked.

I chuckled and so did he. Angie slapped my Guinness down and a fine mist of ale sprinkled my face. I reached for the sweating glass. The man next to me threw the last of his shot glass down his throat. After taking the head off my beer, I pulled Thomas Atherton's photo from my pocket and held it up to the man.

"Have you seen him out on the water?"

The man cast a casual glance at the photo. "FBI, eh?"

"No. Private investigator. His boat was found a couple of weeks ago running on autopilot toward Cherry Point. Only he wasn't aboard."

"He Canadian?" the man asked.

"No. American."

"Then why're ya asking here?"

"I thought someone might have seen something out of the ordinary on the water the evening he disappeared."

The man picked up his empty shot glass and slapped it on the bar. I flinched. He bellowed. "Ange, I'll have another."

Angie must not have heard him. At the far end of the bar, she balanced her breasts on the counter and leaned over to whisper into the ear of a blonde-haired man.

"Ange." The fellow roared, and a hint of Irish brogue surfaced in his voice. "Another, eh?"

Angie whipped around and shot a hot glance his way. "You already had one too many, eh, Walt?"

He grumbled, "Hell, you're too young and too pretty to be my mum. I'll take another."

She waved him off and went back to the patron.

Walt turned to me. "I swear it's not Neptune on her back but the devil," he said.

A moment later a new shot glass on top of a napkin hit the counter with a dull thud. Walt smiled, then turned to grab it. This time he finished the whole drink in one throw.

"'Case she changes her mind," he said. He stared at me, then his eyes narrowed as though through that gesture alone he'd told me all I needed to know. "Seen plenty out of the ordinary on the water." He paused, narrowing his eyes again. "No fish in my nets. No crab in my traps. No money in my pockets. No dead men on the water."

"Didn't say he was dead."

Walt narrowed his eyes. "Not in his boat?"

"Yeah."

"Then he's good as dead."

Walt pushed up from the stool, and with groans and a stoop, he tottered out the door of the Shark's Cove Bar.

"Don't mind that old fool," Angie said. "He's too drunk to know better, and too smart not to drink."

I shook my head and grimaced. She smiled. I thought about asking her what she meant, but I flashed Thomas Atherton's picture at her instead.

"Have you seen him around?"

She grabbed the photo and clutched it close to her face. "Ain't a regular."

"His boat was found in the Strait, only he wasn't aboard."

She handed the picture back. "I heard something about that," she said. "Are you the law?"

"No. His wife sent me looking for him." I took another draft of my beer.

She chuckled. "Why? Sonofabitch ran off with another woman and faked his disappearance?"

I held up a finger. "Now that's a possibility that hadn't crossed my mind."

"Hell. Wouldn't be the first time."

She looked down the bar. "'Scuse me," she said. "Got some other customers to take care of."

I hadn't heard or seen anyone call her, but she drifted back down to the end of the bar, leaning over, resuming her conversation with the same man as before. He cast a quick glance my way, then lowered his head to his drink, nodding slightly as she spoke. He drained the last of his beer, then got up, fading into the shadows at the back of the bar.

I heard a door swing open, then slam shut. I gulped the last of my beer down, then slapped a few bills on the counter and followed him, winding my way past people with drinks or cue sticks in their hands. I dodged a woman about to take a shot, who pulled her cue stick back and nearly caught me in the groin with her elbow. A sign over the back door read, "Emergency exit only. Do not use. Buzzer will sound."

I shouldered the door open, then stepped outside. The only sounds I heard were a creaky hinge and the door slamming shut. The darkness blinded me until my eyes adjusted. The orange tips of several cigarettes glowed in the night. Overhead, a carpet of stars shimmered. I'd stepped into the bar's parking lot, where several men gathered around an older pickup truck. I couldn't tell if the man that Angie spoke with stood among them.

"Excuse me," I said.

Their conversation stopped. One man ground a cigarette butt into the dirt with the sole of his shoe.

"I'm looking for a man who went missing about two weeks ago, out in the Strait. Boat was found but he wasn't aboard. His name is Thomas Atherton. A professor of environmental studies at Western Washington University in Bellingham. Anyone seen or heard anything about him?"

The men shuffled in place. Another cigarette fell to the ground, this one left to burn with a pungent, sour odor.

"Don't know nothing 'bout a fucking professor," a voice said.

"Thanks anyway," I said.

I turned to leave, taking a path that angled down from the bar toward the beach where I'd landed the dinghy. A gentle wind sent a few leaves fluttering to the ground. The chugging of a diesel engine echoed through the cove. Across the darkness of the water, a boat's red light slid by, like the eye of a prowling Cyclops. I could barely make out the silhouette of the *Noble Lady* bobbing gently at anchor under the stars. Suddenly, the bushes beside me rustled. I tried to spin around, but too late. Someone had his hand on my shoulder and the barrel of a pistol jammed into my back.

This guy was obviously not a pro. Having a hand on my shoulder was his first mistake; confronting me on a downhill path his second. I fell to my knees, grabbed his arm and sent him flying over my shoulder. He hit the ground with a dull thud. I pounced on him, jammed my knee into his armpit and flexed his gun hand down so hard his wrist popped and he yelped. He had no strength after that and I took the pistol from him as easily as I'd pluck a flower from a bouquet. His blonde hair flickered in the dim light from the bar. I spun him over, dug my knee between his shoulder blades, and ratcheted his gun hand behind his back. The pistol felt like a small .22 caliber, the kind a woman might tuck into her purse. I barely noticed it in my hand, but I plunged it into the base of Blondie's skull and pushed his face down into the dirt.

"Good way to get killed," I said.

"Me?"

He struggled to speak so I eased the gun back slightly. He turned his head to the side.

"You come around here asking about a missing man. Good way for *you* to get killed. I was just tryin' to do you a favor."

"Sure you were. It's just I can't remember the last time someone stuck a gun in my back as a favor."

"Angie told me to scare you off when you left the bar."

"With her gun?"

"Yeah. She said you seemed like a nice guy asking the wrong questions."

"About a missing man?"

"Small island. Rumors travel fast, eh?"

I pressed the gun a little harder. "What rumors?"

"About Americans. Four men. Buzz cuts. Military types. Rented the Thompson house a few weeks ago. Went tearing out of here one evening a few weeks back on one of two new high-speed, aluminum boats they have. Two boats, four men? No one's ever seem 'em fishing, eh? Boats're tied up at Thompson's dock all day long. Rumors get going that way."

"Did they rent the house before or after that boat was found with explosives aboard, heading for the refinery at Cherry Point?"

"It was all around the same time as I remember."

"Where's this Thompson house?"

"Look, mister, I'm supposed to be helping you out, not getting you into more trouble."

I leaned into him with my knee and he gasped for air.

"Third one on the left after Pollard Cove as you're heading out toward the Sound."

I stood up, and picked the man up as I did. He rubbed his wrist, then started to walk off, but he stopped and spun around.

"You gonna give me back Angie's gun?" he asked. "She'll kill me if you don't."

"Hell, I almost killed you."

I pushed a lever and let the magazine slide into my hands. I shook the bullets loose, and released the one already chambered. Then I popped the clip back into the gun and fired once to make certain it was cleared before tossing it back to the blonde-haired man. His gun hand hung limp at the side of his body, and he caught the pistol with his other hand.

"Thanks," he said, before disappearing up the path toward the bar.

I walked down to the beach and the dinghy, then putted out to the *Noble Lady*. The calm, dark water reflected the starry night sky. And phosphorescence churned up by the outboard engine glowed neon green. As the dinghy's bow broke the surface of the water I remembered Admiral Ritchie getting word to me through my CO that he was doing me a favor by allowing me to leave the coast guard with a general discharge instead of a dishonorable one for insubordination, despite years of meritorious service. Ritchie might as well have had a pistol in my back too.

◎   ◎   ◎

I HADN'T PLANNED ON staying out overnight, so in the morning I had to rummage hard to find something to eat, settling for a heel of bread and cup of instant coffee. A wispy layer of fog sat on the surface of the water. It was nine when I finished breakfast. The sun had yet to crest the high walls of the cove, leaving everything around me in shadows. I lowered the dinghy into the water and headed away from the marina.

Five minutes later, I passed Pollard Cove and started counting houses. The third one on my left was an older stone house with large glass windows, and steps down from the patio to a long, recently rebuilt wood-planked walkway that led to a private dock. Two black pontoon boats with shiny aluminum houses and huge outboards sat threateningly at the dock, looking every bit like unmarked coast guard patrol boats. I tied up behind the boats and hopped onto the dock.

No sooner had I started walking toward the house, when a sliding glass door rolled back and three men stepped out. Each member of this grim trio stood six feet tall or more. Their bulging muscles reminded me that I hadn't worked out in a while. Each had a buzz haircut. The sandy-blonde guy in the middle had on khaki shorts with sandals and no shirt. The dark-haired, barefoot man on his right wore olive green army-issue cargo pants and a matching tank top. He had a large tattoo that covered most of his right biceps. The third man was older, with an angular, weathered face. He had on blue jeans, tennis shoes and a white T-shirt. He spoke first.

"Hey, pal, private property. Where the hell do you think you're going?"

"I thought I might rent this place next summer," I said. "The agency told me to stop by and have a look around. Sorry, I didn't know it was occupied."

Simultaneously, their expressions turned from tight-jawed scowls to slack-jawed frowns. The shoeless man grumbled. "Well, it is."

"Then I'll be going," I said. I turned to leave, and they followed me.

I called back over my shoulder. "Nice boats you got there. Do much fishing?"

"That's what we're out here for," the shoeless guy said.

I doubted that, but I decided to do some fishing of my own. I turned back toward them. "There is one question I have. Not about the house. I'll see that some other time. I've been trying to help this friend of mine who's looking for her ex-husband."

The older man grimaced. "What?"

"Yeah. The guy's boat was crossing the Strait of Georgia headed for Cherry Point. Explosives were found aboard but he wasn't. Just wondered if you fellas might have run across the boat or the man while you were out fishing?"

Their bodies went rigid. The dark-haired guy in army-issue lunged at me, but the older man put an arm out and held him back. A cold gaze set into each man's eyes. If looks could kill, I'd already have been dead three times over. The older man narrowed his eyes and seemed to force a smile over his lips.

"What'd you say your name was?"

"I didn't. But it's Deacon. Reginald Deacon."

"Well, Mr. Deacon. We don't know anything about a missing man. And I think it'd be best if you got in your boat and left."

"Thanks," I said. "I'll be getting back to my sailboat."

I took a harder look at the tattoo on the man in olive green: an eagle perched atop an anchor, holding a trident in one hand and a cocked flintlock pistol in the other. I stepped into my dinghy and headed back toward the *Noble Lady*.

Hairs rose on the back of my neck. I swore I could feel the gaze of the men through their binoculars. These guys *were* pros; that tattooed insignia was the coveted emblem of the Navy SEALs. I veered away from the *Noble Lady* and headed toward the opposite side of the cove, counting at least two dozen boats anchored in front of the beach. I put a large sailboat and two good-sized Bayliners between the men and me, directly in their line of sight.

Then I slowly worked my way back to the *Noble Lady*, using the boats as cover. What were SEALs doing camped out in a resort house in Canada?

Once aboard the *Noble Lady,* I got out my binoculars, climbed into the pilothouse and looked across the cove at the Thompson house. A plume of blue smoke rose from the rear of one of the boats sitting at the dock. Two men jumped into the boat and it zoomed off toward me. I ducked down and sat on the pilothouse floor. I could hear their engines revving as they zigzagged around the boats at anchor, trying to determine which one was mine. The *Noble Lady* rocked in their wake. After ten minutes, the sound of their outboards faded.

I went back downstairs and peeked through the galley blinds. Then I heard the clang and clatter of anchor chains being raised. The large sailboat and one of the Bayliners were preparing to leave. So was a smaller sailboat on the other side of me. Fortunately, I can raise and lower the *Noble Lady*'s anchor without going out on deck. I put on a cap, climbed back into the pilothouse, and kept my head just below the bottom of the windows as I started Miss Perky. Then I flipped the switch on the winch to pull the anchor up.

The sun had finally reached over the cliffs, sending blinding flashes of light off the windows of the homes and boats on my side of the cove. Several more boats weighed anchor, and I followed the small convoy. The large sailboat and a smaller powerboat headed straight down the narrow channel that passed in front of the Thompson house. The Bayliner and two motorsailers cruised toward the Pender Canal.

I followed the Bayliner, and as I turned right into the Canal, I saw the men from the Thompson house jump into their boat and zoom away from the dock. They circled around the large sailboat, like a shark hunting prey.

T ouch any part of a spider's web and the spider will rush there, with poisoned fangs ready for the kill. Barely two miles out of Canada, I touched the American side of Boundary Pass, and it seemed the moment I did a throbbing blue light rushed toward me. Well ahead, the Bayliner and several other pleasure boats had cruised, unstopped, through the spider's web. Apparently, this spider had particular taste in boats, or maybe it just had a particular taste for me.

I studied it harder as it came toward me. Minus the flashing light, the black-and-gray coast guard patrol boat was a dead ringer for the ones docked at the Thompson house. When it pulled up alongside me, Katherine Sullivan stepped from the cabin, an enlisted kid at her side. She had a pained expression on her face. The kid, a big guy with blonde hair, blue eyes, and a Midwestern look, had his hand wrapped around his sidearm. I stepped out of the pilothouse and looked down on them.

"Morning, Lieutenant," I said.

Sullivan stared without replying.

"Sir," the kid said. "Port of origin?"

"Port Browning."

"Port of destination?"

"Bellingham."

"Have you cleared United States Customs and Immigration?"

"I just crossed into the country, and I didn't have time to make the phone call before you showed up."

He looked down at his hand-held computer and began reading from the script.

"Have you ever been boarded by the Coast Guard?"

"Yes."

"When is the last time you were boarded by the Coast Guard?"

"Twice yesterday."

He grimaced. "Twice yesterday?"

"What? Doesn't Station Bellingham file boarding reports anymore?"

"Lieutenant?" He turned to Sullivan.

Both now had the same pained look. She motioned for him to join her in the wheelhouse. We'd drifted into a tide rip, which spun the *Noble Lady* around. At the western end of the Pass, a large freighter had just rounded Turn Point. Sullivan and the young seaman stepped out of the wheelhouse.

"Sir," he said. "We'll need to board your vessel."

I pointed west. "Think it might be a good idea if we got out of that big guy's way?"

The young seaman looked at the tanker. "Yessir," he said.

I stepped back into the pilothouse and drove the *Noble Lady* out of the freighter's path, with the Coast Guard following close behind me. When I took my boat out of gear, the coast guard craft maneuvered alongside me and tied up. I opened my boarding gate and the young man came aboard. His name was Larson. Two other young seamen emerged from the wheelhouse to flank Sullivan, with their hands on their weapons.

Standing on the rear deck, squinting at his PDA screen, Larson began.

"Registration?"

I handed it to him and he passed it on to one of the other men standing on the deck of the patrol boat.

"Driver's license?"

"No."

He looked at me askance.

"Social Security Number?"

"No."

"Date of birth?"

"No."

Larson's jaw tightened. "Sir, failure to comply with the request of a boarding officer may subject you to penalties or fines."

"Son, failure to know the rights of the owner of a boarded vessel may subject you to repeat the Coast Guard's Vessel Boarding and Interdiction Class."

Larson stuck his head out of the boat. "Ma'am, the owner refuses to supply me with a driver's license, social security number, or date of birth."

"He's not required to, by law," Sullivan said. "Besides, I'll vouch for his name and identification."

Larson turned back to me, his face reddened.

"Read the fine print," I said, pointing to the bottom of my copy of yesterday's boarding certificate.

"Boarding report?" Larson said.

"Reports." I handed the slips of paper to Larson.

He looked through them several times. "Three boardings in two days?" His voice rose.

"Go figure," I said.

He stuck his head out again. "Ma'am this is the third time this boat has been boarded in the past two days."

"Continue with your inspection, Mr. Larson," Sullivan said.

Larson walked with me into the boat.

"A lot's changed since 1700 yesterday," I said.

"Look, I don't understand what's going on here," Larson said. "I'm just following orders."

And he did. Meticulously inspecting everything that had been meticulously inspected twice the day before. I signed the boarding report, and he handed me a copy as he left.

"This does not guarantee that you will not be…" He shook his head. "Damn. You know the drill."

"I do."

"You sound like an ex-military man," Larson said.

"Former commander, United States Coast Guard."

"Damn." He shook his head and screwed up his face. "Then what…I mean why…"

"You tell me, son." I shook the boarding report in the air. "Meanwhile, I'll add this to my growing collection."

Larson climbed back into the patrol boat. After untying from me, the Coast Guard sped away. Katherine Sullivan never spoke directly to me, though she stood on the rear deck of her boat and stared impassively my way. I called Customs and Immigration on my cell phone, and they cleared me to re-enter the United States. The Coast Guard didn't stop me again on the way into Bellingham.

◎　◎　◎

I PULLED INTO MY slip at three in the afternoon. I decided to grab a late lunch and hit the weights at the gym later, after recalling those massive biceps on the SEALs. My muscles ached after a good hour's workout, and when I got back to the boat I saw that I'd missed two calls on my cell phone, from the same number, which I didn't recognize.

I dialed my voice-mail and retrieved the messages from Janet Paulsen, reminding me of her gallery opening this evening at eight in Fairhaven. Good thing, because I'd forgotten about it. From the salon window, I gazed at the sunset, painting the western sky a rich salmon color. Then I slipped on a pair of tan slacks and an open-collared shirt the same color as the setting sun.

Fairhaven, the old-town section of the city, was only a twenty-minute walk, which I decided to take even though that meant I'd get to the gallery a little late. As I walked toward town, the fellows in the unmarked car followed. A few blocks up from the marina, I found the paved trail that led through the city, along the waterfront into Fairhaven. In the beginning, the trail was completely exposed and visible from the street, and the unmarked car kept pace at a respectable distance behind me. But the trail made a turn, dipping down beneath the street, where it became invisible to overhead traffic.

Just before the drop, I abruptly changed direction and headed back the way I'd come. The unmarked car made a sweeping U-turn, and as it did I changed direction again, sprinting forward until the trail disappeared from the street. Behind me, I heard car doors opening and slamming shut. I also thought I heard men cursing.

It occurred to me that I was nothing more than a pawn being used by the various agencies with a stake in this case. Whichever agency discovered and apprehended the perpetrator, or perpetrators, behind the Cherry Point bomb plot was not only destined for feathers in their caps, but more taxpayer dollars in their coffers. Some probably wanted me out of the picture so they could go at the case alone, while others wanted to keep an eye on me, hoping I might lead them to Atherton or the OLF or whoever put the bomb on his boat. All of which probably meant I had many big brothers looking after me.

Fifteen minutes later, I was in Fairhaven. With its red brick buildings and faux gas lamps, Fairhaven hearkened back to a different age. As I left the trail and headed up toward the gallery, I looked down Harris Avenue toward the Alaskan Ferry Terminal, where I could still imagine an old wooden steamship, tied up and taking on cargo. I also looked up and down the streets, failing to see my unmarked shadow.

The Seaview Gallery occupied the bottom floor of a renovated turn-of-the-twentieth-century red brick building. A hand-
tooled copper plate, three feet in diameter, of an eagle done in
a northwest Indian style dominated the front window display.
People, holding wine glasses and hors d'oeuvre plates filled with
an assortment of cheeses and vegetables, spilled out the gallery
door. I squeezed through the throng, and inside the front door, a
petite woman in a vibrant blue dress stopped me.

"Charles Noble," I said.

"Yes, Mr. Noble. Janet said to send you into her office when
you arrived." She pointed toward the rear of the gallery.

I walked over the polished hardwood floor, past white walls
and pillars holding artwork; pushing through the deafening
drone of conversation and the competing aromas of perfume
and cologne. I caught brief glimpses of the pieces on display:
Hand-carved wooden masks. Ceremonial canoe paddles. Silver
and copper jewelry. All of it done in the fluid, oval patterns of
northwest coastal Indians. A sign on a door at the back of the
gallery, read "Office."

I knocked, and when the door swung open I was staring into
the light brown eyes of a tall, slender, attractive black woman
with an alluring smile. This woman had hair down to her shoulders. She wore a low-cut black dress and had a silver teardrop
necklace with a ruby in the center. The shiny metal stood in sharp
contrast to her dark chocolate skin. Matching earrings dangled
from her lobes. Our gazes locked for a brief instant, and a tingle
rippled through my body.

The woman smiled. "You must be Charles," she said. "I'm
Vallerie McKee. Please come in."

Janet sat behind a bird's-eye maple desk. When she looked
up and saw me, she placed her hand over the telephone mouth-
piece and mouthed the words, "I'll just be a minute." She had
no windows in her office, but the track lights, beige carpet, but-
terscotch-colored leather sofa and chairs made it plenty bright.
In the large painting, which occupied most of the wall behind

Janet's desk, a Native American woman looked out between two tall cedar trees to an empty canoe drifting on the water.

Janet ended her call and stood to greet me.

"Sorry, people are calling to say they couldn't make tonight's opening." She looked between Vallerie and me. "Have you two met?"

"We have," I said.

"Vallerie's just started as a reporter for the *Bellingham Herald*."

I smiled. "So you're the woman who persisted with the police chief about what happened to Janet and me on the trail?"

She smiled back. "I am, and I've gotten just about every side except yours. Care to tell me about it?"

"I bet you have a tape recorder in your purse," I said.

"In fact, I do."

"I came for the gallery opening," I said. "Not for an interview."

Janet cut in. "Then why don't we all step outside." She walked behind Vallerie and me and pulled the door open. "I need to schmooze my customers. I'll find you two in a bit, and bring some wine."

Vallerie turned to me. "Care to join me, Mr. Noble?"

"Charlie, please."

She held out her hand, and I took it. Outside the office, Vallerie hooked her arm in mine and we strolled around the gallery.

The gallery crowd buzzed. After only a year in the art business, if Janet could pack people in like this, she'd have no trouble succeeding.

"The day after I started, the story about Thomas Atherton broke. It's my first big assignment," Vallerie said. "Do you think the shooting yesterday was related to your work on this case?"

Okay, despite her melodious voice, winning smile, and gorgeous body, Vallerie wasn't about to charm a story from me. "What'd the police tell you about the shooting?"

"They didn't have much to say."

"Sorry," I said. "I don't either."

She smiled. "Shall we look at art?"

"Let's."

We stopped in front of a carved wooden mask with deep eyes, lit from the top, which sank the eyes into dark shadows. Strands of cedar bark hung as hair. Vallerie pulled back slightly.

"Terrifying," she said.

"It's supposed to be. It's a Kwakiutl mask of Tsonoqua, the Wild Woman," I said.

"You say that like you know about it."

"I've visited Kwakiutl villages along the Inside Passage, watched their carvers at work, listened to their storytellers, seen their dances."

"Were you on vacation?"

"No, actually, I was working."

She wrinkled her face slightly. "On a case in Canada?"

"Yes…and No."

"This should be interesting," she said.

I told Vallerie about being in the Coast Guard for almost twenty years, but I didn't go into all the gory details. We made our way forward, stopping to admire a copper plate on which an image of a sun mask had been hammered. Walking deeper into the gallery crowd, the sonic barrage of conversation grew louder, and a heat wave from the many bodies confined in a small space hit me. I hesitated, and Vallerie turned to me.

"Are you claustrophobic?" she asked.

"No. I just got off the water. It's always an adjustment being back on land around this many people."

"I hear wistfulness in your voice," she said. "As though being back on land represents surrender or defeat."

"Not surrender or defeat. Longing. What you hear is longing. To see a horizon. To lose the feel of solid ground beneath my feet. To embark on an adventure."

"Is that why you became a Coastie?"

"Coastie? You've been around Station Bellingham too much."

"Sorry," she said.

"I joined the Guard because, of all the military services, its principal mission wasn't offensive or defensive, but protective. Saving lives. Men and women who risk their lives to save others, mostly boaters, who're either drunk or have done incredibly stupid things to get themselves into trouble in the first place."

"But a lot's changed in the Guard since 9/11, hasn't it?"

I looked into Vallerie's eyes, which scanned my face as though searching for answers beyond my words. I was about to unburden myself when I stopped. "A lot has changed since 9/11," I said. "And that's why I'm on the outside now, looking for new horizons."

"Is it lonely out there...I mean, by yourself?"

"Ever been on a boat?"

"I've cruised, but only with other people."

"Solo cruising seems like the loneliest place. Just you, the water, the sky, the wind, the weather, your boat. Like a moving island apart from the world. But after a few days it's not just you and the elements and your boat. You feel the rhythms of the elements within your body; the throb of your boat's engine an extension of your own heartbeat. And where you first thought to be alone, you experience this inexplicable oneness with everything around you."

Vallerie squeezed my hand. "It sounds entrancing."

"Not everyone's cut out for boating."

"But you are."

"I am. I love being on the water. It allows me to reflect on myself and on life. I think Melville said that 'meditation and water are wedded forever.' It's a marriage that suits me well."

"You're a man of passions and deep feelings," Vallerie said. "That's different, and I like that." Her voice softened.

When wind meets current on the water, dangerous swells can develop. At this moment, wind headed toward current inside of me, and I could feel the swells rise.

We stood in front of a large painting of a lone totem pole decaying deep in a forest. Pale green moss hung from dark green boughs, and a shaft of sunlight stabbed through the canopy to illuminate the pole.

Vallerie pointed to a bear, which dominated the remaining portion of the pole. "I love how these complex images are made by combining such simple shapes."

"I'm certainly not an expert on the art of the Northwest coast," I said. "But I've often thought that the inspiration comes from the water itself. Others have said as much. Look into a reflected image broken up by gentle, rippling waves and you'll find the very same elemental oval shapes that are in this art." I pointed to the painting.

"Whew." Vallerie tugged on my arm. "Do you ever make chitchat?"

"What?"

She smiled. "You know, light conversation. Small talk. Or are you always this deep, this serious?"

"I—"

"Vallerie." It was Janet, juggling three glasses of red wine in her hands. "There's a call from the paper for you. Why don't you take it in my office."

"Thanks," Vallerie said. "I'll be right back."

Janet handed me a glass and we both watched Vallerie glide away.

"She's certainly a gorgeous woman," Janet said.

"She is that," I said.

I sipped some wine. "I'm glad you two met," she said.

I was about to ask why, when Vallerie stormed, wide-eyed, from Janet's office. She rushed over to us and spoke in rapid, hushed tones.

"The lab," she said, her voice pulsing with excitement. "The university's marine science lab has been firebombed."

Janet gasped. "The Shannon Point lab?"

"Yes," Vallerie said. "It happened just moments ago. I'm on my way there to cover it." She turned to me and raised her eyebrows. "Do you want to come?"

I handed my wineglass back to Janet. "I do."

I climbed into the passenger's seat of Vallerie's late-model black Mustang, whose sleek body matched hers well. From Fairhaven, I took her down the back route to the lab. She drove with gusto, devouring the curves along Chuckanut Drive.

On the way, I learned that she'd been an investment broker in New York City, who'd tired of the "rat race" and decided to pursue a dream. Her ultimate goal wasn't to be a beat reporter, even at a large daily. She wanted to be in front of the camera, not behind the printed page. And with looks like hers, I'd invest my money that someday she'd make it there.

I turned toward her. "How long did you say you've been here?" I asked.

"About three weeks," she said.

"You're fast at making contacts."

"Got to be in this business or someone else'll get the scoop. Besides, I'm starting late. This is a second career, and if I want to make it out of the bush leagues I've got to move fast."

"A story like this helps, huh?"

She tapped the steering wheel. "You bet. It's got all the right elements. National security. Drama. Mystery. Great characters."

"It sounds like a movie," I said

"Or a best-selling novel," she said

Police cars, fire engines, and medical vans clogged the narrow artery leading up to the lab, spilling over onto the main roadway. Vallerie swung over to the right shoulder, and my side of the car dropped down a few feet before we jarred to a stop. She pulled a camera bag from the back seat and bolted out of the car. I followed.

An acrid, smoky smell lodged in my nostrils and throat. The pulsing lights from atop the emergency vehicles lit the surrounding trees, whose limbs swayed gently. The scene brought to mind strobes flashing on the sinewy movements of giant graceful dancers in a smoky club.

I followed Vallerie as she snaked her way around the emergency vehicles. Glass and bits of debris crunched under my feet. Ahead of us, the roof and one side of the lab building had collapsed. Fire crews shined huge spotlights and directed two water hoses on the smoldering remains. We reached a yellow police ribbon that cordoned off the site. Vallerie ducked down and lifted it over our heads. A uniformed officer raced over to us.

"Ma'am. No one's allowed beyond that boundary."

"Press." Vallerie pulled a card from the camera bag and flashed it at the man.

I grabbed the camera bag off her shoulder, pointed at it, and smiled.

"Press," I said.

The officer waved us through. Vallerie wandered off to get close to one of the fire crews. I went to look for the local law officers in charge of the scene. On the water side of the lab, along the beach near where Bucky and I sat the other day, two men talked. They flashed a light in the sand, then at the burned-out lab. I recognized the voice and the dimly lit face of the older man smoking a cigarette. His name was Clay Milton, an FBI special agent out of Seattle. The question was whether he'd followed recent developments in my coast guard career.

I called out, "Clay."

He turned and squinted. The burly man with him looked my way and snarled.

"Who the hell are you, buddy?"

"Charles Noble."

"Noble?" Clay said, flicking his cigarette into the sand. "Dave, he's Coast Guard Intelligence."

Apparently, Clay Milton hadn't kept up with my career, and I didn't bother to update him.

"You got here damn fast," Clay said. "Seems like we just called you guys."

"I was up in Bellingham," I said.

"On this thing?" Clay asked.

"What thing?"

"The ghost trawler loaded with explosives headed for the refinery at Cherry Point. Now the lab."

"Did you connect the lab to Cherry Point already?"

"Atherton worked here," Clay said. He tapped a cigarette from his pack. "Twenty years with the bureau. Stopped believing in coincidences a long time ago."

"What happened?" I asked.

"Dave Van Gelder," the burly man said. We shook hands. "Detective, Anacortes Police Department. About an hour and a half ago, residents on either side of the lab reported a loud explosion. An inbound ferry captain apparently called the Coast Guard, having sighted flames. He thought it was a boat fire. We sent a fire unit down here, who discovered the lab totally engulfed in flames. I called the CG back and told them it was onshore. They said they'd be sending an investigating team anyway. Guess that's you, huh?"

I didn't answer.

"Here." Van Gelder clicked his flashlight on and ran the beam up and down three parallel groves that traveled about six feet in dry sand before disappearing into wet sand. "Looks like they came in at low tide but still left some track marks."

I kneeled down for a better look. "They're not from an ordinary inflatable."

"Why's that, Noble?" Clay asked. He lit another cigarette and took a drag. The air was so thick with smoke from the fire that all he needed was to inhale deeply.

"Track marks're too deep," I said.

"Coulda been loaded with something heavy," Van Gelder said.

"Could have," I said. "Where are the footprints?"

"Yeah, that bothered me too," Van Gelder said. "Don't see any."

"They could have easily erased their track marks in the sand," I said.

"Coulda," Van Gelder said.

"Anyone in the building when it went up?" I asked.

"Don't know," Clay said. "Got in touch with the night janitor, who said that graduate students sometimes worked late on weekends. We're checking with the university. Saturday night, you know. We haven't been able to reach anyone in authority yet."

Suddenly, a loud beep jumped from Van Gelder's jacket pocket. He reached in, emerging with a walkie-talkie, which he pressed to his face.

"Van Gelder, here…okay…okay…send 'em around back. We're standing here on the beach shooting the shit."

He shoved the walkie-talkie back into his pocket, then turned to me. "Did the CG send a shipload to investigate?"

"What do you mean?" I asked.

"Two more guys from District Thirteen just arrived."

I clenched my fist, but I spoke calmly. "I'll go see who it is."

I walked back toward the lab building, dodging the spray from a fire hose that arced over the charred remains. The officer who let Vallerie and me through passed by me, escorting two men, whom I didn't recognize.

On the other side of the building, Vallerie held court with a gray-haired man wearing a sweatshirt and jeans, who seemed thoroughly charmed by her presence. I walked behind her and hooked my arm in hers. She flinched. I leaned into her and whispered, "Time to go."

She cut her eyes at me. "I haven't finished interviewing Chief Williams. Besides, I'll need you to take some pictures."

I turned to the chief and put my arm out. "Excuse me, Chief." Then I pulled Vallerie aside. She shook free.

"What the hell are you doing?" she asked.

"You want a story?" I said. "The real story isn't here."

"Of course it is," she said. "What do you—"

"Noble." I heard Clay Milton's voice calling out from the other side of the building, and I think Vallerie heard it too, because she stopped talking. And when I pulled her toward the road leading up to the lab she didn't resist.

"Trust me," I said. "The real story's not here, it's in Bellingham."

I walked Vallerie past the fire chief, who looked askance at us.

"Sorry, Chief Williams," Vallerie said over her shoulder. "I've got to go. I've got your card. I'll call you to finish the interview, and send someone for photos."

"Noble." Detective Van Gelder called for me this time.

I hustled Vallerie under the yellow ribbon and back along the line of emergency vehicles. As we neared the main roadway, she asked, "Are you in trouble?"

"I will be if we don't get out of here fast."

"Why didn't you say so?"

"You were too busy getting a story."

"Here." Vallerie shoved a remote control unit with the car keys dangling from it into my hand. "Press the button once to unlock the doors. You drive."

When I squeezed the button, the car beeped and the head-lights flashed once. I swung in behind the wheel, jammed the keys into the ignition and gunned the engine. The tires skidded trying to find traction, kicking up a cloud of dirt behind us. But when we made it to the surface of the blacktop, I swung the wheel hard around and we shot down the road. We passed Van Gelder and Milton standing on the side of the road. Milton jabbed an angry finger at us, yelling choice words that I'm sure I would not have wanted to hear.

"Trust me," I said again to Vallerie. "The real story's back in Bellingham."

Her giddy laugh surprised me. "Seems like the real story's behind the wheel of my car."

e headed toward the freeway, and I explained to Vallerie what happened back at the lab. I also asked her to call information for the telephone numbers of Melissa Buchanan and Matthew Voltmann. Neither was listed.

"You're a grad student," I said. "It's Saturday night. You've been working hard all week. Where do you go?"

"To a watering hole," she said.

"No. You're a Birkenstock and granola grad student, working hard all week. Where do you go?"

"In Bellingham?"

"Yeah."

"Don't know."

I sped along the darkened roadway, past the lights of houses reflected in Lake Samish. Then I snapped my fingers and turned to her. "You go to a smoke-free, alcohol-free watering hole."

"Damn," Vallerie said. "They've got one in Bellingham?"

"Uh huh."

"What do they serve to drink? Carrot juice?"

"Guess we're about to find out."

◎   ◎   ◎

WE PARKED IN DOWNTOWN Bellingham and walked a few blocks toward the Wild Horse Café. A line of college-age students leaned against the outside wall of the club, cigarettes dangling from their lips. I swept the blue cloud from around my face as we entered. Kind of defeats the purpose of going to a smokeless club in the first place.

Inside the long, narrow building a rap group performed live. All of the young men wore baggy pants, and the lead singer looked about seventy pounds overweight. To either side of him, two backup singers puffed into microphones, creating an explosive, dueling rhythm between them. And on top of this, someone added a scratchy beat of whines and whirrs from a record spun by hand on a turntable. A sea of heads bobbed up and down.

I leaned in to Vallerie and put on my best street accent. "Yo, dey don't look like dey from da 'Hood, but dey tryin' to sound like dey from da 'Hood."

She chuckled.

"Elvis syndrome," I said.

"What?"

"White folks talk about us like dogs, then try to sing like us when they get on stage."

She laughed and shook her head. "Or look like us when they go to a beach or tanning parlor."

"Dat's what I'm talkin' 'bout."

Vallerie laughed again.

"Do you want to work the crowd?" I asked her.

"Do I have a choice?" she asked.

"You're young and attractive, dressed almost like you fit in."

"Is that a compliment?"

"Uh huh."

"Thanks. Who'm I asking for, again?"

"Melissa Buchanan. Bucky. And Matthew Voltmann."

"Does he have a nickname?"

"The Dr. Ruth of amphipods."

"What?"

I laughed. "Just ask for Matthew."

Vallerie sauntered off into the crowd. I headed for the bar and the pudgy older guy standing behind it, stroking his dark goatee. He narrowed his eyes and wrinkled his face as I approached.

"What'll it be?" he asked.

"Guinness on tap?"

"What are you, a comedian? You want beer, we got Clausthaler, Kaliber, or O'Douls. All alcohol-free. You don't look like a student. Whaddya really here for?"

"Guess my cover's blown, huh? Information," I said. "I'm trying to locate two graduate students. Bucky Buchanan and Matthew Voltmann. Know 'em?"

He paused for a moment. "Are you the police?"

"No."

"Then I don't have to say anything to you."

"No, you don't. But the university's marine science laboratory was firebombed tonight, and they are graduate students who work there."

"Fucking ecoterrorists."

"Maybe. But we won't find out unless we talk to these two students."

"What's with the 'we?' Thought you said you weren't the police."

"My partner and I." I pointed toward the crowd. "Tall, attractive news reporter in a black dress. We're investigating the firebombing, and the incident at Cherry Point a couple of weeks ago."

"Guy's boat headed toward the refinery with explosives?" the bartender asked.

"Uh huh, that incident," I said. "And these graduate students worked for him."

"Oh. Now I see. You think they were involved. What? Do you work for Homeland Security?"

I pulled out my wallet and flashed my private investigator's badge and license at him. "I'm not at liberty to go into the details of my employment."

He winked, nodded. "Oh, I see. One of them. Look I never heard of this Volt…Volt—"

"Voltmann."

"Yeah. This Voltmann character, but this Bucky. She a girl?" He held his hand out, palm down. "Kinda short. Kinda cute. Kinda spunky."

"Uh huh."

"She's been in a few times. Haven't seen her tonight, though."

"You know where she lives?"

"Sorry, pal, can't help you there."

"Any regulars around who can?"

"Ask DJ Groove Finger. He might know."

The bartender pointed toward the front of the club. Off to one side, a wiry young kid with matted blonde hard hovered over a turntable as though concentrating on a science experiment.

"DJ Groove Finger?"

The bartender shrugged. "Look, I don't name 'em, I just book 'em. And the college kids love this guy."

The rap group was going on…and on…and on…about a guy who left his girlfriend in the care of his best friend while he went out to "take care of bid'ness" only to return to find his best friend "taking care of bid'ness" with his girlfriend. DJ Groove Finger had his index finger on the record, spinning it back and forth in time to the rapper's words. Making my way through the crowd, I bumped into Vallerie from behind and whispered in her ear.

"Wanna dance?"

She twirled around with her eyes narrowed and her claws out, ready to pounce.

"Oh, it's you," she said. "No hits for me. But I've been hit on every second try."

I smiled. "I don't like their taste in music, but at least the young men of today still have good taste in women."

"It wasn't just the men."

"Hmmm. I guess the young women have good taste in women too."

"Come." I grabbed Vallerie's hand and pulled her through the crowd. "We have to talk with DJ Groove Finger."

"Who?"

I pointed. "The guy destroying those LPs over there."

It sounded like the rap group had begun a new song, but I found it hard to tell since the beat stayed pretty much the same, and so did the lyrics. Someone beat up on someone else for messin' with the first someone's girl. Then this first someone started beatin' up on the girl. Okay, so my parents didn't like my taste in music either. And I'm sure someone's parents didn't like Bach.

I elbowed my way to a spot just below the riser where DJ Groove Finger sat, dragging Vallerie behind me. A chorus line of scantily clad young women, sweat glistening on their skin, looked up at the DJ, squealing every time he rubbed the record one way, then the other.

I dropped Vallerie's hand and grabbed a woman by her shoulder to move her aside. When she turned around, I backed away. She had so many visible piercings—eyebrows, earlobes, nose, lips, tongue—it looked like her face had been riveted, which made me wonder about all the places she'd pierced that I couldn't see.

"You wanna dance?" she said in a dreamy voice.

"Not now, sweetheart. I need to speak with DJ Groove Finger."

I tapped DJ Groove Finger's leg several times, but he kept right on bobbing his head with his eyes closed, pushing and pulling the LP with his finger. So I reached up and put my hand on the record. I must have pushed the tone arm because the needle scraped across the surface, making a raucous noise through the speakers. The women around me moaned and screamed. The crowd went wild. DJ Groove Finger opened his eyes, his finger picking up the rhythm after my interruption.

"Yo, Man, that's cool what you did there."

I flashed my badge. "Can you talk and play?"

He nodded.

"I need your help. There's trouble at the school."

"Someone here flunk a class?"

"Someone bombed a laboratory and we can't find two of the graduate students that work there. Thought you might know them. Bucky Buchanan and Matthew Voltmann."

His eyes flashed wide. "Bucky, hurt?"

"I don't know. And I won't know unless I can find her."

"She's good people. Real good people. Hold on."

He held up one hand and kept spinning the LP with the other. Then he reached for a microphone.

"Okay. Okay." His voiced boomed over the speakers. "Give it up for Biggy D and the Bad Boyz." DJ Groove Finger made an exaggerated clapping motion over his head. The rap group turned to him with grimaces on their faces, but the crowd broke into applause. He spoke in rapid fire. "I'm taking my finger off the groove while we take a little break. Biggy D and the Bad Boyz will be right back, but first DJ Groove Finger has a favor to ask. I need the 4-1-1 on Bucky Buchanan. And I know someone out there wants to give it up for me."

Within moments a line of people, mostly nubile young women, were in front of the DJ's riser and we had an address and telephone number for Bucky. As I turned to leave, a supple body plowed frontally into me. I looked down upon a pair of breasts and arms covered with tattoos. A young woman raised her head and slowly rolled her eyes. "You're leaving already? We haven't had a chance to dance to the DJ's funky groove."

Vallerie buried her head in her hand and stifled a laugh.

I gently peeled away the young woman. "Maybe next time," I said.

She pouted and skulked away.

"Looks like you missed your calling," Vallerie said.

I wagged my finger at her. "Don't go there."

B ucky's apartment sat on a hill just below the university, overlooking Bellingham Bay. The orange lights of the marina and the industrial buildings along the waterfront twinkled in the background. A southerly breeze blew in a damp chill. Vallerie ran her finger down the list of residents, but I grabbed her hand before she pushed the button next to Bucky's name.

"Front door's open," I said.

We pushed through the door and walked up the stairs, which creaked under our weight.

"She lives on the second floor," Vallerie said. "But we're here kind of late. Don't you think this is a bit intrusive."

"Do you want a scoop?" I asked.

"You've got a point," she said.

We walked down the second-floor hallway. A steady beat of bass thumped the first apartment door we passed. At the end of the hall, we found a door with a hand-drawn cartoon of a big-toothed beaver holding a diploma labeled "PhD" under its arm like a lance.

Vallerie grimaced. "Bucky Beaver? Kind of juvenile for a grad student?"

"After DJ Groove Finger, I can think of a lot more raunchy images she could have on her door."

Vallerie wagged her finger at me. "Don't go there."

I couldn't find a doorbell, so I knocked. And we waited. No one answered so I knocked again. And we waited more. Then I noticed fresh scratch marks on the door lock's metal strike plate. I pointed to Vallerie's purse.

"Have you got a tissue or a handkerchief?"

She handed me a tissue. "Breaking and entry?"

I carefully wrapped the tissue around the doorknob, twisted, and pushed. The door swung open. "Not tonight."

I waved Vallerie in. After her footsteps clicked several times on the hardwood surface, I heard dull thuds as her feet encountered an object lying on the floor.

"Damn," she cried out.

"Are you alright?"

"I stepped on something. Can you find a light?"

"Stand where you are and don't move," I said.

With the tissue over my fingers, I groped along the wall until I found a light switch. I expected the worst, but when I flipped the switch, I saw Vallerie trapped in a pile of dirty clothes. She twisted around to free herself.

"Yuck," she said. "This place is trashed."

I stepped over the mound of clothes and walked into the small living room where the window looked out to the water. Books lay strewn over the floor like a deck of oversized playing cards dealt haphazardly from a dealer's hand. Above a lamp keeled over onto an olive green sofa, a large gash in the seat back bled yellow foam stuffing. On a small wooden desk by the window, a computer monitor sat with its cords dangling in space. I looked but I didn't see the case housing the body of the computer, just a lone keyboard lying on the floor.

"Shall we try the bathroom?" I asked.

I kicked open a door off the living room. It swung back, clearing a toilet by less than an inch, rolling bottles over a white tiled floor. I stuck my head in and checked the tub. Fortunately, I didn't find anything there.

Through a second door from the living room we entered Bucky's bedroom, where a dresser stood, missing two drawers. One drawer was overturned on a pile of panties and bras. A strong, cloying fruit-and-powder smell hung in the air. Bucky's white bed linen was stained yellowish brown from a pool of perfume that drained from a tipped-over bottle. Back in the living room, we stepped over books. Vallerie stopped and looked around.

"Who did this?" she asked.

"Someone's looking for something." I pointed to Bucky's desk. "Computer's missing. A document. Data. A name. Something they thought Bucky had. Anyway, aren't you supposed to have a little pad and pen out, scribbling down notes?"

"Tell me again what the story is," Vallerie said.

"The university's lab where Thomas Atherton worked was firebombed this evening, and the graduate student who worked with him…Well, I don't how to end that sentence."

"Yeah. I've got that much about the lab. I'm just not sure where this figures in." She swept her hand around the living room.

I stepped into the kitchen and switched on a light. A potpourri of smells assaulted me. Dried food and spices spilled from open white cabinets onto a butcher-block countertop and down to the floor. I sidestepped a pile of uncooked brown rice to reach the refrigerator. Photos and notes attached by magnets littered the refrigerator door. Next to a snapshot of Bucky, about four years old and buried in the sand up to her neck, I found a list of graduate student names, addresses and telephone numbers, Matthew Voltmann's among them.

ON THE DRIVE ACROSS town to Matthew's place, I told Vallerie everything I knew about the sex life of amphipods. She didn't seem impressed until I got to the part about the bulging eyes of male amphipods, and sex happening billions and billions of times every moment in the oceans. When we stopped at a red light, she turned and smiled.

"With the women flaunting their stuff and the men's eyes bulging, they should call that club the Wild Amphipod."

We both laughed.

Matthew lived at 1298 Yew Street Road. Yew Street Road? What kind of name was that? The city planners couldn't make up their minds whether it was a street or a road, so they named it both? The road, or the street, wound its way up into the hills just east of Bellingham. Coming down the back side, the house numbers plunged suddenly from 1302 to 1292 and, around the next bend, Yew ended in a tee with another road.

We turned around. Vallerie popped the door of her glove compartment and handed me a flashlight. I shined it on front doors, and on the luminous white-on-blue house numbers staked into the ground. It didn't help. 1298 fell in the middle of a dark gap of trees off to our right. With a name like Yew Street Road, I should have guessed Matthew's address wouldn't be easy to find. If, in fact, he lived on Yew at all.

We drove past where his house should have been, stopping at an empty volunteer fire station to turn around again. Coming back down Yew a second time, I saw a lawn sign that read, "Dancing Dolphin Pottery."

"Stop," I said.

"But there's nothing here," Vallerie said.

I pointed to the sign across the street. Vallerie pulled over to the opposite side of the road.

"Dolphins eat salmon," I said. "Salmon eat herring. Herring eat amphipods. Matthew studies amphipods. So maybe that sign is telling us where he lives."

Vallerie sighed. "What the hell type of logic is that?"

"About as good as the logic that named this Yew Street Road."

I got out and ran across Yew. To the right of the sign, a dirt road disappeared into the trees. I waved Vallerie over with the flashlight. After bumping along the dirt road, then bouncing across a small wooden bridge, the car's headlights illuminated a cabin in the woods off to our right. A few hundred yards beyond the cabin, lights blazed on the bottom floor of a large house.

I had Vallerie stop so her headlights pointed at the cabin door. She stayed in the car, while I walked the short path to the cabin. With the car's engine off, I heard a brook babbling, and overhead stars twinkled through the boughs of tall trees. Reggae music, which sounded like Bob Marley, thumped softly from inside the darkened cabin. I raised a wooden door handle, which lifted a wooden bolt inside.

The door creaked as I pushed it open. And when I stepped inside, I heard a *whoosh*, like the sound of a bird's wings, then I felt the crushing pain of an object smashing down on my head. I crumpled to the floor. The room began to spin, and I started to black out.

I squeezed my eyes closed tightly, trying to prevent myself from losing consciousness. My head throbbed with pain, and I felt a warm, sticky trickle of blood when I touched it. When I realized I wouldn't black out, I opened my eyes and rose to my feet. My knees wobbled under me. I stumbled toward the window, while in the background, Bob Marley sang, "Ambush in the Night."

Through the open window, the babbling brook swallowed the sound of footsteps racing through the woods, and the night embraced whoever attacked me.

I left Bob Marley wailing and went out to Vallerie, but she wasn't there. I looked up toward the large house, and saw her on the porch, talking to someone in the lighted doorway. So I went back into Matthew's cabin, opened the door and found a light switch.

The cabin was in shambles, and near the door a board lay on the floor, with a bloodstain smeared on it. I closed my eyes and rubbed them, the pain so intense all I really wanted was to lie down and sleep, but I forced myself to look around. A calf-high metal box with the guts of a computer lay on the floor near the cabin's only window, as though whoever thumped me abandoned it in order to escape.

I yanked a handkerchief from my pocket and winced as I pressed it over the wound on my head. With my free hand, I dragged the computer back to a desk where the power cord, and cables from his monitor, modem, and printer dangled like the cut ends of arteries from which a heart had been severed.

Between sharp spasms of pain, I reattached the power cord and monitor, then turned the computer on. After a beep, the main screen appeared with a background picture of a male and female amphipod mating. I crouched in front of the screen. A doorbell rang from the computer speakers, and at the bottom of the screen a smiley face jiggled up and down. Then a stilted electronic voice announced, "Matthew, you've got mail." I clicked on the smiley face.

The last message to Matthew had been delivered an hour and a half ago. The subject line read, "NEWS RELEASE." The message warned, "YOUR LABORATORIES, YOUR REFINERIES, AND YOUR PIPELINES WILL NOT BE SAFE UNTIL YOU STOP POISONING OUR OCEANS. WE WILL STOP THE GEORGIA STRAIT PIPELINE FOR THE HEALTH OF OUR PLANET. THE OCEAN LIBERATION FRONT."

"Charlie?"

My body jerked badly, sending a firestorm of pain shooting down from my head. I leapt to my feet.

"I didn't mean to scare you," Vallerie said. Then she gulped. "My God, you're hurt. What happened?"

"I walked in on someone trying to escape."

Vallerie hung her head down and shook it. "While I was busy trying to get a story from the people who rent Matthew the cabin. Sorry, I should have been here to back you up and I wasn't." She sighed. "Was it Matthew?"

"I never saw who hit me."

She nodded up toward the house. "Jim and Carol said he came by about an hour ago and told them he'd be gone for a few days. Something about needing to do some field research."

I tried to respond, but instead I squeezed my eyes closed with the pain.

"Hell, we can talk about this later," Vallerie said. She grabbed my arm and walked me out of the cabin toward her car. "Sit in the car. I'll go back up to the house and get some ice."

I leaned back in the car seat, and when Vallerie returned I took the ice-filled towel from her and pressed it against my head. She wanted to drive me to a hospital. After a few minutes, the cold numbed the pain enough so I could at least think.

"Call the Bellingham police department," I said. "And ask to speak with Detective Ben Conrad."

She whipped out her cell phone and pressed 9-1-1, but I grabbed her hand before she could hit "Send."

"Call information and get the number for the police station," I said. "Then call the station and tell them to put you through to Ben Conrad. Say it's an emergency."

She got through to Ben and told him what had happened. While we waited for him to arrive, I told Vallerie about the e-mail Matthew received, and she apologized several more times for leaving me alone.

Red lights soon pranced through the trees as two police cars made their way down the dirt road and pulled up alongside us. Ben stepped from an unmarked white car and walked over to my window. He shined a flashlight on my head.

"You need medical attention for that? I can get EMTs out here."

I waved him off. "No. I'm okay. But you'd better take a look at what's on the computer inside the cabin."

He walked into the cabin, while a uniformed officer got out of the other car, came over and proceeded to take a statement from me. Not long afterward, Ben stepped from Matthew's cabin tapping his flashlight in his hand. He sauntered up to the car.

"How'd you know to come here?" he asked.

"Hunch," I said.

"Good hunch. What do you make of it?"

"Once wasn't enough. OLF wants to show they can strike whenever, wherever they want."

"You think this Voltmann kid's involved?"

"I do."

"Sounds to me like someone needs to find these crazies."

"You're right. Someone needs to."

"You get any more good hunches, maybe you should let me know first in case you need some backup."

Vallerie took a deep breath, and I could feel her on the verge of saying something. I put my hand on her leg to hold her back. "Thanks," I said to Conrad.

"Did you tell the feds and the guys from Anacortes yet?"

"No. I thought I'd give it to you first."

He raised his flashlight to his head and saluted me with it. "Noble, I owe you one."

Conrad walked toward the large house. Vallerie and I drove off.

"I've got to find the OLF," I said.

"Where? It's not like they have offices that you can visit."

"I don't know where yet. I'll have to triangulate it."

"What?" she asked.

"Triangulation. A basic navigation problem."

"Oh," Vallerie said. "You mean using two known points to find a third, unknown point?"

I nodded my head, though it hurt. "Uh huh."

"And the two points you know are Bucky and Matthew."

"That's right."

"If you find them, you'll probably find the OLF."

"Something like that," I said.

"It sounds good," she said. "But do you know where either Bucky or Matthew is?"

"No. That's a problem, isn't it?"

"And you're sure Matthew and Bucky are involved with the OLF?"

"I'm not sure of anything," I said. "But someone was after their computers. Maybe Bucky and Matthew were trying to remove them so no one would discover what they know. Or maybe someone else already knows what they know. Maybe after Matthew got that e-mail from the OLF, he knew he'd be the target of an investigation. Any way you slice it, they're involved. The only question is to what extent. And the only way I'll find out is by finding them."

"Well, we won't find them tonight." Vallerie sighed. "I'm beat." She checked the dashboard clock. "It's not quite two in the morning. I still can make the deadline for tomorrow's edition." She winced. "Though I'm not sure yet what the real story is, I'll at least write an article on the firebombing of the lab and the disappearance of the two graduate students."

I touched her leg again. "Hold off on Bucky and Matthew."

"After I ran around with you all night looking for them?"

"I didn't say don't run the story. I just said hold off until I...we have more."

"On one condition. I'm the first to get whatever you find, even before Conrad gets it."

My head hurt too much to argue. "You're on," I said.

When we pulled up to the marina, two guys came to life in an unmarked car at the corner of the parking lot. Vallerie noticed them too.

"Friends?"

"Shadows," I said. "Ever since I first started working on Atherton's disappearance."

"Who are they with?"

"The department of None of Your Damn Business."

Vallerie stiffened. "Excuse me. After I spent all night running—"

"No. Not you. That's what they told me when I asked."

"Sorry...Let me get this. You're chasing leads but you have no idea where they're headed. And you're being followed by people but you have no idea where they're from. Isn't that kinda like a dog chasing another dog chasing its tail?"

"Gee, I never thought about it quite as concisely as that. These guys are working for some federal agency. FBI or DHS. They want to find Atherton, and they're probably hoping I'll lead them to him."

Vallerie chuckled. "Like I said. A dog chasing another dog chasing its tail."

"You want me to make the introduction?" I pointed to the unmarked car. "I'm sure they'd appreciate hearing that directly from you."

"I'll pass," she said.

I opened the car door and walked down the gangway toward the *Noble Lady*.

I awoke close to noon the next day. After breakfast, I walked up the gangway, waved to the guys in the unmarked car. Damn, they had a boring job. I fed two quarters to a vending machine in front of the marina restaurant, and pulled out the day's newspaper. The headline read, "Fire Destroys University Marine Lab," and underneath that, "Ecoterrorism Suspected." The byline read, "Vallerie McKee." I tucked the newspaper under my arm and headed back down to the *Noble Lady*.

I pulled my guitar from its case, running through warm-up scales and exercises. I spent twenty minutes playing the first three measures of the Prelude, watching my posture and my breath, before daring to play the entire piece. And when I got to that difficult passage my fingers locked up again, so I went back to the basics of a few measures, posture, and breath.

After practicing, I called the university and asked to speak with Melissa Buchanan but the operator directed me to the security department instead. I hung up. I pulled out a pencil and pad and yanked the door of the refrigerator open, jotting down what provisions I'd need for four or five days away.

Then I called Janet and asked if she had time to meet me this afternoon. We agreed on Tony's, a coffee shop down the street from her gallery, at four-thirty, which left me plenty of time to shop. Something about being on the water stimulates my appetite and my culinary instincts. After shopping, I rolled a cartload full of groceries down to the *Noble Lady* and packed the refrigerator full. By then it was time for a brisk walk to Fairhaven to see Janet. The guys in the unmarked car tailed me, but I didn't bother giving them the slip.

Inside Tony's, Janet sat on a stool at the end of a counter that spanned the length of the side window. She jumped down from the stool when she saw me, walked over and squeezed my hand.

"We don't have to sit at the counter," she said. "But it's my favorite spot for watching people."

"It's fine with me."

We walked to the front counter and ordered lattes. I got mine straight. Janet had a list of modifications.

"Half soy milk, half rice milk—"

The woman behind the counter finished her order. "Mocha, easy on the chocolate, a dab of whipped cream, a sprinkle of cinnamon. You got it."

Janet smiled and nodded.

"Must be a regular," I said.

"It's my drug of choice."

"What? The soy milk? The rice milk? The chocolate? The whipped cream? The cinnamon? Or the coffee?"

"Hmmm. Come to think about it, all of the above." She had a mischievous twinkle in her eyes.

We carried our lattes back to the counter. Outside, two kids on skateboards zoomed by, and across the street a man in calf-high leather boots and a Mounties hat strolled along. Fairhaven was the closest thing Bellingham had to an area of the city that resembled Greenwich Village.

Janet delicately scooped a little whipped cream from the top of her drink, placed the spoon in her mouth and extracted it slowly.

"Umm. I'm jealous," she said. She licked the spoon.

"Of whom?" I sipped my latte.

"Vallerie."

"Why?"

"She called this morning and said you showed her an exciting time last night."

"Did she tell you what we did?"

"After going to the lab? Not really, but I kind of figured it out by reading the morning paper. I got the impression that Vallerie enjoyed being with you."

"Oh."

With the edge of her spoon, Janet parted the remaining whipped cream, then dipped the spoon underneath, emerging with a tiny white island floating in a sea of mocha. "I think she's had you in her sights for a while." She stuck the spoon in her mouth and pulled it out slowly again.

"How's that? She's barely been in town for a month."

"She's the one who first told me about you."

"How could she have known?"

"It's a small town. News travels fast." Janet tapped her spoon lightly on the rim of her cup. "After Thomas's boat was found heading toward Cherry Point, she interviewed me. When I mentioned wanting to hire someone to help find him, she said your name came up in the investigation."

"That's strange."

"She thought it was strange too. A black man in this town, living on his boat, working as a private investigator. She asked me if I knew you."

"Interesting gal," I said.

"A lot of interesting single women here would enjoy spending time with you."

"Is that prophecy?" I took a healthy gulp of my latte.

"No, it's an observation from watching the dating scene over the years."

"It's been years since I dated seriously," I said. "After Sharon's death it was hard thinking about a long-term relationship with another woman. I didn't feel ready to open up emotionally again."

"A long-term relationship. Is that what you want?"

"I want to circumnavigate the earth on a boat, and I don't want to do it alone."

Janet mused, the smiled. "'Come see the world with me.' That's not too shabby for a pickup line. It sounds like you might be ready to venture out into those scary waters again."

"I don't really know, but it sounds like this might be the place to find out. Apparently there are more single women than single men in town?"

"From what I see and what I hear."

"Was Thomas a flirt?"

She frowned, then let her spoon dive deep into her cup. "Not really. Thomas was brilliant and women who find intelligence a turn-on always wanted to be around him. But he lived in his mind, and unlike you, he found it difficult to engage around his feelings. It's sad to think that his mind may have gotten him into trouble."

"I don't quite follow you."

"He believed so much in certain ideas like environmental stewardship, particularly when it came to the sea, that it wouldn't surprise me if someone exploited him. Thomas could have easily been blind to ulterior motives."

"Someone like the Ocean Liberation Front?"

"Yeah."

"How much do you know about Bucky Buchanan?"

"A little. When she first came to Huxley as a grad student, we had her to dinner several times until it became uncomfortable for us to be around Thomas together."

"She's Canadian, but do you know where she's from?"

"Nanaimo. Comox. Somewhere on Vancouver Island. But her family also had a place in the San Juan Islands. I don't remember which island. Why?"

"Vallerie didn't tell you?"

"Like I said, she didn't say much about last night."

"We went by Bucky's apartment after leaving the marine labs. It had been ransacked. Matthew's place also. And now they're both missing."

"Let me guess. You want to find her?"

"I do."

"Why? Do you think she'll lead you to Thomas?"

"That thought had occurred."

"The thought of them together..." Janet shook her head. "I know...it's been over a year, and we both need to get on with our lives. I should let go of finding Thomas, pay for your services, and concentrate on running the gallery."

I waved her off. "Don't worry about paying me. I intend to find him. I joined the Coast Guard because what I enjoyed most was helping people who'd gotten into trouble. I miss that. And if I can't find that being a private investigator, I'll have to look for some other kind of work."

Janet stared out the window and took a long sip of coffee. Finally, she turned to me. "I admire your commitment and dedication. And I also intend to pay you for your time. I've thought about it. Do you have any space on the *Noble Lady* for a great piece of northwest Indian art?"

"If I don't, I'll make space," I said.

◎　◎　◎

THAT EVENING, THE SUNSET painted the sky orange. Evening can be a wonderful time to cruise, and I thought about leaving. I didn't have a solid plan, but I'd poke around the San Juan Islands to see if I could turn up anything about Bucky and her family. The phone book listed twenty-one Buchanans spread throughout the islands. At least, that'd give me something to do.

I raised the engine hatch and dropped down into the holy place. The transmission and engine levels were fine, but when I popped the cap on the coolant reservoir and stuck my finger in, I noticed it had dropped nearly a half-inch below my second knuckle. A good sign that I was losing coolant. So I topped the reservoir off with water and looked for leaks, but I couldn't find any. I turned the engine over and let it run for a few minutes, popped the reservoir cap, and sure enough the coolant level was down again. One more time, I topped the coolant off. Then I crawled on top of Miss Perky and leaned over, straining to look.

Ah hah. A trickle of green-tinged water ran out a weep hole and down the back side of my freshwater pump, which meant it had blown a seal and I wasn't leaving until the morning.

I settled in for the evening, fixing myself a goat cheese, baked garlic, pear, and walnut salad. I walked into the forward berth and lifted the mattress, exposing the *Noble Lady*'s wine cellar. I pulled out my finest, most expensive bottle of merlot, a Washington State Red Mountain Reserve 2000. Then I turned up a CD of Andrés Segovia playing the guitar. Listening to El Maestro, I relaxed into the realization that some ideals one can only strive for, knowing full well they will never be achieved.

Halfway through the merlot something bumped the *Noble Lady*, not hard but enough to rouse my suspicion. I doused the lights, cut Segovia, and reached for my pistol. I crouched, moving out of the galley to the rear deck. Whatever it was bumped the boat again. It could have been a log. I crawled onto the aft seat and peered over the stern. In the dim light, I made out a woman, paddling a kayak, who appeared to have run into the *Noble Lady*. Her yellow boat glowed under the marina's lights.

I swallowed a laugh and pushed the canvas aside. "Can I help you, Ma'am?"

She looked up, then said, "Sir, it's Lieutenant Katherine Sullivan."

K atherine Sullivan held onto her paddle with one hand and
the *Noble Lady*'s swim step with the other. I tucked my
pistol between my waistband and the small of my back.

"Permission to come aboard, Sir?"

"You want to come around to the dock? It'd be easier for you
to get out."

"No, Sir. I think it's best for me to stay waterside. Less
chance of being seen."

I unsnapped the canvas from its frame and extended a hand
to Sullivan over the gunwales. She grabbed my arm and pulled
herself out of her boat onto the *Noble Lady*'s swim step. Sullivan
reached down for a line from her kayak, whipping it around a
cleat on the *Noble Lady*. She swung one leg then the other over
the gunwales, and I snapped the canvas back in place.

I walked through the rear door, then turned to her, waving
her forward. "Come in, Lieutenant, and tell me what this is all
about."

"In a moment, Sir. First, I need to get out of my gear."

I held the door while, in the shadows of the rear deck, Sullivan unzipped her life vest and tossed it on the backseat. Then she unhooked her spray skirt, letting it fall to the deck, and pulled off a windbreaker. She stripped a wide-brimmed hat off and ran her fingers through her hair.

"Permission to use the head, Sir?"

"You've certainly boarded the boat enough times to know where it is, Lieutenant."

She walked past me into the *Noble Lady,* disappearing down the steps, then into the head. I closed the door behind me and sat at the galley table.

When the door to the head creaked open, Sullivan emerged wearing jeans and a white spandex top, both of which accented her figure nicely. Her dark hair, which I'd only seen tucked into a bun under her hat, now fell below her shoulders. Two silver pendants dangled from her earlobes. The blue stone set in the middle of each looked like lapis lazuli and matched the color of her eyes. Her reddish brown lipstick and hint of eye shadow brought out the darker tones of her skin. Though I could not imagine why she was here, one thing I didn't need to imagine: Lieutenant Katherine Sullivan was indeed a very beautiful woman.

She pointed to the settee wrapping around the galley table. "May I sit, Sir?"

"Yes, Lieutenant. And since I'm no longer an officer in the Coast Guard, you don't need to call me 'Sir.' You can call me Charlie."

"Yes, Sir," she said. Then she smiled. "Sorry, Sir...um...I mean sorry, Commander...um...I mean...Charlie."

"Lieutenant, what are you doing here?"

"Sir." She laughed self-consciously, then crossed her legs. "Sorry. It's hard not to think of you as Commander Noble. I could probably be court-martialed for this, but I had to come to see you. I don't like what District's doing to you and I don't understand why they're doing it."

"I presume you're off duty, Lieutenant?"

"Yessir. Whew." She held up her hand. "Yes, I am...but, Sir...damn." She dropped a fist onto her thigh. "I mean, if you want me to call you Charlie, then you have to call me Kate. That'd make it a whole lot easier. Deal?"

"Deal. Would you like some wine, Lieutenant?" I chuckled. "Sorry...rewind. Would you like some wine, Kate?"

"Yes." She smiled. "Yes, I would."

I poured her a glass of Red Mountain Reserve and another for myself. Katherine grasped the wineglass by its stem and held it up to the light; the dark red liquid was the same color as her lips. She lowered the glass, swirling the wine, then taking a delicate sip, which she rolled on her tongue. She reached for the bottle and twirled it around to read the label.

"Red Mountain Reserve 2000. Good wine. Tastes like black cherry with a hint of chocolate." She looked at me, frowned, then sighed. "You're on a watch list. Any patrol boat encountering the *Noble Lady* has standing orders to stop and board her, regardless of the last boarding."

I took a sip of wine. "Tell me something I don't know."

"The orders are straight from District, and they began the afternoon you showed up at the station asking about the boat we intercepted heading for Cherry Point."

"Yes, you could be court-martialed for telling me this."

"I commanded the patrol boat that intercepted that Grand Banks. I ordered a man to risk his life to board it. I joined the Coast Guard to do these things. To protect our country. To save boaters. I didn't join to play games or participate in cover-ups." She took another sip of wine. "The Grand Banks is still sitting at our dock. The explosives were removed. But after that, no one's been aboard to inspect it. It's been declared off-limits to all station personnel. And we've been informed we are not to speak about the incident to anyone other than District investigative officers."

"That's all standard procedure."

"Yes. But initially this was viewed as a terrorist threat. Scuttlebutt was that maybe it was even a foreign terrorist attack masquerading as domestic ecoterrorism. Then the brakes were put on the investigation, and we were given only two new orders: to fire upon any non-responding vessel that comes within 300 yards of Cherry Point; and to interfere with your free movement on the water. Someone at District doesn't want the investigation to proceed. They don't want you involved. And I don't understand why."

"You're probably right, but you're also risking your career by coming here to tell me. What are you, six or seven years out of the academy?"

"Four."

"Maybe up for another promotion soon. That's not bad. You're on a good career track." I shook my head. "You shouldn't be here."

She raised her wineglass to her lips, but I didn't see her take a swallow.

"Sometimes it's nice just to feel the liquid on your lips and tongue," she said. "To smell it. To taste it without swallowing." She sighed. "I know my job is to follow the orders of my superiors. But there are orders of a higher calling: Integrity. Honesty. Following the dictates of one's own conscience."

"Those are tough orders to follow when you're in the military."

Kate set her glass down and stared at me. "Is that why you're not in?"

I grabbed the stem of my wineglass, rocking the base back and forth on the table. Tiny waves of red liquid collided before the wine began to circle around the eye of a miniature whirlpool. My CO's voice popped back into my head: "You've got two choices, Commander: Change your threat assessment report to give him what he wants, or change your threat assessment report to give him what he wants."

I stared down at the swirling wine. "Perhaps," I said.

Suddenly, Kate rested her hand gently on top of mine, and I raised my head to the earnest look in her eyes.

"I need to know," she said. "You see, you were my hero. That day, after you walked out of our class at the academy. I said to myself, 'He's the kind of officer I want to be.'"

"And you will be, but not by doing this."

"I will be because when faced with tough choices, I made the right ones."

"For your career."

"No." She pointed to her chest. "For myself. Just like I think you did."

"What makes you think that?"

"The man I saw in front of my class that day. An honest man with integrity." She took a swallow of wine. "My dad served in the Coast Guard. A Lieutenant Commander. He flew rescue helos out of Nome, Alaska, then closer to home over the Great Lakes. My mother was Native American. Part Inuit, part Kwakiutl. I put up with a lot to earn my bars. Just like I'm sure you did. At the academy, they called me 'Squaw.' After I graduated, 'Ensign Pocahontas.'"

I nodded my head. "Been there with the N-word," I said. "It's sad. Most people don't even know that African Americans have served in the Coast Guard since the 1700s, when slaves were aboard ships as seamen, stewards, and cooks."

"I didn't know that," Kate said. She stared into her wine. "When I was fourteen, my dad died on a mission to rescue a merchant ship breaking up in a gale on Lake Superior. Wind whipped the waves to twenty feet. Nothing for a Bering Sea pilot. Daddy was ordered back to base, but he refused to go. He managed to drop a swimmer and several rafts, but a rare peak wave clipped his tail rotor and he couldn't pull out. The crew and the swimmer survived."

"That was your father?"

"Damn right."

"I'm sorry. I remember the incident well."

Kate had tears in her eyes. "'Sweetpea,' he'd say to me. 'You follow orders until the orders conflict with what you know to be true in here.'" She touched her chest again. "Something about this investigation doesn't ring true in here."

I raised my glass, taking a sip of wine and rolling it around my mouth with my tongue. I told Kate about the catch-22 face-off with Vin Ritchie. And why I'd decided to act on my conscience and not my career. After I finished, she raised her glass toward me.

"Just like my dad," she said. "I knew you were that kind of man. But why would Ritchie want you off the Cherry Point investigation?"

"Anger. Spite. Vindictiveness. Protecting his turf. I don't know. But I do know, Lieutenant...I mean, Kate...when you get back on duty you need to keep your head down and follow orders."

She took a deep breath, held it, then let it out. "I'll do that, Sss..." She laughed. "I still want to call you Sir. I'll do that, but I want you to know, the next time I board the *Noble Lady*, where I really stand."

"Thanks," I said. I stood up. "Can I help you into your boat?"

"Not so fast." She took a surprisingly big gulp of wine. "Permission to speak freely?"

"Isn't that exactly what you've been doing up to now?"

"Yes, Sss..." She caught herself. "Yes, but this one's harder." Kate uncrossed her legs and shifted her body, sitting ramrod straight now, reminding me of how we were forced to sit in the academy's mess hall. She cleared her throat twice.

"I'm just going to come out and say it."

I waited. Kate took another gulp of wine. And I waited some more. Her face flushed.

"Damn," she said. "I'm embarrassed and I'm not sure how to say this." She straightened her body again. Then, as though barking orders to her crew, she said, "I find you really attractive, Sir. And if the Commander is not otherwise engaged, I'd like to know if there might possibly be an opportunity to get to know him better at some future date?" Then as though talking to herself, she said, "There...I said it." And she lunged for her wine.

I hid behind my wineglass, so my grin wouldn't show. After gaining my composure, I looked at Kate and said, "Did you just ask me if we could date?"

She nodded slowly. "I believe I did."

"Old guy like me. I'm flattered that a beautiful young woman finds me attractive. But you've—"

"You're not old. You're only forty. I'm twenty-eight. Is that a problem?"

"Under ordinary circumstances? No. I was about to say that your future lies in the Coast Guard, mine in another direction I'm still not sure about. It would be a bad career move for you to be seen anywhere near me. Certainly not in Vin Ritchie's district."

"This isn't about a career," Kate said. "It's about wanting to be with a man I can trust and respect. Someone who shares values important to me. Someone with more going than 99 percent of the guys I meet. You never said if you were already seeing someone."

"You mean, 'otherwise engaged'?"

"Yes, Sir." She snapped to attention, playfully.

"No. My wife died five years ago."

Kate gasped. "I'm so very sorry. I had no idea."

"Thank you."

"If you say to me, 'Absolutely not. Never,' I'll drop the matter and never mention it again. Otherwise, I'll presume it's not unreasonable to hold out a beacon of hope."

"Do you always hide behind military-speak?"

"Only when I'm as damn nervous as I am now," Kate said. She fiddled with her wineglass.

I smiled. "I never say never."

She smiled back. "That's good enough for me."

She pushed away from the settee and stood. "Permission to kiss the Commander?"

I narrowed my eyes.

"On the cheek," she said.

"Permission granted."

After the kiss, Kate slipped on her paddling gear, I helped her back over the gunwales. She slid into her kayak, looked up, and asked, "When's the next time you're leaving port?"

"Tomorrow," I said.

"Then I guess you don't have a choice. Our first date'll be in the middle of Bellingham Bay."

"Lieutenant, I'll say this much. I like your style."

"Thank you, Sir." She saluted me smartly, then paddled off.

I picked up a new water pump at eight the next morning. By ten I had it installed, and by eleven Miss Perky was warmed up and purring. I unhitched the mooring lines, threw them aboard, then I jumped on and climbed up to the pilot-house. When I spun the wheel hard left and gave Miss Perky short, hard cracks of forward and reverse, she turned in her own length. Soon we were running down the fairway, and out of the harbor.

Once in the bay, I looked behind me at the coast guard dock but I didn't see any small patrol boats. I grabbed the binoculars and scanned the bay ahead. For the first time in recent days, I actually looked forward to being boarded by the CG.

I didn't have to wait long.

Halfway across the bay, a black speck trailing a white rooster tail screamed from behind Eliza Island. The patrol boat appeared to be cutting straight across the bay, when suddenly, like a hound dog picking up a scent, it carved a sharp turn and careened toward me, its flashing blue light barely visible in the afternoon sun.

I pulled the *Noble Lady*'s throttle into neutral and walked out on deck, throwing several fenders overboard. The patrol boat zoomed to a stop, and I held on while a small tsunami from its wake passed under my hull. Seaman Crenshaw stood on the rear deck. I tried to find Kate, but sunlight glinting off of the wheelhouse windows made it impossible to see inside.

"Sir, port of origin?"

"Bellingham. Seaman Crenshaw, you wanna toss me line?"

"Sir, port of destination?"

"Friday Harbor, Seaman Crenshaw. It'd save you some time while we're playing this game if you tossed me a line."

He grimaced and clutched his pistol. "Sir, when is the last time you were boarded by the United States Coast Guard?"

"The last time you boarded me, Seaman Crenshaw."

He wouldn't make eye contact. "Sir, please shut down your engine, we will need to board your vessel now."

"The engine's been off since before you got here. Lines, Seaman Crenshaw, toss me the lines."

Loss of control. Coast guard boarding parties are taught at all times to maintain control of a boarding situation through tone of voice, demeanor, facial expression, physical position, and show of weaponry. I knew it would irk Crenshaw if I tried to dictate the pace of his spiel, but what the hell, at least it would amuse me. He finally tossed me lines and I secured the two boats. I reached my hand over the boarding gate to help him aboard, when Kate popped out of the wheelhouse.

"Seaman Crenshaw, I will do this boarding and inspection," she said.

"Yes, Ma'am. Does the Lieutenant want me to accompany her?"

"No, Seaman Crenshaw, please stand by inside the wheelhouse."

"Yes, Ma'am."

Kate grabbed my hand and stepped aboard. She wore her hair tucked up under her cap. Her dark blue uniform revealed little of what I'd seen of her last night. She walked into the galley, placed her PDA and clipboard on the table and grinned.

"All of your equipment in working order, Sir?"

"Yes. Do you wish to inspect it, Lieutenant?"

"Hmmm." She placed her index finger on the side of her face. "Perhaps at a later date."

She punched some keys on her PDA, and a printer attached to it spit out a boarding receipt.

"This receipt shows that you've been boarded and inspected by the Coast Guard and you check out fine," she said. "But it's no guarantee that we won't board you in the future. Do you understand, Sir?" She smiled mischievously.

I pretended to frown. "I think so, Lieutenant."

She strolled out of the galley and stepped through the boarding gate, back onto her patrol boat. She barked, "Mr. Crenshaw, grab our lines and let's get back to the barn."

Crenshaw stepped from the wheelhouse, a puzzled look on his face. I untied the boarding lines and threw them back across to the patrol boat.

Before she sped away, Kate smiled and said in a crisp, professional tone, "Sir, thank you for operating cautiously and safely."

I climbed back into the pilothouse and fired up Miss Perky. I'd been to Friday Harbor so many times, I probably could have smacked the *Noble Lady*'s rump and she'd have galloped there on her own. But I pointed her toward the south tip of Lummi Island, and in no time we were whipping through riptides at a place called Devil's Corner. Fortunately the current was going our way.

While cruising northwest along the coast of Cypress Island, I heard a pair of bald eagles trade cascading, fluted calls. Then, with a great swoosh of air, one leapt from a tall snag, diving sharply, gracefully unhinging its talons from beneath its body, and reaching what seemed to be only a few inches below the water's surface. Another prodigious flap of wings brought it rising into the air again, a writhing fish beneath it. It flew past the snag and its mate called out, then took flight to join it.

Once through the narrow gap between Cypress Island and tiny Towhead Island, I turned on the Vessel Traffic System channel, where the controller reported a southbound tug and barge off the Clark Island light. When crossing Rosario Strait, my general formula is if I can see large traffic, I wait. The Clark Island light was about eight miles away, and I guessed that tug traveled about twelve knots an hour, which gave me forty minutes or so to make the crossing. I chanced it.

I pushed Miss Perky up to 2400 rpm and kept an anxious ear fixed to the VTS channel. I first saw the bow of the tug rounding Lawrence Point on Orcas Island, then thirty seconds later not one but two barges.

Crossing active shipping lanes, there's a point of no return, and though there's almost always room to maneuver to avoid a collision, this type of crossing is nerve-wracking to me. The tug captain checked in with VTS, reporting his speed at fourteen knots and estimating Tide Point, near me, in about twenty minutes. I could still turn back, or stop and let the tug and barge go by, but I decided to press on. I kept the *Noble Lady* on autopilot and stepped outside to watch the tug and barge as we crossed paths, nearly a half-mile apart.

The route to Friday Harbor squeezes through one of two small passes. Peavine Pass is short but narrow. Obstruction Pass, wide and tortuous but interesting. With the current about to shift, that meant I'd hit either pass near slack water, so I decided to take the interesting route. The current in Obstruction Pass pushed the *Noble Lady* around, but nothing beyond what she could handle. At the end of the pass, sunlight sparkled off a copper statue, one of several pieces of avant-garde metal sculptures erected by a private landowner on a point at the west end of the pass. Traveling this way always reminded me of breezing through a modern art gallery.

Friday Harbor is nestled deep into a cove along the northeast side of San Juan Island. The town is perched on a hill above the port. As you enter the cove, a complex of buildings off to the right house a University of Washington marine science laboratory.

While moored at another island last year, I met four young female graduate students collecting samples of sea anemones from beneath the dock. I didn't remember their names, but I did remember they worked out of the Friday Harbor lab. It seemed like a good place to start asking about Bucky, so I headed over to their docks and tied up behind a sixty-foot NOAA research vessel. But when I stepped off the *Noble Lady,* a security guard in a green uniform came running down the dock, waving his arms, his holstered gun bouncing off his overweight frame.

He pulled his gun out, leveled it at me and yelled. "Hands in the air."

Another guard, who also looked out of shape, raced down the dock with his gun drawn. By the time they'd reached me both men had bright red faces and labored breathing. I raised my hands, afraid that with any more stress one of these two gray-haired men might suddenly collapse, accidentally discharging his weapon.

The first guard kept his gun trained on me, but spoke over his shoulder. "You okay, Sam?"

Bent over with both hands on his thighs, it took Sam a moment to catch his breath. "Uh huh. Let's cuff him and bring him in."

"You don't need to handcuff me," I said.

"Turn around," the first guard said. "You're trespassing on the private property of the University of Washington."

The second guard waved his pistol and chimed in. "Better do as Pete said."

Then the reason for all this silliness dawned on me. "On high alert because of the firebombing of the marine lab in Anacortes?"

"You know about that, huh?" Pete asked.

"I'm investigating it."

Sam squinted. "Sure you are. What kinda investigator cruises in an old rig like that?" He pointed to the *Noble Lady.* "Probably couldn't even do ten knots."

"Seven to seven and a half."

Sam chuckled. "Like I said. What kinda investigator cruises at seven knots? Bad guys could do loopety-loos around you and still get away. Let's take him inside and call the police."

They cuffed my hands behind my back and walked me up the gangway toward the main building. I didn't resist. At least this assured me of gaining entrance to the lab. Inside the building, Pete and Sam sat me in a chair opposite the receptionist's desk.

"Cheryl," Pete said. "Call the police and tell 'em we apprehended an intruder trying to gain access from the dock."

Cheryl, a sensibly dressed, fit, graying brunette in her late forties, looked hard at me. I raised my eyebrows and shrugged my shoulders. Then she looked at the guards.

"Are you sure you want me to call the police?"

"That's what I said," Pete said.

"Ask to speak with Sheriff Sykes," I said.

Everyone turned toward me.

"Tell him that Charlie Noble's here on an investigation of the firebombing of Huxley's marine lab."

Cheryl picked up the phone, and punched in one number when Pete yelled, "Stop." He turned to me. "Are you really here on an investigation?"

I pointed to the phone. "Ask Ed Sykes, if you don't believe me."

"How d'ya know Ed?" Sam asked.

"I helped him draw up the Maritime Safety and Security plan for Friday Harbor."

Sam whistled low.

Pete grimaced. "You did?"

Cheryl held up a hand. "Wait a minute." She slid open a drawer and pulled out a thick coil-bound booklet, thumbing rapidly through the first few pages. "Here," she said.

Pete walked around to the other side of the desk, took a pair of reading glasses from his top pocket, unfolded them and slipped them on the end of his nose. He snatched the heavy volume from Cheryl, muttering aloud, "Well I'll be."

"What's it say, Pete?" Sam asked.

"Developed in conjunction with Commander Charles E. Noble, USCG."

Pete forgot to pull off his glasses, and tripped hurrying back around from Cheryl's desk toward me.

"Sorry, Commander," he said. "Very sorry, but you were right. We're on heightened security here since the firebombing. No one's to enter this facility without an ID tag."

He jiggled a key in each handcuff, which popped open.

"I'll call Dr. Rondell," Cheryl said. "To tell him you're here."

Pete and Sam slunk out the door. Cheryl went back to her computer screen. I sat and waited, feeling infinitely better knowing that Pete and Sam were in charge of security at such a vulnerable, sensitive target.

A few minutes later, a bearded man walked into the reception area, wearing an open collar shirt, jeans, and glasses hanging from a silver chain around his neck. He stuck out his hand and we shook. "Simon Rondell," he said. "I apologize for the manner in which you were treated, but I'm afraid we're not experienced with security here at the lab."

"I can see that," I said.

"The university insisted on locating security guards here after the firebombing in Anacortes. How may I help you?"

Rondell had a stiff manner that suggested more comfort with marine organisms than people.

"I'm trying to locate a graduate student who worked at the Anacortes lab, who's been missing since the firebombing. Her name's Melissa Buchanan, but she also goes by the nickname Bucky. Do you know her?"

"Bucky?" He paused. "Other than Buckminster Fuller, I don't know any Buckys."

"'Bout a year ago, I met a team of four female grad students from this lab collecting samples over on Stuart Island. I don't remember their names, but I'd like to find them and ask them about Melissa. It's got to be a small community of female marine biology grad students."

Rondell held up his hand. "Sorry, but without prior authorization from the university, I'm unable to release the names of any students, or allow you to speak with them." He pointed. "Cheryl will give you the Seattle number to call for more information. Now if you'll excuse me, I have an aquarium full of squirming critters that need me."

Rondell pivoted and walked down the hall. I turned to Cheryl, who was busy scribbling on a yellow Post-it pad.

She tore off the top sheet and handed to me, shaking her head "I've been working here for twenty years. Nothing's like it used to be. Sorry we can't be of more help."

I folded the small sheet and slipped it into my shirt pocket as I walked down the university's dock. When I reached the *Noble Lady*, I pulled out the yellow note. I read it and smiled. Then I turned around and waved toward the main building. I don't know if Cheryl saw me.

She'd given me a name, "Erica Greeley," and Erica's number here in Friday Harbor.

From the University of Washington's marine sciences lab, I moved the *Noble Lady* the short distance over to the Port of Friday Harbor marina and tied up along the concrete pier on the inside of the breakwater.

I called Erica Greeley on my cell phone. Her voice-mail picked up, offering several seconds of whale calls, then the message, "Hope you're having a whale of a day, leave a message at the tone." I left my number and asked her to call me back about Bucky. Then I hiked the long distance from the visitor's dock to the port office, where I paid for a night's stay.

I paused on the steps leading down from the office to take in the picture-postcard view: A few cumulus clouds hung in the cobalt blue sky. Soft light from the late afternoon sun illuminated the tallest peaks on neighboring islands, where some trees—set amidst the ever-present dark green foliage of the Northwest—had already begun turning yellow and red. Then a huge green-and-white car ferry turned the corner and lumbered into port. Below me, a sea of masts and gleaming hulls spread out. Overhead, two seagulls squawked at each other. I took a deep breath and held it, succumbing to the enchantment of being around boats and water.

With a few hours to kill before dinner, I started walking back down the docks, when the sound of whales on Erica Greeley's voice mail message played again in my mind. I spun around and headed quickly back up the ramp, past the port office. I tried taking the long flight of stairs up to the city two at a time, but I only made it halfway and slowly walked the rest. At the top of the staircase, I turned left and headed a few storefronts down to the Whale Museum.

Inside the museum, a young woman with a round face and sun-baked red cheeks sat behind a desk. She looked at a wall clock and frowned. "We close in fifteen minutes. That doesn't give you much time to see the exhibit."

"I've been here many times," I said. "Today, I stopped by to see if you could help me find a friend I heard had just gotten back on the island."

"Who's that?"

"Bucky Buchanan."

She perked up. "Bucky's back?"

I smiled. "That's what I heard."

"Terrible what happened to her lab."

"Uh huh."

"Do you think the Ocean Liberation Front did it?" she asked.

"I don't really know," I said.

She shook her head, jingling her silver whale-tail earrings. "Like, I don't think so. Firebombing. Explosives. Too much risk to innocent lives," she said. "Chaining a ship in port. Freeing fish from nets. Harassing the navy when it's doing underwater sonar testing. That's more the OLF's style."

"You know where I could find Bucky?"

"How d'ya know her?"

"Herring," I said. "I'm doing an investigation of the herring population near Cherry Point."

"It's sad how they've been decimated by pollution."

"Do you know that for a fact?"

"Like, you're doing the study. What's the data show?"

I grimaced. "Right now, not much."

"Like, what do you mean?"

I held up my hands. "Lab's gone. Computers are gone. Years of work gone. Thomas Atherton's gone. Not much."

"Yeah, I guess so." The edge of her lips twitched. "I heard about Thomas. Damn. Bucky must have been upset. Like, she worshipped him."

"It's one of the reasons I want to catch up with her. She seemed very upset the last time I saw her."

"You know, Bucky wanted to go to school at the University of Washington so she could work at the lab here."

"Oh. What happened?"

"Even though she went to UW as an undergrad, she didn't get into the graduate school." The young woman sighed. "It made her pretty angry at first. Then she found Huxley and Thomas, and it didn't seem to matter that she wasn't here...Like, I've been yapping too much. That's why they have me here at the Museum when I'm working, instead of out with the whales. Division of labor, you know. Like, I'm the one who really likes being around people as much as being around the whales. With some, Bucky for instance, it's different. She likes the whales more. If she's on island, she'll be around them. Over at the point."

"Lime Kiln?"

"Yeah. But not where the public views the whales. Like, she walks north toward the kilns and follows a path out toward the water. I've been there with her a couple of times. In fact, we started calling it Bucky Point. It's small. Nothing but a rocky ledge. Still, when the pod swims by, you have a ringside view."

"Thanks. I'll try to find her tomorrow."

I turned to leave, and as I pulled the front door open, the woman called out, "I get off at three tomorrow afternoon. I could go with you."

"That's kind, but I need to leave tomorrow afternoon so I'll go out to the point in the morning."

I pulled the door open again.

"One last thing," the woman said.

I turned around. She'd pursed her lips and squinted.

"The trail out to Bucky Point. It can be hard to find..." She put a hand to her chin. "I think it's the second kiln you come to. Turn toward the water there and you should find it. I never did get your name."

"Noble," I said. "Charles Noble."

She straightened her body. "What a regal name... Mine's Erica." She patted her chest. "Erica Greeley."

"Erica," I said. "Nice to meet you. You're exactly the kind of person I was hoping to run into."

◎   ◎   ◎

I AWOKE THE NEXT MORNING to *Bling Bling*, a gleaming white yacht at least a hundred feet long, docked across from me in front of the U.S. Customs kiosk. I lifted a few weights that I had aboard, downed a high-protein smoothie for breakfast, then practiced my guitar for a little while. At nine, I called a cab to take me to Lime Kiln Point, then I walked up toward the port's office to wait. In the backpack slung over my shoulder, I'd tucked a bottle of water and my 9 mm pistol.

Celtic harp and fiddle music played in the taxi, a van built to carry three rows of passengers. We drove through town, then dropped down in the mist to a road on the floor of a lush, dark green valley that cut across the island.

At the far end of the valley, the road rose and we turned south. A moment later a panoramic view of the ocean opened. Strong southerlies buffeted the sea, raising whitecaps along the length of Haro Strait beneath us. And across the strait, a fast-moving bank of clouds dwarfed the city of Victoria and the chain of islands off Vancouver Island.

Two miles along this winding, windswept route, the van pulled up to Lime Kiln State Park and I climbed out. At the entrance to the park, a sign told the hard-to-imagine story that the Industrial Revolution was fueled, in large part, from this idyllic spot. Lime is used to make products as varied as steel and paper and concrete. And during the nineteenth and early twentieth centuries, if you were west of the Mississippi you most likely got that lime from close by the spot I now stood on. At least that's what the sign said.

The van pulled away, leaving me in the mist. I headed down a paved trail that wound through cedars and Douglas firs on its way to Lime Kiln Point Lighthouse. Through the trees, the red roof and white sides of the light tower stood out against the gray fog swirling around it and the foamy sea lapping at its base. I bypassed the trail down to the lighthouse, continuing on to the limekilns. A short distance later, the trail rose above a pit, home to a restored limekiln that looked like a Buddhist pagoda with a huge hole in the middle. I continued on the trail until I came to the broken remains of another limekiln.

I smelled salt spray, but I didn't see an obvious trail out toward the water. So I pushed aside tree limbs and stepped over fallen logs, picking my way around moss-covered rocks until I came to a knob of land ten feet above the sea. Crashing waves sprayed me with a fine mist. I didn't think I'd reached Bucky Point. Then I looked to my right and up.

One ridge over and thirty feet above me, Bucky sat on a point of land, cross-legged with her eyes closed like a diminutive Buddha dressed in a blue fleece jacket. I couldn't get to her from here. I'd have to go back inland, then work my way out to the point.

Suddenly, I heard three short, sharp explosions like distant cannon fire, and then, not more than fifty yards off shore, a huge orca leapt completely from the sea. And, as though forgetting momentarily the laws of gravity that bound it, the whale hung suspended in space before falling back with a prodigious splash. Other tall dorsal fins surfaced around it. I should have left, but the sight of the whales mesmerized me. And when I finally turned to leave, I looked up at Bucky, who was looking down at me. For a few moments, we stared at each other.

I cupped a hand around my mouth. "Bucky. Wait."

But I was too late. She stood up and ran back along the ridge and I lost sight of her. I hustled back toward the limekiln and looked down the trail toward the lighthouse. She hadn't gone that way, so I ran along the trail that continued on from the lime-kilns. But I didn't see her moving in that direction either.

I stopped and listened. Up ahead, on the water side of the trail, I heard rustling in the dense brush. I swung off the trail, crashing through the branches and fallen leaves, until I saw a speck of blue fleeing as fast and surefooted as a mountain goat over an expanse of moss-covered rocks.

I couldn't see a path, so I followed the general direction Bucky took. I moved through a thicket of cedar trees, ducking under one bough, only to have another whip across my cheek when I raised my head. I kept moving as fast as I could, high-stepping over fallen limbs and trees where possible, clambering on exposed, slippery patches of damp moss, always with an uneasy sense of a steep drop to the rocks and the ocean below.

Ahead of me, Bucky kept moving too, as though traveling along a road that she alone knew. I paused for a brief moment to survey the terrain, and when I softened my vision slightly I saw it: A barely lighter shade of green. The cut ends of tree limbs here and there, long ago severed and since healed. A stretch of earth without many rocks jutting from it, when all around, mossy rocks stuck out.

She *was* following a road. Maybe it was once a logging road, or one that moved limestone. Now nature had all but reclaimed it, except for those who knew. I continued along the old roadbed, as it dipped down then climbed over an area where crumbling rock lay everywhere. It looked like a landslide had occurred, trumping the signs of human incursion.

Bucky emerged from the next wooded area, running along a rocky bluff, when suddenly she stopped and looked back, then ahead several times. As though she'd hit an invisible force field that prevented her from going further. But once out of the woods, I saw what held her back: A chain-link fence spanning the distance from the edge of the bluff to as far inland as I could see. Here, human incursion had trumped nature.

Bucky looked back at me again. I was less than a hundred yards away, and closing fast. Sweat pushed out from my forehead and under my arms. Bucky looked up at the fence, then back at me. She ripped off her blue jacket, tying it around her waist. Then in a flash, she leapt for a handhold, scrambling to the top, covering the barbed metal crown of the fence with her jacket, and swinging her small frame over to the other side. She climbed down a few links, then let herself drop to the ground, bouncing up and scampering away.

When I got to the fence, I read the large green sign. "Private Property. Keep Out." I whipped my backpack from my shoulders and slung it around one arm. I reached as high as I could, calling forth reflexes from my youth, when I regularly scaled chain-link fences to gain access to locked schoolyard playgrounds and other forbidden sites. I pulled myself up, searching with one foot then the other for a toehold. The fence rattled as I climbed.

But when I was ready to lay my backpack over the sharp metal prongs on top, a muffled crack sounded, followed by a sharp ping off the fence. I hung by my hands and feet like an insect on a wall, stunned by the light.

At first, I thought the owner of the property was protecting his dominion. But the shot came from behind. I turned to see two men emerging from the woods, one with a handgun, the other kneeling with a rifle. I dropped ten feet to the ground as another shot sent the fence ringing. I'd present nothing but a huge target scaling the fence now.

I crouched low and scurried along the fence. The man with the pistol rushed my way, while the one with the rifle stayed in place. I guessed he had a sniper's scope and wanted me in the open where he could take a clean shot.

Fortunately, the other man could not come directly at me as I ran. A deep crack in the rocky surface between us meant he'd have to get to the fence first, then follow me out toward the edge. I tried to keep rocks between me and the gunman, and when I couldn't I dove to the ground and slithered along. I pulled my gun from my backpack and fired a shot at the man, now close to the fence. That stopped him in his tracks.

The rifleman fired several shots in my direction, the first two high, the next two low. This guy was a marksman, trying to bracket his shots and hit me that way. So I backed away from the fence and ran more of a zigzag pattern, stopping occasionally to fire in the direction of the man with the handgun.

Bullets whistled around me as I crawled to the end of the fence and peered over the edge of a rocky ledge with a long drop down to the sea. If I climbed the fence here, the rifleman would nail me. If I waited, I probably could take out the second man, but I hadn't brought another clip of ammunition and I only had three rounds left. So I shoved my gun into the backpack, jammed my arms through the straps, grabbed the bottom corner of the fence and let my body swing over the ledge. I didn't look down.

The rifleman kept firing but he didn't have a clear shot. I let go with one hand, reaching around to the other side of the fence. I saw the second man coming my way. My arm muscles strained as I pulled myself up a few links. My leg flailed in space as I tried to gain purchase on the bottom of the fence, and when that didn't work, on the rock ledge.

The second man was about fifty yards away when I finally jammed a toe into a small crack in the rock, swung my other hand around, pulling myself up and onto the ledge. I rolled away from the fence, grabbing my gun from the backpack and firing a shot through the fence at the second man coming at me. He ducked and I ran for the cover of several large rocks, which afforded me protection as I made my way back to the overgrown roadway.

I turned back to look. The second man had climbed over the fence and he waved the other man forward. When the rifleman got to the fence, he heaved his rifle over the top and his partner caught it. Then he scaled the fence, dropping down to the other side.

ucky was nowhere in sight, so I followed the remains of the old road as best I could, moving fast, keeping well out of sight of the two men behind me. My feet snapped underbrush and my shoulders scraped low-hanging branches. A sharpshooter and a point man working as a team? The face of the guy who'd gotten closest to me flashed across my mind. I'd seen him before with a SEAL emblem tattooed on his biceps, standing on the dock of a vacation home in Port Browning. They weren't after me. They'd used me to lead them to Bucky. And now that they'd found her, I was just in the way. But why were two SEAL guys after Bucky in the first place?

I didn't have time to meditate on an answer. I just kept moving as fast as I could. Behind me, branches cracked. The SEAL guys were moving fast too. I veered inland, deciding to bushwhack until I reached the main road. Not only could I travel faster there, but also it'd throw them off Bucky's trail. I thought I'd be traipsing through more woodlands and brush, but I soon came to the manicured back lawn of a huge estate, which I hoped was

RED HERRING

a summer home with nobody in. I ran along the edge of the cut grass, making good time. I didn't see the two guys behind me.

When I reached the main road I headed north in the direction Bucky had run. I came to a sign for Smallpox Bay and the entrance to San Juan Island County Park. Dotted with blue and red dome tents and fifth-wheel campers, the park bordered the water. A rainbow assortment of kayaks lined the beach, their shiny hulls gleaming in the sun.

Suddenly, as though an order had been given to hundreds of lemmings, en masse, dozens of people broke out of tents and campers, rushing toward the beach, some stepping into spray skirts as they ran, giving them the look of a troupe of glissading dancers adorned in neoprene tutus. They furiously dragged their kayaks into the water and everyone paddled off as though a starter's gun had been fired. Spouts in the bay beyond the kayakers told the tale: the orcas had arrived.

I remembered Erica Greeley at the Whale Museum say, "she'll be with the whales." In front of me, a man stood beside a long trailer with several kayaks laid on padded racks, and spaces for many more. The sign next to him read, "Rentals by the Day."

I whipped my wallet from my pocket and ran over to him.

"One," I said.

"Hundred dollar deposit. Thirty-five dollars for the day." He winked. "You're a big guy, I've got just the boat for you." He pulled down a kayak from the top of his rig. "Ever paddle before?"

"Uh huh. I need a spray skirt, a hand pump, a life vest, paddle float, and a paddle."

He shook his head and smiled. "In a hurry to catch the whales?"

"I am."

I hoisted the kayak on my shoulder and as I turned around to face the beach, I saw a car barreling down the road.

"Hey, we close at five," the proprietor said.

I didn't bother to turn and speak. Instead, I waved with my free hand as I ran toward the water carrying the boat on my shoulder. I slapped the kayak down in shallow water, stepped into my spray skirt and life vest, and hooked the other safety equipment under the bungee cords crisscrossing the front of the boat. I slipped into the seat and paddled out from shore before stopping briefly to fasten my spray skirt around the top of the cockpit, effectively locking myself in.

I dug my paddle into the water, spinning the boat around once before heading out of the bay. The car speeding down the highway was now parked at the top of the campground, and the two gunmen were running toward the beach with rented kayaks bobbing atop their shoulders.

Beyond the mouth of Smallpox Bay, I looked right. Against a gray sky, paddles rhythmically beat the water and the air. The clutch of kayakers looked like a flock of waterfowl trying to take flight.

Outside of the kayakers, tour boats carrying less ambitious passengers plied the waters, listing to one side as people crowded the decks to gape at the whales. Small geysers erupted among the kayakers and around the tour boats as the pod of orcas swam steadily north.

I couldn't see if Bucky was among the throng, but when I twisted my head and glanced behind me, I saw the two guys had not reached the mouth of the bay yet. The wind was blowing close to twenty knots from the south, pushing me as I paddled. The next time I turned to look, I saw both men rounding the mouth of the bay, heading my way. I picked up my paddling pace.

The next puffs came not from the whales but from the tour boats. Tiny clouds of exhaust smoke disappeared into the mist. Then the boats picked up speed, and shrank to be small specks against the background of the sea and the islands of British Columbia in the distance. The whales had gone. All together, the kayakers executed an about-face and the flock of them headed toward me, churning water with their paddles, slapping down the back side of small waves as they struggled into the wind.

I kept paddling, aiming my kayak at the middle of the group, and five minutes later the fastest of them whizzed by—or so it seemed. In reality, I was whizzing by them with the assistance of this stiff breeze. I scanned right and left, looking for Bucky but I still didn't see her. Perhaps I'd played this hunch wrong. Then, off to my left, I saw a blue jacket and a paddler who didn't sit high in the boat. I angled in that direction and came upon a group of all-women kayakers in double kayaks, led by a guide in a blue paddling jacket.

"The pod's gone," the guide said as they passed by me.

"I'm looking for a woman out here, short, red-haired," I said.

"What type of boat's she paddling?"

"I don't know."

"Sorry, but I'm Mother Hen. I keep my eye on my chicks and the whales and not much else."

I threaded through the group of doubles and turned to look for the two guys behind me, but all the boats on the water, now spread out over a wide area, made it hard to find them quickly. Then I saw two splotches of color three hundred yards away, going against the grain of the other kayakers. I thought about hiding among this group of women and heading back toward Smallpox Bay. But after passing through the final wave of kayakers, I saw another small fleck of blue against the shoreline, still moving north.

I spun my boat in that direction and plowed the water with my blades. The two guys must have seen me, because they picked up their pace too. If that was Bucky, it was now a race to see who could reach her first. The wind helped and, when I looked over my shoulder at the two gunmen, I realized their inexperience in kayaks would help too. I didn't doubt their strength, but they looked like windmills as they paddled, which meant they used the muscles in their arms more than their backs. Muscles that would tire more quickly. That reminded me to concentrate on my paddling stroke, not just for short-range speed but also for endurance. I kept the paddle blades low to the water, cork-screwing my body from side to side. The muscles up and down my spine rippled.

Slowly, I gained on Bucky. The closer I got the more I admired the seeming effortless fluidity of her stroke, which made it appear that she and her boat were one. She turned around briefly, casting a glance at me, then further behind at the two men in pursuit. She lowered her head, bringing her whole body to the task of paddling. Though she might not have the strength of the men behind her, she clearly outclassed us in skill.

Suddenly, Bucky disappeared as though swallowed by the shoreline.

enry Island sits off the northwest tip of San Juan Island, like a lone jigsaw puzzle piece that refuses to be fit in. Between the two islands, Mosquito Pass flows like a fast-moving saltwater river propelled by the tide one way, then the other. Bucky had turned up the pass.

Ten minutes later, I followed her into the pass, the sensation underneath my kayak like paddling into a stream of molasses. The current ran hard against me, and my arms strained with each stroke. Ahead of me, Bucky struggled in the current too. After several minutes of fighting the current, I turned around to the sight of the two gunmen heading up the pass behind us.

Suddenly, Bucky angled in close to shore and she shot ahead like a cannonball. Smart gal. She'd found a back eddy flowing against the current. I got to that point and I angled in too. My body jerked, the feeling like stepping on a moving walkway after strolling along. But as I neared a sharp bend in the pass, the ride petered out.

Then Bucky surprised me again, cutting away from the shore and angling straight across the main body of the current. She leaned her kayak into the onrushing current, stretched her paddle out, slapped, then skimmed the flat side of the blade over the surface of the water. She shot over and back down the pass behind me, to a point where she was opposite the two gunmen.

When I reached the place where Bucky left the shore, I followed her. Though I didn't have anywhere near as good a low brace stroke as she did, at least I knew what to expect. Crossing the eddy line, it felt like a huge hand reached out to pull the rug out from under my kayak. I threw my body upstream, leaning the boat over, and hit the water with the flat side of the paddle. It worked. I stayed upright and I, too, shot back across and down the pass.

The gunmen didn't wait to reach the same point. Instead, they moved out after Bucky from a faster part of the back eddy into the main stream. It cost them dearly.

Apparently, neither of them knew about bracing to cross an eddy line. The first one flipped the moment his boat hit the main current. He popped to the surface, clutching wildly for his boat. The second tottered back and forth like a seesaw, his paddle held high in the air. He didn't go over, but the current flushed both men and their boats far downstream. The man in the water was in trouble if his partner also didn't know how to perform an on-the-water kayak rescue.

Bucky, meanwhile, had found a back eddy on the other side of the pass, and she sped along to the east end. I followed not far behind her until we both entered the calm, protected waters of Roche Harbor. She looked behind her once, but she didn't turn into the harbor. Instead, she continued across the harbor to a gap, which led to Spieden Channel on the other side of San Juan Island. I let her go and turned into Roche. I had a good idea of where she was headed. My muscles ached. My stomach growled. And I wanted to get back to the *Noble Lady* while those two guys were still figuring out how to get back to shore.

I paddled into shore at Roche Harbor, passing rows of multimillion dollar yachts, each of which could have been named

Bling Bling. I called a taxi and then I called San Juan County Sheriff, Ed Sykes. I told him he might want to look for two navy SEALs struggling with their kayaks in Mosquito Pass. Ed told me not to worry about returning my boat. He knew the rental operator. If I left my kayak at Roche, he'd send one of his deputies to pick it up and return it to the man.

The taxi deposited me at Friday Harbor late in the afternoon. I rushed down the docks and fired up Miss Perky the moment I hopped aboard. Once she began to purr, I threw off the dock lines and backed away from the pier. After I'd cleared the breakwater and the mouth of the harbor, I pointed the *Noble Lady* west toward Stuart Island and put her on autopilot. Then I climbed back down into the galley for something to eat.

I wound my way through Johns Pass, pulling into Prevost Harbor on Stuart Island's east side just after sunset. I tucked the *Noble Lady* into a small nook behind a large reef near Satellite Island. It's a hidden anchorage in the middle of a popular spot, and an anchored boat is easily missed here.

The following morning, I awoke early to a squawking blue heron perched on the side rail of the *Noble Lady*. After making a smoothie, I flopped the dinghy into the water and putted over to the main dock, walking across the isthmus of the island to Reid Harbor. Reid's a long, finger-like indentation in Stuart Island with plenty of room to anchor but no place to hide. At the head of Reid Harbor, several kayaks lined the beach. The sleek, yellow boat looked like the one that Bucky paddled.

Orcas travel a regular circuit following salmon and other prey. People are habitual too. In the heyday of the sixties, a hippie commune thrived at the mouth of Reid Harbor, and I could have easily imagined Bucky there. But those days had long since passed, and Stuart Island now boasted homes for the affluent.

I looked toward the beach. If that was Bucky's kayak and she was on this island, I knew another place she might be. I headed back across the isthmus and took the dinghy to the weatherbeaten, older public dock at the west end of Prevost Harbor. The tide was down, and I tied the dinghy to the bottom of a rusting, barnacle-covered ladder. I climbed up to the dock and walked past a small white building, which served as a boathouse for the few residents at this end of the island.

From the dock, I walked along a public road that gained elevation quickly, and I turned back for the spectacular view of Mount Baker rising above the lowlands and the sea. The road, with its growing cover of orange and brown leaves, skirted the edge of a grass landing strip, used by island locals. Several small planes gleamed in the morning sunlight.

Beyond the airfield, the road plunged deep into a cedar and fir forest where, down a small ravine, vines and moss devoured the rust-eaten, bullet-ridden skeleton of an abandoned 30s-era car. Then, on this clear, sun-filled day, came peek-a-boo glimpses across Haro Strait to the islands that dotted British Columbia, before the road dropped down into more cedar and fir, ending at the tip of Stuart Island and the Turn Point Lighthouse.

Lime Kiln Point might be where the public went to see orcas, but those who wanted a more secluded shore-side meeting with these masters and commanders of the Inside Passage came here to Turn Point instead.

I'd helped to rebuild this lighthouse on my first tour of duty with the Coast Guard out here. The waters whip around the point, creating tide rips for almost a mile out that orcas and dolphins feed in. I walked down the path from the road to the lighthouse, cutting across the high, yellow grass. I stopped suddenly behind a tree.

Bucky sat at the edge of a cliff, cross-legged, her eyes closed. One tough little Buddha, only this time with no place to run. I crept closer, then called to her.

"Bucky, I'm not here to hurt you."

She sprang up with a fierce look in her eyes. "Stop. Don't come any closer." She held her hand out toward me, while looking back over her shoulder, down the cliff.

I inched closer. "I'm here to help."

"No you're not. You're here to bring me in. I'm wanted for the firebombing and for the explosives on Thomas's boat."

"I don't think you did it."

"Bullshit. Then why have you been following me?"

"Because someone's out after you."

"Stay right there," she said, looking over her shoulder again.

"Your apartment was ransacked, so was Matthew's. They're looking for you, or something they think you or Matthew have."

She held up the backpack. "This," she said. "They...you want this. Thomas's data that proves the destruction of the herring habitat at Cherry Point."

"All the more reason why you're not the one who firebombed the lab or threatened Cherry Point."

"Sure, like the government's gonna believe me."

I took another step in her direction. "We can figure out a way to make them believe you."

"I'm warning you, stay back or I'll jump."

Once again she looked over her shoulder. I didn't believe her. She turned away from me. I jogged toward her. But before I could reach her, Bucky leapt off the point.

I stopped, unable to fathom that Bucky would take her life just like that. Then my ears perked up to the sound of an outboard motor. I raced to the edge of the cliff. Damn. I slammed a fist into my thigh. She'd planned all this beforehand. Hadn't I described her as a great actress in the tradition of Tallulah Bankhead? Bucky had jumped down onto a ledge with a steep drop toward the water. And two young people in a high-speed inflatable were at the bottom to meet her.

She looked up and smiled, waving to me as they zoomed around Turn Point. I raced around to the other side of the lighthouse and watched her disappear. Like an orca, Bucky was traveling a familiar circuit. But some comfort came from knowing there really was only one place she could travel from here.

I weighed anchor from my Prevost Harbor nook and cruised the *Noble Lady* twenty minutes across Cowlitz Bay to Waldron Island, tying up at the island's only public dock, in front of an old wooden boat named *Skipjack* with a U.S. Post Office decal affixed to its pilothouse window.

Hospitable is not a word that describes Waldron. There's little windward protection. The anchorages aren't great. The rocks and reefs pose navigational hazards. And the residents—less than a hundred—prefer it that way. The island is one of the last true American frontiers: four and a half square miles surrounded by water, without electricity, stores, or development.

If I wanted to hide out this is where I'd go. But how do you find someone in a close-knit island community notorious for jealously guarding its secrets? A twenty-minute cruise wasn't enough time to work out the details. So I decided to do what I'd gotten good at lately: making myself obvious and obnoxious, then seeing who took a potshot at me.

I walked to the top of the dock, where a sign above a small wooden building read, "U.S. Post Office, Cowlitz, WA." A woman with long gray hair and a long, floral-patterned dress came out of the building, heading for her dark blue pickup truck. When she saw me, she did a double take, eyed me up and down, and then walked over.

"Barbara Freemont," she said. "And you are?"

"Charles Noble."

"What's your business here on our island, Mr. Noble?"

"I'm out cruising, and I've never stopped here. I like out-of-the-way places, where most people don't travel."

She raised her head toward the dock. "That your boat?"

"The *Noble Lady?* Yes."

"Hmmm. Least it's not a big, fast boat. You know there's not much here for boaters."

"I'm not looking for much," I said. I swept my hand around to the water and islands in the distance. "'Cept maybe the view."

She narrowed her eyes. "Road's public. That's about it. You can walk it before you leave. Everything else is private. We like our privacy here. Folks don't cater to off-islanders nosing around."

"I'll remember that."

She eyed me up and down again, then turned, her dress swirling around her as she walked over to her pickup.

I headed up the only road I could walk before leaving. A sign pointed to the Waldron Island School. I took the turn, and the chance, walking down a tree-lined dirt path. I came to a large wooden building with solar panels and lots of skylights set amidst the cedar shingles. I peered into a window.

Inside the one-room building, a tall woman stood before a semicircle of seven children, a book in her hand, a map of the Middle East behind her. She looked up from her book and saw me. She flinched. I must have startled her, but she waved me in.

I swung the heavy door open and walked into the classroom, which caused a collective gasp to rise from the students, who appeared to range in age from five or six to thirteen. One young girl with long brown hair and big eyes squealed.

"Are you a Bedouin?" she asked.

"No, I—"

"He's not a Bedouin," a blonde-haired boy wearing over-sized glasses said. "He's an African American."

"But Bedouins *are* Africans too," the girl insisted.

"He's African American," the boy said slowly.

"Still African." The girl didn't back down.

The teacher cut in. "Mr. ..."

"Noble," I said. "Charles Noble."

"And you're here on what business?"

"I'm sorry if I disturbed your class. I was just walking up the public road and—"

"I'm Denise," she said. "And the children are always glad to meet an outsider." She turned to her class. "Why don't you introduce yourself to Mr. Noble?"

And they did. The girl fond of Bedouins was named Amy, her antagonist a boy named Todd. Their classmates were Sarah, Rod, Jacob, Nigel, and Marla.

"We're studying Arab culture," Denise said. "Hence the interest in Bedouins. We were comparing the Bedouin way of life to life here on Waldron Island. I'm reading some poems by the thirteenth century Persian poet Rumi. Have a seat and listen."

I didn't see any chairs, so I joined the children sitting cross-legged on the floor. Denise tapped a button on a CD player, and a buzz that sounded like a cloud of bees began, followed by the twang of a Middle Eastern stringed instrument, then a flute, then the haunting, tremulous chants of a male voice. The children sat in rapt attention, enthralled by the music. Denise lowered the volume slowly, then, over the music, she read a poem about being shipwrecked and finding the true course of one's life by hanging on to a single surviving plank.

After the poem, she asked the children to talk about finding surviving planks in their lives. Sarah told about her mother, suffering from cancer, and how tending to their family vegetable garden helped her through the ordeal. Todd said he'd made friends with a deer, which he fed each day after school, and that helped him weather his parents' divorce. These kids might live on an island, but they hadn't lived sheltered lives.

Denise dismissed class and the children scattered, some jumping on bikes, others taking off down the dirt road. I walked over to Denise, a woman well into her forties, dressed in black culottes and a long, ruffled white cotton shirt. Burnished silver earrings with a finely etched Celtic knot pattern hung from her ears. She studied me before speaking.

"What are you really here for?" she asked.

"I'm investigating the firebombing of Huxley's Marine Science Laboratory in Anacortes."

She raised her eyebrows. "Firebombed? What's that got to do with Waldron Island?"

"I think one of the graduate students from the lab might be here, and I need to question her."

"Who's that?"

"Melissa Buchanan. She also goes by the name of Bucky."

Denise pursed her lips and shook her head. "Not a resident, that's for sure. Are you law enforcement?"

"No. I'm working independently of the police and the Coast Guard and the FBI and a host of other interested agencies."

She narrowed her eyes. "I don't understand. If you're not working for a government agency, then why are you looking for this Bucky person?"

"Too many unanswered questions."

"And this Bucky has answers?"

"Maybe. If not, maybe she can lead me to people who do."

"So it's more than just her you're looking for here on the island?"

"Maybe. Know anything about a radical environmental group called the Ocean Liberation Front?"

Denise remained expressionless, though the corner of her mouth twitched.

"You know, Mr. Noble," she said. "Folks on the island don't like off-islanders nosing around."

"So I've been told."

"There's a Bedouin verse that captures the essence of Waldron." She spoke slowly. "I against my brother...I and my brother against our cousin...I, my brother and our cousin against the neighbors...All of us against the foreigner." She stared expressionlessly at me again. "You'd do well to remember that on this island. Now, if you'll excuse me I have to prepare my classroom for tomorrow."

◎　◎　◎

I'D HEARD THAT BOATS moored on Waldron's public dock were often found drifting, with their lines cut. So to have a restful sleep, I moved the *Noble Lady* around to Mail Bay, a small cove on the east side of the island.

The following morning I was back at the public dock. I tied up early and walked to the school, this time with my guitar in hand. I met Amy as she entered the building. Today she wore a red sweater over her blue jeans. She held onto a backpack slung over one shoulder.

Amy frowned. "Bedouins don't play the guitar."

"What do they play?" I asked.

She frowned again. "A funny instrument called an u...u..."

"Oud," I said.

This time she smiled. "Yeah. That's it. An oud."

Denise barreled through the front door, her eyes narrowed, breathing hard. "What are you doing back here?" She asked in a low, tight voice.

"I—"

"He came to play the guitar," Amy said.

"Mr. Noble, I need you to—"

I put up a hand. "You're studying the Arab culture and the Middle East, right? Then give these kids something they can really relate to."

"What, rock 'n roll music?"

"No, a history lesson on how the guitar migrated out of Africa into the Middle East, on to Europe, and finally to America, where it was first used to play blues and rock 'n roll."

She raised an eyebrow. "You can do that?"

"Give me an hour and a half with your class."

"You're on." She pointed at me. "But if I catch even a whiff that you're a phony, I'll have you thrown off this island just like that." She snapped her fingers.

"I believe you would."

I stood at the back of her classroom while the students filed in. They held hands and collectively repeated an oath about honoring the earth. Then, Denise turned to me. "You remember Mr. Noble, who visited our classroom yesterday. He's returned today with his guitar to talk about...well, I'll let him take over."

"Do you have some chalk?"

"Here." Denise slapped a piece in my hand, scowling behind a mask of skepticism.

I pulled out my guitar and turned to the class. "I want to introduce you to my friend." I ran my hands down her body along her curves.

The class laughed.

"Anyone know where the guitar came from?"

The kid who insisted I wasn't a Bedouin raised his hand. "Elvis," he said.

The class chuckled again.

"Actually the guitar came from Spain, where before that people played a similar instrument called the lute, and the lute came to Europe from the Arabs of North Africa where it was known as the oud or *al-ūd.* So deep in the history of the guitar, way before rock 'n roll, is the music of the Arabic cultures that you're studying."

On the blackboard, I wrote, "Oud, *al-ūd,* Lute, Guitar."

"Let's listen to some of the guitar's music," I said.

I found a chair in the corner of the room and sat down to play a repertoire similar to the one I played at my first lesson with Mr. Oller: *Lagrima,* then a bit of *Recuerdos del Alhambra,* whose wandering tremolos were meant to capture the bubbling, spouting fountains that graced the courtyards of the old Arab castle in Granada, Spain. Afterward I played a version of the *Capricho Arabe* by Francisco Tarrega, which sounds as though it came from the Casbahs of North Africa.

The kids began dancing and swaying. One young girl rolled up the bottom of her blouse and claimed to be a belly dancer. I moved from Spain to Germany, where I played a Bach boureé. The kids were a great audience. Not one even batted an eye at my flubbed notes. After my short classical repertoire, I treated them to some jazz and blues, ending with a version of the rock song "Light My Fire" by guitarist José Feliciano that brought the morning full circle, back to Spain.

When I finished, Denise had a smile on her face. She invited me to join the class for lunch. After eating, I said good-bye and got up to leave. She walked me to the door. She handed me a paper and pen.

"Here," she said. "I can pass along a note to someone who might know about this woman you're looking for."

"Thanks," I said. And I scribbled a short note to Bucky.

"Wait on your boat," Denise said. "If no one makes contact with you by tomorrow morning, leave."

"I'll do that," I said.

She eyed me sternly. "What you did for the kids was really nice. But you'd better not do anything that hurts this island or the people who live here." Then she turned to go back in to her class.

When I walked past the post office, Barbara popped out wearing jeans and a straw hat, looking every bit the country bumpkin. She smiled.

"Thanks for playing for our kids," she said. "They mean everything to us."

I laughed. "This is a close-knit island."

"So close," she said. "We need each other and sometimes wound each other because of that need. On a small island, inter-dependence can be a bitch to survive."

With my wrists and forearms tired from performing, I sat at the galley table reading and humming the Bach Prelude instead of playing it.

The "putt putt" of a diesel engine grew steadily louder and I looked up to see the black hull of *Skipjack* chugging into the dock. I closed the music and stepped off the *Noble Lady* to help the skipper tie up. A man with a heavy white beard and navy blue skullcap pushed the pilothouse window back and eyed me as he glided by slowly. Then, like a turtle, his head disappeared into the darkened boat. With a puff of blue-gray smoke from his exhaust and a complaining whine from his engine, he spun the boat on a dime and angled in toward me.

The bow of the *Skipjack* glided to within inches of the *Noble Lady*'s stern. My body poised to push back the old wooden double-ender, when another belch of smoke accompanied the rev of the engine thrown into reverse. The old man's maneuver reminded me of territorial marking.

"Need a hand with the lines?"

No response.

Then the man, probably in his late seventies, stepped out of the cabin and onto the dock with his mooring lines in hand. Like an hombre hitching his horse to a post, he whipped the lines around the dock rail. He leaned into the cockpit and wrestled with a large canvas sack marked "U.S. Mail – Official Use Only," which he slung over his shoulder and walked off.

I stepped back onto the *Noble Lady*.

Not long afterwards, someone knocked softly on the galley window, which surprised me because I hadn't heard the dock creaking under footsteps beforehand. When I parted the blinds I didn't see anyone either. Then I stepped onto the rear deck and looked out. Amy stood on the dock with a bouquet of wildflowers. She ran her hand along the teak cap rails, then wrinkled her nose.

"Bedouins have camels, not boats."

"But camels are nothing more than four-legged boats that travel on sand rather than water."

She paused to think, then she frowned. "That's silly. Maybe you're not a Bedouin after all."

I pointed to the flowers. "Where'd you get those?"

"From our garden. Do Bedouins like flowers?"

"I don't know about Bedouins, but I do."

"Good." She extended the flowers toward me. "'Cause I picked them to say 'Thank you' for playing your guitar in our class."

I took the flowers from her. "That's really kind of you."

"There's more," she said. "The parents of the kids at school are making dinner for you. It's called a pro…pro…"

"Progressive."

She smiled. "Yeah, that's it. A progressive dinner. It starts at my house and I'm supposed to meet you here at five and bring you home. You know, this is all very special. We've never had a Bedouin over for dinner."

◎ ◎ ◎

I MET AMY at the head of the dock at five. She grabbed my hand and led me up the public road like a small tug towing a large barge. When we passed by the post office, the bearded captain of the *Skipjack* had a key in the door, closing the post office for the evening. He turned to us, smiled and waved. Apparently being with Amy also bought me immunity.

Amy lived in a log-cabin not far from the school. A small brown and white dog wove through several neatly stacked wood-piles to greet us. I bent down to pet him.

"Do Bedouins have dogs?" she asked.

"I bet they do," I said.

She squeezed my hand. "I like Bedouins, like you" she said.

I liked Amy. Sharon would have liked her too.

The cut wood filled the air with the sweetness of cedar. When the front door to Amy's house swung open, it surprised me to see Denise, the schoolteacher, standing there with a red apron on.

"Hi," she said. "I'm not only the schoolteacher, I'm also Amy's mother. We wanted you to see another side of Waldron and to thank you for giving to the kids."

The house vibrated with the raucous sounds of children playing and the background hum of adult conversation. Amy tugged on my hand.

"Do Bedouins like being around other people?"

"I don't know. What do you think?"

"I think being a nomad makes them lonely. Wandering through the desert, moving from place to place, makes them sad."

She dropped my hand and disappeared into the crowd.

"She's really fixated on Bedouins," Denise said.

"I can see that."

"When she heard they were nomads and moved sometimes daily to a new home, it touched her deeply. I got divorced when she was two. She's seven now, but we've moved so many times since the divorce that I've lost count."

Denise set out fresh vegetable soup, salad, and bread for the first course of the progressive dinner. I sat with my bowl and salad plate, listening to the residents tell stories and jokes about the first European settlers on Waldron: fighting the British for control of the island, running rum from nearby Canada during Prohibition, or living in such dire poverty they didn't even notice the Great Depression.

After soup and salad, I hopped into Denise's pickup with Amy and we bounced inland along a dirt road to an A-frame home set in a large clearing. The new host and hostess were Joel and Elizabeth Conner, who'd moved to the island fifteen years earlier. He'd been a social worker in Los Angeles, she a public defender. The pink, cut halves of a large baked salmon lay on their table, garnished with grilled red peppers, zucchini, carrots, and onions.

While we feasted, Joel and Liz told a story of the darker side of island life. How a few years back, a man, no longer living on Waldron, convinced authorities that Joel was a drug kingpin. Then, early one morning, police, FBI, DEA, and ATF agents raided the island. Marijuana plants were seized from some residents. But they only found a smoked butt on Joel's porch. Some islanders did jail time.

Barbara, from the post office, sat among the group and said softly, "All the sheriff had to do was clip his business card to one plant, and the lot of them would have been destroyed in the morning."

Bitterness and recrimination still reverberated from that raid. I guess interconnectedness *was* a bitch to survive.

It was almost nine and very dark outside when we moved on to another home for dessert: homemade sweet potato pie a la mode. The ice cream was homemade too. After we finished, someone handed me an old steel-stringed Gibson guitar with a cherry sunburst finish. I pulled a pick from the neck. Guitars, banjos, and even a mandolin came out. We played and sang for a while, and though I didn't know most of the songs, I followed along with the chords until the steel strings chewed my fingertips raw.

Finally, the party broke up. Denise told me to wait for her in the pickup, while she gathered Amy, who'd fallen asleep in a back room. I sat in the passenger's seat, looking up at a night sky speckled with stars. I picked out a satellite moving across the face of the Milky Way. The driver's door swung open, and I turned to see a young man behind the wheel. My body stiffened. He spoke in a whisper.

"Your note said you wanted to help Bucky."

"Yes."

"Then we need to talk."

He started Denise's truck and I pulled my door closed. We bumped along the road. And through the sideview mirror I watched as the night enveloped the soft yellow glow from the windows of the Conners' house.

The pickup's chassis chattered as we crawled along dirt and grass. On an unfamiliar island, switching locations three times at night had turned my sense of direction upside down. We must have been somewhere inland, because I couldn't see lights from any nearby islands. I stuck my head out the window. We also appeared to be heading north, from the position of the Big Dipper. A branch scraped the hood and I ducked inside just before the needles of a cedar bough whipped past my window.

The driver kept his eyes fixed on the road.

I turned to him. "My name's Charlie Noble."

He said nothing. He slowed the vehicle and strained to look ahead, tapping the brakes then spinning the wheel right. The engine whined and the tires skidded as we clawed our way up an incline. When the road leveled off, he stopped the truck but left the engine running. Finally, he turned to me and said, "Get out."

I opened the door and jumped down into the night, shielding my eyes from the headlights as the driver backed down the road. Suddenly, footsteps approached me from behind. I turned but could see nothing. A woman's voice called out.

"Put your hand on my shoulder and follow me."

From her voice, I placed her in her twenties. From the angle of my arm on her shoulder she stood about five-six. Her long, silky hair fluttered over my fingers as we walked. Slowly, my eyes adjusted to the darkness, but I only made out two human forms leading me on a path through the woods. We walked for nearly twenty minutes, when ahead I saw a faint glow of light, which grew steadily stronger until the windows of a small structure came into view. I expected to find a cabin, but when we got to the door I realized that I was entering a geodesic dome.

The person in the lead knocked twice, paused, then knocked three times again and the door swung open. Inside, five young people sat in a circle on the floor. Flames flickered from a stone fireplace behind them. Bucky was not among the group. But what surprised me even more was a section of the rounded walls lined with LCD screens and a bank of computers and electronic equipment. My mind busily collected pieces of a jigsaw puzzle, shoving them together faster than I realized. I spoke impulsively.

"Are you folks the Ocean Liberation Front?"

N o one flinched. A hand patted the floor.

"Have a seat, Mr. Noble," a voice said.

Everyone pushed back, and I took my place among the group. The couple that escorted me to the dome did not enter, leaving two men and three women sitting cross-legged with me on the floor.

In the dancing shadows of the flames, I found it hard to make out faces, but all of these young people had slender bodies. One woman appeared to have matted hair grown into dreadlocks. The scent of marijuana drifted over from the young man to my right. Across the circle, a tall woman with long hair, a flowing dress, and the cloying smell of too much lavender, rose to speak.

"I'm called Hera," she said. "And we are fighters for this planet." She swept her hand around the circle. "The earth is under attack. Our oceans are the lifeblood of this planet." Hera spoke with a deep, resonant voice in slow, measured, almost hypnotic tones. "All around us the oceans are being poisoned because of stupidity and greed. Millions of tons of raw sewage are pumped into the oceans daily. Runoff from farmlands and cities and pollution from fossil-fuel vehicles have created hundreds of square miles of dead zones in offshore waters. Fish have such high levels of toxic chemicals that people are warned against eating them. Some species have been fished to the brink of extinction. Global warming is raising the temperature of our oceans, melting glaciers and creating unprecedented climate changes. And—"

I thrust my hand forward. "An explosion which could have killed or injured hundreds and produced a monumental environmental disaster was narrowly averted. A professor and two graduates student are missing. A building for research to support your claims has been destroyed. How does any of this advance your cause?"

Hera's eyes flashed wide, flames capering in them. "We're facing an environmental catastrophe and people will not listen. They want to drive their SUVs and live in their oversized homes regardless of the environmental costs. They want to use chemicals to increase crop yields and to fatten animals, so they can also fatten corporate bottom lines. And this greedy, selfish lifestyle is devastating the planet."

"And ecoterrorism is going to make people listen?"

Hera sucked in a breath. Her nostrils flared. "We...are... not...terrorists."

"Then what *do* you call such acts?"

"Direct action. Sabotage."

"I fail to see the difference."

"Throughout history, sabotage, vandalism, looting, arson have been tools of political, social, and economic change. No one calls the Boston Tea Party terrorism, it's patriotism. We applaud the Abolitionists and the Suffragettes, yet they resorted to violence to achieve their ends. And you of all people..." Hera pointed to me. "As a black man you should know that violence was integral to the struggle for freedom in this country and in places like South Africa."

"No." I shook my head. "The Civil Rights Movement in this country was nonviolent."

Hera laughed. "Lynchings. Water cannons. Attack dogs. Beatings. Assassinations. You call that nonviolent?"

"No. The movement itself was nonviolent."

"Black Panthers. Riots. Looting. Burning down buildings and stores." She ticked off the items on her fingers. "Nonviolent?"

"But only a small group participated in that."

"We're a small group too. And just as the violent actions of the Black Panthers made it easier for others to listen to more moderate voices like Martin Luther King's, maybe direct action by groups like us will make it easier for others to listen to more moderate voices calling for environmental change before it's too late."

Around the circle, heads nodded. And while I didn't want to admit it, Hera obviously understood the value of the "good cop, bad cop" routine.

"I didn't come for a history lesson, or to hear the gospel of environmentalism preached to me," I said. "I came to find Bucky. She's in trouble. Maybe I can help. But only if you tell me where she is and exactly what happened with Atherton, Cherry Point, and the university's lab."

"Humph." Hera shook her head. "Here to help her, or to turn her in to the authorities?"

"Look, people have been shooting at her…and at me."

"You're a former coast guard intelligence officer. Why should we trust you to help Bucky? Why should we tell you what we know?"

"Who are you, the Queen Bee?" I pointed around the circle. "Don't any of you have an opinion? Aren't you allowed to speak?"

Everyone else kept their heads down. No one answered. The fire lit Hera's smile.

"We're a collective," she said. "We speak with one voice, and I've been voted to be that voice tonight."

"Well, right now I may be Bucky's last best hope. If the Coast Guard or FBI finds her first, she'll be in jail. And some of the men out looking for her don't take prisoners. They want the data that she has on the Cherry Point study. They could care less about her life. You've already risked enough by bringing me here. For chrissakes, you're hiding out on an island, which is great until someone like me discovers you. Then you're surrounded. So let's cut the bullshit and the political diatribe and get real. Tell me where Bucky is and tell me what happened."

Hera's body stiffened. She pointed to me. "Don't—"

"I'm here."

A collective gasp arose from the circle and all heads turned toward a door that opened along a curved wall of the dome. Bucky stepped from the shadows and walked slowly toward the circle. She stood behind Hera, placing both hands on the tall woman's shoulders. A moment later, another voice called out from behind the door.

"So am I." It was Matthew Voltmann.

"Let's tell Mr. Noble what really happened," Bucky said.

"Sister," Hera said. She grasped Bucky's hand. "Are you certain?"

"Tell him, Hera."

Hera's hand dropped to her lap and she looked down, shaking her head slowly.

"The truth, Mr. Noble, is that we don't know much. The night his boat was found heading toward Cherry Point, Thomas had planned to visit us secretly. He wanted to tell us about the results of his environmental impact study."

Bucky jumped in. "The data showed that damage to herring stocks from industrial pollution was much worse than anyone had imagined. Thomas thought there was a real danger that the species of Cherry Point herring would go extinct within a decade if nothing was done, or even sooner if the pipeline was built."

"The consortium that had filed the court challenge was afraid we were contemplating a direct action against pipeline construction, which might interfere with their case," Hera continued.

"So Thomas agreed to come here," Bucky said, "to talk to the OLF about his results and to reassure us of the likelihood that any judge hearing the case would place a stay on the construction of the pipeline once the data was presented in court."

"But he never made it," Matthew said. "Right before he left Bellingham, he met with Bucky and me. He told us he'd been receiving death threats. He handed us the only copy of his data and told us to keep it safe, in the event that he didn't return from his meeting on Waldron Island."

"We listened to VHF radio and heard the Coast Guard intercept Thomas's boat as it headed toward the refinery," Hera said. "And then we heard that the boat was wired with explosives aboard, and a note from us."

Bucky cried. "We don't know what happened to Thomas."

Hera said emphatically, "The OLF didn't commit these crimes."

Suddenly a bright red light flashed atop the wall of electronic equipment, and an irritating off-key buzzer sounded.

"Shit." A young man in the group jumped up and ran to the wall. "Intruders."

He jabbed at buttons and typed furiously on a keyboard. After some beeps, a few screens came to life. The buzzer stopped.

"How do you know?" I asked.

He spoke quickly while scanning the monitors. "We've got the area wired. In-ground sensors. Infrared cameras in trees. They'd never be able to take out everything. It's all wireless. Connected back to here. There…there they are," he said.

I sprang up. The kid at the computers tapped a monitor where shimmering, rainbow-like figures moved across the face of a darkened screen.

"Infrared's got one…two…three…four. Four men. Look at their arms." He pointed to the screen. "They're carrying weapons, and moving this way."

Behind me the buzz grew louder. I didn't have the heart to tell these kids they might be up against navy SEALs or an FBI SWAT team. Hell, not just these kids. I was now up against whoever came after them too.

"How far away are they?" I asked.

"Five hundred yards, tops. We've only got a few minutes to evacuate."

"Come on, Brad," Hera said to the fellow at the computers. Her voice was high-pitched now, excited. She tossed a motorcycle helmet across the room and Brad caught it.

"What's the evac route?" I asked.

"ATVs," Brad said. "They're coming up a hill after us. We'll take the ATVs downhill by another route to a cove, where we'll pick up our boat."

"Only way out?" I asked.

"No—"

"Brad. No. He could be one of them," Hera said.

I turned to Bucky and Matthew. "Are you two going with them?"

Bucky had a helmet in her hands. She turned between Hera and me.

"Come on, Bucky, Matthew, we don't have long," Hera said.

I yelled. "Is there another way out?"

No one answered.

Brad hit a few switches and the screens blacked out. The only light now came from the fireplace. Then someone threw water on the fire. It hissed, and the smell of steam and smoke spread through the room. In the darkness, I heard the others running across the room toward the door. I started to follow their footsteps, when an arm reached out and grabbed me.

"This way," Matthew said. "Bucky and I will show you another way out."

Bucky pulled out a flashlight and tugged me toward the door from which she and Matthew had come. She held the door open and shined her light inside, illuminating a small closet with clothes hanging along a wooden dowel. I hesitated.

"Hide here?"

"No," she said. "It's a closet with a false floor that leads to a tunnel."

Matthew lifted one end of the coatrack. A latch popped and beneath my feet a trapdoor swung open. I stepped away from it, backing against the closet door. When Bucky reached down to pull the trapdoor up, a rush of musty, cool air hit me in the face. From outside, the muffled sounds of small engines faded. Then suddenly, gunfire and men's voices erupted.

"It's a ladder down," Bucky said. "Be careful, the rungs are slippery and damp."

Bucky disappeared, then Matthew, leaving small dancing shafts of light from their flashlights behind them. I pushed the trapdoor further up just as the door to the dome burst open and someone sprayed gunfire around the room. The trapdoor rested on my head as I climbed down the ladder. After a few rungs, a latch above me snapped into place. Then I heard the closet door open and clothes pushed back.

"All clear. All clear," a voice yelled.

"Damn," another voice said. "Fucking kids escaped on ATVs. Let's go. They can't get far."

Footsteps stormed from the dome. I joined Bucky and Matthew at the bottom of the ladder. She could almost walk standing, but I had to crouch and push myself along the rough, irregular dirt walls.

"What is this?" I asked.

"There used to be a lookout cabin here. Rumrunners used the tunnel to escape from the law. We built the dome over the original cabin site, and kept the tunnel access just in case a time like this came. The tunnel leads about a quarter mile down the hill, but it turns and exits onto a path on the other side of a ridge. They won't find us."

And they didn't.

We emerged from the tunnel at the bottom of a ravine and fought our way through thick vines that guarded the opening. For the next hour, Bucky and Matthew led me on a tortuous path downhill, until we finally exited onto the main road and ran toward the dock. When we neared the post office, I held them back and pointed to the beach. Starlight barely illuminated a dark form lying on the sand. When it didn't move for several moments, I grabbed Bucky's flashlight, shining it on a camouflaged inflatable tied by a long rope to a piece of driftwood. We ran over to it. Bucky whipped a knife from her pocket, cut the line and pushed the inflatable out into the water, where it drifted away from shore.

"Welcome to Waldron Island," she said.

We ran to the *Noble Lady,* and a few minutes later we chugged away from the dock, turning the corner at Point Disney. Tonight the name fit. It did feel as though I'd just been on a horror-filled Disneyland ride. I headed down President's Channel, with Bucky and Matthew sitting behind me in a pilothouse lit by only the soft, green glow of the radar screen and the red and blue lights from the instruments. Way in the distance out the window, on the other side of a dark expanse of water, the orange lights of the refinery at Cherry Point brightened the sky, and a thick column of smoke rose from the main stack.

"Sorry about Hera," Bucky said. "She can get carried away."

"The truth is, she's partially right," I said.

"About what?" Matthew sounded incredulous.

"The crazy way that since 9/11 some in this country label everything terrorism, forgetting that one person's terrorist is another person's freedom fighter, believing that there's only one way to see a situation—our way. Terrorism's the new bogeyman to keep people afraid. It's a lot easier to control them that way."

Matthew laughed. "Be careful."

"Of what?" I asked.

"You're starting to sound like one of us. We may have to recruit you."

"It'd never work."

"Why?" Bucky asked.

"I have problems with authority, especially the kind where you sit in a circle allowing someone else to speak for you."

Bucky and Matthew sat in silence. I ran without lights, which only made our voyage seem that much more eerie.

Suddenly, Matthew burst out, "You're pretty close to shore."

"Don't worry," I said. "I'm watching my depth sounder and my chart," I said. "I'm keeping us in the radar shadow of the islands. That way, vessel traffic radar won't pick us up."

"Are you taking us back to Bellingham?" Matthew asked.

"No," I said.

Bucky gasped. "Then where?"

"A safe house."

"Where?"

"You'll find out when we get there."

I crossed over to the Orcas Island side of President's Channel to stay out of the line of sight of the Village Point radar tower for as long as I could. Then I headed out from Orcas toward Fossil Bay on Sucia Island just before the Parker Reef light. Off to my right, the orange glow of Bellingham lit the night sky.

Sucia's a gem of an island, maintained by the state as a recreational destination for boaters. Boats anchor and dock there year round. Except for the caretaking family, no one lives on Sucia. Jerry and Wanda stay in a cabin in Fossil Bay with their three girls. Over the years I'd been boating, I'd gotten to know and like them. They also owned the *Wanda K*, a large steel tug that sat in the middle of the bay. During the summer, Wanda and the girls baked sweet rolls and served coffee from the tug to a line of happy boaters in dinghies, awaiting their morning fix. And when the bay was completely filled with boats in the summer, they let me tie up to their tug.

I crept into Fossil Bay, slowing down even further as I neared the *Wanda K*. I turned around to Bucky and Matthew.

"Go out on deck and throw the fenders over the side. Then go back to the boarding gate. When I pull up to the tug, you hop off. The tug's forward door is always open. You'll find blankets and a place to sleep inside. I'm not tying up, so wait until I tell you to jump. I'll go over to the dock and tell Jerry and Wanda you're here."

"Like this is the safe house?" Bucky asked.

"Uh huh. Stay inside. Don't turn on any lights. Don't walk the decks. Jerry and Wanda will bring you food tomorrow. Keep Thomas's data with you. I'll be back for you when it's safe."

I slowed the *Noble Lady* to a crawl, while Bucky and Matthew lowered the fenders over the side. And then I nudged up to the *Wanda K,* throwing the *Noble Lady* into reverse so her tail swung into the other boat. Just as the fender kissed the side of the tug, I called down to Bucky and Matthew.

"Now. Jump aboard now."

And they did.

I glided past the tug and headed over to the dock, where I secured the *Noble Lady*, then walked up the ramp and over a trail through wetlands to Jerry and Wanda's cabin. Their old, blind dog Ozzie barked as I neared the place. I tapped on the door several times. A light came on, and Jerry cracked the door. The former coast guardsman, rubbed his eyes, then smiled. I told him the situation. He assured me they'd take care of Bucky and

Matthew. Then I walked back to the *Noble Lady,* untied her from the dock and, though tired, I headed back to home port.

A band of early morning light lit the eastern sky as I rounded the south end of Portage Island. Across Bellingham Bay, Mount Baker lifted her snowy white crown above the steadily brightening hills. Crabbers skidded hither and yon, hauling traps from the water. Halfway home, another flashing blue light appeared across the bay, headed straight toward me. I slowed down, then shut off the engine and drifted. Within moments, the coast guard patrol boat arrived. No pass for me this time. Kate Sullivan wasn't in command. Someone barked over the hailer, "United States Coast Guard. Please stop your engine now."

I was already sitting atop the boarding gate when the patrol boat roared to a stop. A man whom I'd not seen before leaned from the back deck. He wore three red chevrons and an arc on the sleeve of his work shirt, the insignia of a chief petty officer. His name patch read, "Hanrahan."

"You just out this morning, drifting?" he asked.

"No, Chief. Waiting for you."

He sneered and then proceeded with the familiar litany of idiotic questions. When I refused to give him my driver's license or social security number, he glared at me. Then he came aboard with a young seaman. But they found nothing, and the Chief handed me yet another certificate of boarding before we separated boats and went our own ways.

A WEB OF SUNLIGHT streamed through the spaces between my closed window blinds, trapping mostly dust. I rubbed my eyes and sat up. Last night seemed like a dream. After being boarded by the Coast Guard, I must have made it safely into the marina and docked the *Noble Lady.* Scary. I hardly remembered any of it. I grabbed the clock, moving it in and out until my bleary eyes focused. Damn. My eyes flashed open wide. I had a lesson with Mr. Oller in thirty minutes. I threw on clothes, gulped down a smoothie and raced over to his house.

A small sign on the front door let students know that he was in session and asked them to please come in. I gently shut the door behind me, hoping he wouldn't hear me enter and end his current lesson precisely on time. I moved a backpack from the couch onto the floor, took a seat, and popped the latches on my guitar case. But I had only practiced for about five minutes before a door downstairs swung open, and I hastily returned my guitar to its case. A young woman crested the stairs ahead of Mr. Oller. I stood, and we faced each other.

She wrinkled her face. "You look familiar," she said.

I noticed the tattoos down her arms and the dark blue wavy lines peeking just above the collar of her blouse. "Apparently we both like classical guitar, and also DJ Groove Finger," I said.

She smiled and nodded. "That's right. You never gave me a dance." She pointed at me. "I'll get my dance next time."

Mr. Oller, dressed in his suit and thin tie, stood patiently while the young woman retrieved her backpack. Then he escorted her to the door. He turned around and walked back toward me. He ran his hands down his arms and over his chest.

"I don't understand young people today," he said sadly. "But at least with some I share a common language of the guitar." He rolled the "r." "Come," he said, waving me forward.

Downstairs, in Mr. Oller's studio, I played the beginning measures of the Prelude several times, while he watched. "Relax. Breathe. Be aware of your body while playing," he said.

This time he sat and spoke without touching me. Then I ventured to play the whole piece. My anxiety rose as I reached the challenging measure. Sure enough, my fingers jammed again. Mr. Oller smiled and nodded.

I huffed, then rested the guitar across my lap. "I can't seem to get past this measure," I said. "Every time I approach it, I lose a sense of where I'm going, and my fingers get confused."

"Good," Mr. Oller said. "And the more you try to attack that measure directly, the more confused you will get. Remember, we have to practice here." He held up his hands. "And here." He pointed to his head, then to the picture of him with Segovia. "El Maestro said to me once, 'Frederico, when you are confused over a piece of music, do not practice it over and over again. For all you will be doing is practicing your confusion.'" Mr. Oller's face lit up. "So, we drop the Prelude and move to another part of the suite."

He grabbed sheet music from a pile beside him, and placed it on my stand. Then he turned to the back of the folio, and tapped. "Two short minuets, which are not hard to master."

He reached down and opened his guitar case, pulling out his instrument. And for the first time I got to hear Mr. Oller play. He didn't need the music. He took a deep breath, closed his eyes, and let his fingers caress the strings.

The first minuet was airy and light, the second heavy and grave. Listening to him play the two minuets reminded me of being on the water in conditions that changed from flat calm with clear skies, to fogged-in with lumpy seas. When he finished he placed his guitar back in its case, pointed to the first minuet and said, "Now you try."

I managed to sight-read my way through the first two lines of the first minuet, and it didn't sound too bad. We worked on the ornamental trill in the fourth measure for the rest of the lesson. And when we were through, Mr. Oller turned to me. He interlaced his fingers, moved his hands back and forth, and said, "It's a suite. All in one key. All the parts, all the themes are connected. If you're confused in one area, move to another, and what you learn there will help resolve your confusion."

On the drive down to Seattle, I couldn't help but think that lessons with Frederico Oller would make me a better classical guitarist, a better private investigator, and...well a better person too. I didn't believe the OLF had anything to do with Atherton's boat or the firebombing of the lab, and it was time for me to move on to those who might benefit from the rest of us believing that they did.

Overhead, patches of blue poked through holes in the mottled gray sky. And in the rearview mirror, I watched an unmarked car trail me all the way down Interstate 5. The compact Seattle skyline dominated the view ahead, until Mount Rainier uncovered around a turn in the freeway, dwarfing any human architectural achievements. Still, among Seattle's concrete, steel and glass, the Bank of America Tower stood out at nine hundred sixty-seven feet, the tallest building in the city. The curved, polished, dark granite surfaces of the tower reminded me of an ocean wave turned on end. And the Bank of America Tower also endeared itself to me by reason of its local name, BOAT.

Pipeline Development, Inc. had headquarters on the top floor of the BOAT and, in keeping with Mr. Oller's suggestion, I was moving on to another area of this investigative suite in hopes that it would resolve my confusion.

BOAT took up a city block, and, to my surprise, police barricades cordoned off all of Fifth Avenue in front of the tower. I drove by, turning to see a group of several hundred people on the street outside of BOAT, placards raised on thin wooden posts bobbing up and down.

I parked in an underground garage several blocks away and walked back, slipping under a police barricade. A line of motorcycle officers surrounded the protestors, whose signs read, "Stop the Pipeline," "PDI Will Straightjacket the Strait," and "Herring Have No Voice."

A woman's angry voice blared over a public address system. "They've lied to us, and when they couldn't lie they've falsified data. The pipeline will further contaminate Cherry Point. Herring will die. Salmon will die. Orcas will die. And eventually we'll have our own Dead Sea. We have to stop the pipeline. We have to stop the pipeline." The crowd joined in the chant, and "We have to stop the pipeline" reverberated off the granite face of BOAT.

I thought I recognized the speaker's voice, and when I got closer to the podium I saw Hera, the woman from OLF, speaking today under a banner that read, "Citizens United to Protect the Strait." SEALs or FBI—I wasn't sure which, but apparently OLF managed to outwit the pursuit on Waldron Island. I had to hand it to these kids. They played a pretty mean game of "good cop, bad cop."

A smaller group of counter-protesters stood opposite the larger group, separated by police in riot gear who'd carved out a narrow walkway between both groups, for people entering the tower. The counter-protestors heckled and spit out obscenities. Funny, I recognized some of them as well, from the workers I tangled with at the PDI construction site.

While I was still fifty yards from entering BOAT, a bull-horn squealed and a police officer barked to the protesters and counter-protestors, telling them to separate and to move back from the building.

That's when a bottle rocketed across the neutral zone, from the counter-protestors' side. A young man caught the bottle and hurled it back. Then, two officers barged into the crowd after the protestor, creating a gap in the police line. Protestors and counter-protestors simply swarmed through, headed toward each other. Fists and signs flew in all directions. I tried to duck out of the way, but I came face-to-face with one of the men from the PDI construction site, who recognized me.

"Fucking messenger boy," he said.

He threw a punch at me. I sidestepped him, grabbed his arm, twirled him around and flung him into a line of advancing police officers. Then I quickly ducked underneath the brawl and fought my way toward BOAT. The revolving doors spit me out, inside the building. I looked back to see that the police had separated the warring parties and quickly re-established order.

Suddenly a hand clapped my shoulder. I turned to see a security guard glaring at me.

"Hands behind your back," he said. "You're trespassing on private property."

"I'm here to see Mark Roderick, security director at Pipeline Development, and I got caught up in that melee outside."

The guard, a rotund young man who looked well fed on fast foods, halted, seemingly unsure of what to do next. It helped to have been responsible for maritime safety and security throughout Puget Sound, which meant I got to know the security directors of large corporations with assets, and therefore potential targets, on the water. It may have also helped that, rare for me since leaving the Coast Guard, I had on a suit and tie. Though I'm sure they looked crumpled from fighting my way in.

"Call him," I said. "And tell him Commander Charles Noble, United States Coast Guard, is here to see him."

"Wait here," the guard said. He walked over to a long desk in the middle of the lobby and spoke to another man, who picked up a phone. A few minutes later, the guard strolled back over to me.

"Sorry, Commander," he said. "Sign in, then pick up a visitor's tag. You know, this building was originally a target on al Qaeda's 9/11 hit list. We have to be cautious about whom we let in."

The elevator took a while to reach the top floor. When I stepped off, I looked for a men's room to tidy up. Through the small window above the washbasins, I glimpsed a stunning view of the top of the Olympic Mountain range. An urban myth held that the women's restroom on this floor was voted best in the nation because it had floor-to-ceiling windows looking out on the same scene.

I came to a set of floor-to-ceiling cherrywood doors with silver letters that read, "Mark A. Roderick, Director of Security, PDI Corporation." I'd been to see Roderick once before for a meeting on underwater pipeline safety. The former FBI agent came to work for PDI in the days post-9/11, when security suddenly became a concern of every major corporation.

The door opened into a large reception area done in cherrywood, with several large brightly colored glass flower vases placed around the room on cherrywood pedestals. The vases, full of flowers, appeared to be the work of famed local glass artist Dale Chihuly.

The receptionist, an older woman in a dark blue dress with pearls dangling from her neck and from her ears, sat at a low table in front of a wall bearing the three massive silver letters, PDI. She popped her head up from a computer screen, gasped, then collected herself. Maybe she thought I was one of the demonstrators who'd managed to slip past the police.

"May I help you?" she said.

"I'm here to see Mr. Roderick," I said.

She frowned. "Is he expecting you?"

"Commander Charles Noble, United States Coast Guard, retired," I said.

She squinted at me above her glasses, unimpressed. "Oh, you called from downstairs." She punched a button on her telephone and said, "Commander Noble's here." Then she said "Yes" a few times before hanging up. She turned to me. "Have a seat."

Instead of sitting, I walked over to a large, glass case housing a scale model of northern Puget Sound, Vancouver Island, and the smaller American and Canadian islands in between. A heavy, dashed black line revealed the projected course of the pipeline as it snaked through the mainland of northwest Washington, then exited at Cherry Point to travel across the Strait of Georgia to Vancouver Island.

I hadn't studied the model long, when a voice behind me said with the hint of a southern twang, "Commander Noble, what brings you to PDI?"

I turned to see Mark Roderick, a man in his fifties with a receding hairline and round cheeks that held a permanent blush. We shook hands.

"The PDI pipeline project," I said.

"Hell." He pointed out the window and down. "Seems that's brought everyone to PDI today." He turned to the receptionist. "Linda, hold my calls while I talk with Commander Noble."

Roderick had a corner office with a commanding view of the Space Needle, the Olympics, and Puget Sound. I sat in a plush black leather chair in front of his glass-top desk, uncluttered except for a computer screen, a sleek modern telephone, and one folder marked "Pipeline Protest."

"Helluva time you picked to pay a visit," he said. "Damn protestors. I don't have long. But tell me, Commander, what can I do for you? I heard you weren't with the Guard anymore. Hey…" He snapped his finger and pointed at me. "Are you looking for a job?"

I waved him off. "No," I said.

"'Cause if you are, I'll hire you before you step out of my office." He tugged on his lapels. "Best move I ever made, leaving the Bureau. Great hours. Great pay. Great benefits." He swept his hand around the room. "And look at these goddamn accommodations. Never see something like this in the FBI. Just keep that in mind. Are you trying to make it as a solo security consultant?"

"In part," I said.

"I know a coupla fellows who left the Bureau to do that. First few did pretty well. It's a tough road now. Too many indies competing with each other. Okay, let me stop jabbering. You're here about the Georgia Strait pipeline project. How can I help?"

"I'm part of the investigation into that boat the Coast Guard intercepted heading for Cherry Point with explosives."

Roderick's eyes widened. "You've got my attention now."

"It seems pretty clear that the OLF wasn't behind the boat, or the subsequent firebombing of the Anacortes laboratory."

Roderick whistled low. "Are you sure? We've got security cams on the demonstration right now, sending feeds to the FBI to see if their facial recognition software can identify any potential OLF members in the crowd."

"I helped apprehend and interrogate two OLF ring leaders."

"And where are they now?"

"In safe custody, I'm told."

"If the OLF isn't behind these bombings, then who is?"

"An individual or institution with something to gain from making it appear that the OLF is."

Roderick shifted in the seat behind his desk. "And you're telling me all of this because…?"

"PDI stands to benefit from the perception that Thomas Atherton and the OLF intended to bomb the Cherry Point facility to stop the construction of the pipeline."

"How?"

"Thomas Atherton was working on a new environmental impact statement, but now he's missing and so is his data, and the suit filed a few weeks ago to stop the pipeline hangs on the results of that study. And—"

"And with Atherton's data lost, you think PDI will have an advantage in court," Roderick added.

"Could look that way," I said. "PDI, acting in its own self-interest, stacked the deck."

He frowned, then pointed out the window. "You should be out there, with those half-cocked kids."

"I'm not taking sides," I said. "I wanted to give you a heads-up so that you could clean house if you need to, before someone shows up to clean house for you."

"Fuck." Roderick pounded his desk. "Not sure you did me a favor."

"How's that?" I asked.

"After 9/11 it was fashionable for big companies to hire a high-profile director of security. All of this is swell." He swept his hand around his office. "But the truth is that I'm mostly window dressing. The CEO and the Board still make major security decisions behind closed doors. And you're talking a possible criminal conspiracy: PDI trying to influence the outcome of a case by interfering with an environmental impact study, maybe even planting a bomb, destroying a laboratory. Hell, if word got around PDI that I was looking into that, it'd probably cost me my job."

"And if PDI is involved, it'd probably cost you your job anyway."

Roderick stared at me and breathed hard. "Look, I gotta get back to dealing with this protest."

I stood up to leave, but before I reached the door, Roderick called out.

"Commander."

I turned around.

"I'd be careful if I were you," he said. "The corporate world's as brutal as the military, maybe even more so because no one here even bothers to pay lip service to notions of honor, integrity, and fair play. Word like this gets around, it could make some pretty powerful people pretty angry."

"Thanks," I said. I closed the door behind me.

If some pretty powerful people got pretty angry, that'd mean I guessed right.

I got back to the *Noble Lady* about seven that evening and no sooner had I pulled out my guitar than my cell phone rang.

"Charlie," the woman said. And then she began to sob.

It took me a moment to recognize Janet's voice.

"What's the matter?"

"They found Thomas." She broke into another round of sobs.

"Where?"

"His body," she said. "They found his body floating near Spieden Island."

"Are you at home?" I asked.

"No," she said. "I'm still at the gallery."

"I'll be right over."

I ran up to the parking lot and jumped into my car. Vallerie opened the door when I got to Janet's gallery.

"She's not doing well," Vallerie said.

I walked past the masks and artwork, on my way into Janet's office. She sat beneath the picture of the Indian woman and the lone canoe. Janet's eyes were red. I moved behind her desk and leaned on the edge. I reached out for her hand. "I'm sorry," I said.

She sniffed back tears. "He didn't deserve this," Janet said. "Thomas was a good man. He didn't deserve to die like this."

"Tell me what you know," I said.

"I'd just hung the 'Closed' sign in the window, when my telephone rang," she said. "It was the Coast Guard. They said two kayakers…reported finding…" She tried to force the words out between deep breaths and heaves, but grief got the best of her and she started crying again.

I squeezed her hand. "It's okay," I said. Then I turned to Vallerie, standing on the other side of the desk. "Do you know what happened?" I asked.

Her eyes were moist. "I got a call from a coast guard information officer, who said that two kayakers came across a body floating in the waters near Spieden Island," she said.

"How did they know it was Thomas?"

"Apparently his wallet was still in his pocket."

"Time of death?"

"They didn't say."

"Cause of death?"

"I don't think the medical examiner had seen the body yet. My understanding is that it had to be taken to…"

"Friday Harbor," I said.

"Yes," Vallerie said.

I squeezed Janet's hand again, then looked at Vallerie. "Will you stay here with her?" I asked.

"Where are you going?" Vallerie asked.

"To find out more about Thomas," I said.

Janet squeezed my hand, then looked up at me and shook her head. "You don't have to," she said. "I know where Thomas is now."

"This is no longer just about him," I said. "It's about doing what's right; about discovering the truth."

◎   ◎   ◎

WHEN I GOT BACK to the harbor, I called San Juan County Sheriff, Ed Sykes, at home. He said the kayakers came across Atherton's body earlier in the afternoon. He also said that he might know more tomorrow because the coroner was performing the autopsy as we spoke. We agreed to meet for breakfast.

Fifteen minutes after I hung up with Sykes, the *Noble Lady* was warmed up and ready to go. I chugged out of the harbor, trying to guess how long it would take before the Coast Guard intercepted me. I figured the guys in the unmarked car called in my movements, and somehow that information made its way over to Station Bellingham. I guessed twenty minutes, but it took a half hour before a blue light raced from the coast guard boat shed, heading my way. I shifted into neutral and let the *Noble Lady* drift on dark waters. Orange city lights lined the shore, stars lined the night sky.

The coast guard patrol boat came to a stop alongside me. Kate Sullivan wasn't in command, Chief Hanrahan was.

"Throw me a line, Chief. You're late," I said.

Hanrahan didn't have a sense of humor. Like an automaton, he launched into his questions and inspection. And a half hour later, he handed me another boarding certificate.

Piloting the *Noble Lady* at night is an intimate experience, with the cabin bathed in a soft glow of reds, blues, and greens; with visibility limited, and my awareness focused on the sound of her engine and what her dials, meters, and screens tell me.

At night, even large boats pass by, not as threatening hulks, but as curious red and green eyes slipping through the mantle of liquid darkness. And while it's disorienting and sometimes frightening to feel so blind, piloting at night is about trusting your boat and yourself.

I pulled into the Friday Harbor marina well after midnight and took my favorite spot along the concrete dock on the inside of the breakwater.

◎   ◎   ◎

I AWOKE EARLY THE next morning, hanging on to the flotsam of a dream. Something about Vallerie McKee in a bikini waving me ashore, while Janet Paulsen tried to pull me under the water. And when I struggled to the surface, Sharon smiled from the rear deck of a forty-two-foot Krogen, which disappeared into the fog. Then suddenly, Katherine Sullivan zoomed from the fog in a coast guard patrol boat and plucked me from the frigid waters. I bet a Freudian psychologist would have a field day with that dream.

When I told the waitress at the Spinnaker Restaurant I was meeting Ed Sykes for breakfast, she showed me to a waterside booth with a commanding view of the harbor and the mountains of Orcas Island, backlit in early morning light. A ferry captain let out two short, sharp horn blasts that I'm sure awakened anyone still sleeping. Moments later the three-story green and white giant glided by. The whump, whump, whump of its heartbeat vibrated the restaurant's windows and my body.

"Thought you were getting out of the investigation business."

I turned to see Ed Sykes standing beside me. I rose to meet him. I had to, because he stood several inches taller than I. His graying blonde crew cut gave him the look of an aging drill sergeant. His face had the leathery, cracked texture of a fisherman's, but his sparkling, bluish-gray eyes hinted of a mischievous kid still lurking inside. We clasped hands, then gave each other a quick hug. He slid into his seat across from me. Our waitress glided up to the table and we placed our orders. I went with crab cakes and eggs. Ed ordered a salmon omelet. We both had orange juice to start, instead of coffee.

"Did you ever find those two SEALs?" I asked.

"Damnedest thing." Sykes shook his head. "We found their kayaks, spray skirts, and paddles onshore, but not a trace of them. No sign that they tried to hike out either. Obviously, they didn't drown. It looked like someone plucked them from shore."

"They could've radioed for help."

"From where?"

"Canada," I said.

"Canada?"

Between sips of juice, I brought Ed up-to-date on my investigation into Atherton and the OLF. The waitress slid our plates on the table.

"It's the first I've heard about the feds raiding Waldron Island," Sykes said. "It's my backyard. You think they'd give me a heads-up. Maybe even let my guys tag along."

"I don't know that it was the feds," I said. "It could have been the SEALs."

"Hell, that doesn't make any sense. SEALs are military, and the military's not supposed to be used against civilians in this country."

"That was pre-9/11," I said.

"Yeah, I guess you're right. The way things are now all you need to do is yell 'terrorist,' then anything goes. The law be damned."

"What did the coroner's report on Thomas Atherton show?" I asked.

"The body had deteriorated from bottom feeding, most likely by crabs." Sykes looked at my plate. "You sure you want to hear this now?"

I nodded and took a bite of crab cake. "I can handle it."

"The coroner said he probably died of cold-water-immersion shock. But he also said it didn't look like Atherton went into the water willingly."

"Tell me more."

"You probably know a drowning victim's body initially sinks, then as it decomposes it releases methane gas, which fills up the body cavity like a balloon, causing it to rise to the surface two to four days later. The coroner's report cited bruises on the vic's wrists and arms."

"From a fall off the boat?"

"Not on both arms. Coroner said it indicated a struggle."

"So someone threw Atherton overboard."

"Without a life jacket," Sykes said. "From all the saltwater in his lungs, the coroner thought he probably succumbed immediately."

"The shock of the cold water triggered an automatic brainstem reflex to breathe?"

"Yep. Like sucking in a breath when you're scared." Sykes stabbed a piece of salmon in the middle of his omelet.

"Only there's no air, just frigid saltwater."

"Hell of a way to go," Sykes said.

"They say it's a peaceful way to go," I said.

"That's the rumor. Ever wonder who started it? Someone who drowned then came back to life? Hope I never find out firsthand." Sykes laid his fork down. "Anyway, we're treating Atherton's drowning as a murder." He stared at his plate, frowned, then pushed it away. "Damn, now I've lost my appetite."

I pushed a breadbasket over to Sykes. "Have some bread and a glass of water, until you get it back."

"You know, you could've called instead of coming all the way over from Bellingham," Sykes said.

"And miss the chance to go cruising?"

He pointed at me and winked. "You got a point there."

Sykes picked up his fork and resumed eating.

◎   ◎   ◎

IT WASN'T YET EIGHT when Sykes and I finished breakfast. After a quick shower at the marina, I warmed up the *Noble Lady* and headed out for the three and a half hour trip back to Bellingham.

Make that four hours, with the mandatory Coast Guard boarding and inspection, which I didn't mind so much this time because along with my certificate I got a smile and a quick hug from Kate Sullivan.

Once in port, I called Vallerie to see if she'd have lunch with me. I knew she was anxious to find out more about Atherton. I took a brisk twenty-minute walk to meet her at a Thai restaurant not far from the marina.

Geraldo, the Mexican owner, greeted me as I entered. Butri, his Thai wife, seated me at my favorite booth in the far back corner. Vallerie hadn't arrived yet. She walked in a short while later, dressed in fitted, chocolate-brown slacks the color of her skin, and a white blouse. I took a sip of water and stood up to shake her hand, but she insisted on a full-on hug.

Butri brought only one menu, placing it in front of Vallerie, who narrowed her eyes. "Did you already order?" she asked.

Butri cut in. "No. No. Mr. Noble always get same thing. No need for menu. Always number 32. Four stars."

Vallerie smiled, and it brought back memories of her standing onshore in my dream. "Hot guy," she said. "Number 32? What's that?"

"Garlic prawns."

"I'll have the black beans, broccoli, and chicken. Four stars." Vallerie said.

"Hot gal," I said.

Butri lifted the menu and scurried toward the kitchen, returning almost immediately with two bowls of egg-drop soup. Vallerie pushed the bowl aside and pulled out a pad crammed with notes. I told her about my breakfast meeting with Ed Sykes. Afterward, she shook her head.

"So it looks like Thomas Atherton was murdered."

"It does, and I need your help," I said.

"With what?"

"Background information on PDI."

"The company that's building the pipeline?"

"Uh huh."

"Do you think they're behind Atherton's murder and the bomb threat to the refinery?"

"I think they stand to gain in court from the perception that they are the innocent victim of an ecoterrorist plot."

"What kind of background information are you after?"

"Everything you can get on Phillip DiAmbrosio, the president of PDI. Where he was born. What college he went to. Names and connections of the PDI Board of Directors. What other boards they serve on. Major stockholders. Subsidiaries, if they have any. Every big project PDI's been involved in for the past twenty years—"

"Whew." Vallerie raised her hands. "I get it. You want an intelligence profile on PDI, is that right, Sir?" She deadpanned.

"Something like that," I said.

"Don't you have this backwards?"

"What do you mean?" I asked.

"I'm the investigative reporter." She pointed to herself. "You're the investigator." She pointed to me. "I'm supposed to tell *you* what to look into. But I bet this is how you proceeded in the Coast Guard, with a staff under your command. Only, you're not in the Guard any longer."

Butri slipped the soup dishes from the table and replaced them with our entrees. She set a steaming hot, covered bowl of rice between us. Vallerie ignored me, filling her plate with rice and then her entree. I dug into my dish, planning how I'd get the information on PDI myself. After a few bites, Vallerie laid her fork down and looked up from her plate.

"I'll see what I can do, Sir," she said. She saluted me, unable to hold onto her stern face, which quickly lapsed into a grin.

After lunch, I had Vallerie drop me off at Village Books in Fairhaven. I browsed through their basement boating section, waiting for her to leave. Then I walked upstairs and checked the front window. The car that had been shadowing me for more than a week was parked across the street. I went downstairs and slipped out the bookstore's back door, heading across Fairhaven Commons and taking a circuitous route that eventually led me back to the marina.

The unmarked car wasn't in the parking lot when I arrived, so I jumped into my car for another trip to Seattle.

Rear Admiral Vincent Ritchie and I didn't have much in common other than a love of boats. Several years back, he discovered his wife sleeping with a junior officer and the messy divorce left him without a home and living on his boat. This sounded like a great sacrifice except that Vin Ritchie's boat was a sixty-two-foot Nordhavn, basically a small luxury ship.

I pulled into the Shilshole Bay Marina just before six. Above the navy blue waters of Puget Sound, I was treated to a view of the saw-toothed, snowcapped peaks of the Olympic Mountains silhouetted in the dying, orange rays of the sun.

I didn't know exactly where Ritchie kept his boat, but it would be easy enough to spot. So I got out and walked the docks. The marina segregated slips by size. I bypassed docks with smaller boats, turning down a row of slips with a catamaran of at least sixty feet at the head. At the end of the row, I saw it.

The Nordhavn's superstructure squatted above the rear of the boat, which combined with the very long foredeck to give it the "all business" look of a miniature freighter. But the shiny dark blue hull and gleaming white pilothouse, separated by a thick red stripe, left no doubt that this boat was for pleasure as well. One thing I'll say to Ritchie's credit: he used the boat. Once to the South Pacific, and several times through the Panama Canal, then across the Atlantic.

Ritchie, a short, stocky man, stood on the dock, polishing the hull of the *Admiral's Gig*.

I walked up behind him. "Admiral. May I speak with you?"

He didn't bother turning around. I suppose he could barely make out my reflection on the hull.

"I'm off duty, son. Can't you see that?" he said in a croaking monotone.

"I realized that, which is why I came to see you off base, and after hours."

He kept buffing, still without turning around. "State your business, and be brief about it."

"My business has to do with the attempted bombing of the refinery at Cherry Point."

Ritchie tossed his polishing rag onto the deck of the *Admiral's Gig* and spun around. His eyes widened, then narrowed. "Noble? What the hell are you doing here?"

"I came to ask you a few questions about the incident."

He stared at me "You did, did you? It's a coast guard investigation. What business is it of yours now?"

"I work for the ex-wife of the owner of the Grand Banks that the Coast Guard intercepted off the refinery."

"Yeah. I heard something to that effect. She hired you to find her husband." He laughed. "Well, some kids in kayaks did your job for you. Guy turned up a floater yesterday."

"I'm aware of that, Admiral. But his death is now being investigated as a murder."

"That so? Suppose you're the investigator?" He chuckled low.

"Admiral, the District would benefit from the belief that it needed to protect against a small-boat attack like the one supposedly mounted against Cherry Point."

clyde w. ford

"Supposedly? You already lost that battle, Noble. Give it up. There's no *supposedly* about it. Someone wired a GB with explosives and pointed it at the refinery. If it wasn't for one of my heads-up coast guard crews, Cherry Point would be toast now."

"Admiral, exactly what kind of explosives were found aboard that GB?"

Ritchie smirked. "You think I'm going to tell you?"

"Why did a fast vessel out of Canada rendezvous with that GB before it headed toward the refinery?"

The admiral's jaw flexed but he remained silent, though his eyes steamed with scorn. I steadied myself against his gaze.

"What was a SEAL team doing camped out across the border in Canada, near where that vessel came from?"

"You don't know what you're talking about. And you damn sure don't know what hornet's nest you're poking into." A mist of spittle flew from his mouth.

"Then tell me, Admiral."

He pointed at me and barked. "You know your fucking problem, Noble? You always rode a goddamn high horse. You never understood how the military works. World's divided into good guys and bad guys. You're either on one side or the other. After 9/11, we're at war with the bad guys and there is no middle ground. The Guard's charged with protecting the coastline of America. That's 13,000 miles of ocean. It's not like being on land. Anything can slip through that border. Hell, I could paddle a goddamn bathtub full of explosives over from Canada and land on U.S. soil. My job is to make sure nothing that could harm us gets through that border." He pointed out to the Sound. "And if some goddamn ecoterrorists make it easier for me to grab more boats and more bodies, then it's not me who benefits, it's every goddamn American who can sleep more soundly at night because the men and women of the United States Coast Guard are better able to do their jobs."

246

Ritchie's face was beet red by the time he finished. I took a deep breath. "You're right, Admiral, the Guard's duty is to protect America, not to mislead it, or deceive it. Certainly not to participate in criminal activity in the name of Homeland Security."

Ritchie sucked in a breath. "You're out of line accusing the United States Coast Guard of criminal activity."

"No. I'm out of uniform because the United States Coast Guard forgot that it's also supposed to defend the truth."

"This discussion is over," Ritchie said.

He grabbed his cloth and resumed polishing the *Admiral's Gig*. I turned and walked back down the dock. I hadn't gone far, when Ritchie hollered at me.

"Noble."

I spun around.

"Don't you know that we're at war? And in war the first casualty *is* the truth."

It was my turn to point at the Admiral. "We are at war, Admiral. Only sometimes I'm afraid we don't know who the real enemy is."

"That's why you're out of the Guard, Noble," Ritchie said. "You couldn't figure out who the real enemy was." He shook his head in disgust.

I turned and walked back up to my car. Ritchie had one thing right. I didn't know what hornet's nest I was poking into. That's exactly why I was poking a stick at him. And there was still another nest that needed poking.

WHEN I PULLED INTO the marina parking lot I blinked my lights at the guys in the unmarked car, in case they hadn't noticed my return. Then I walked down the dock to the *Noble Lady,* but when I stepped onto the rear deck my body stiffened.

The bottom of the plastic cover on the water side was rolled up, as if someone had tried to enter. I checked the cabin door lock.

It didn't look tampered with. I swung up onto the foredeck, tugged on the pilothouse door, and peeked inside. No one had gained access that way either. I unlocked the cabin door, stepped inside, and switched on a light. Standing in the doorway, I peered back onto the rear deck, where I saw a small slip of paper. I stooped down to pick it up.

The terse, hand-written note read, "Black Wave??? Why are they interested in you?"

I whipped out my batch of boarding certificates and found the ones signed by Kate Sullivan, which I laid on the galley table next to the note. I'm not a handwriting expert, but the penmanship looked the same to me. I pulled out my cell phone and called Vallerie to arrange for breakfast first thing in the morning. I finally understood why navy SEALs had been popping up all around me.

◎   ◎   ◎

I met Vallerie at the Old Town Café.

"B," I said to Sean as he hovered over the table with his green pad in hand. He pulled a pencil from behind his ear.

Vallerie wrinkled her face. "You're not very adventurous when it comes to menus, are you?"

"I know what I like," I said. "That doesn't change."

"What's B?" she asked.

"Pancakes with a side order of sausage."

"And real maple syrup," Sean added.

"What's 'A'?" she asked.

"Two eggs sunny side up, split order of black beans and home fried potatoes with sourdough toast," Sean said.

She laughed, shaking her head as she did. Then she closed the menu and handed it to Sean. "I'll have A," she said.

"What do you have on DiAmbrosio and PDI?" I asked.

"As much as I could find in a day, Sir."

I held up my hand. "You can drop the 'Sir.'"

She sucked her teeth playfully. "But it sounds so authentic."

Vallerie pulled out a file folder full of hand-written notes and what looked like printed sheets from Internet sites.

"PDI began operation in 1975, shortly after Phillip DiAmbrosio returned from a tour of duty in Vietnam," she said.

"Which branch of the service?" I asked

"Not in the service."

"Diplomatic?"

"No." She held up her hand. "Hold on. I'm getting there."

"Intelligence?"

"Yes. CIA. And PDI has made a specialty of government contracts. Nicaragua. El Salvador. Grenada. Panama. The Gulf. You name the hot spot, after the fighting PDI was there."

"We bomb 'em, they build 'em…with taxpayer's dollars, of course," I said. "Let me guess, they're in Iraq working on pipeline reconstruction?"

Vallerie flipped through her notes. "Third highest paid contractor there."

"So who runs security for them in Iraq?"

"What?" she asked.

Sean, in his usually graceful style, slipped breakfast in front of us, almost unnoticed.

"Most contractors hire independent firms to provide security for their workers in Iraq," I said.

"Sorry," Vallerie said. "I didn't track that down."

"Did you come across the name 'Black Wave?'" I asked.

She shook her head. "Black Wave? What's that?"

"A private security firm that contracts with corporations like PDI. Sometimes with the Pentagon. Black Wave hires ex-SEALs, Special Forces, and CIA types for jobs the government or private firms would rather not admit they need done."

"They don't sound like folks to meet in a dark alley."

"They're not. Believe me, I've already met them there. They play for keeps."

Vallerie sucked in a breath. "You think they had something to do with Thomas Atherton's death?"

"Yes, but it's who they're working for that matters. These guys are only guns and muscle for hire."

I spread butter over my pancakes, then poured syrup. Not enough to drown them, but enough to make them sweet. At least one thing seemed clear: The guys I thought were SEALs weren't. They were contract labor for Black Wave.

Vallerie speared a home-fry with her fork, then thumbed back and forth through several pages of notes. "Black Wave..." she muttered. "Black Wave...here." She tapped her finger on a page. "You asked about PDI's Board of Directors. Martin Gillespie sits on it. Gillespie's the CEO of Black Wave, Inc."

I pointed my fork at her. "He's also the former ambassador to Nicaragua, who allegedly covered up our involvement with right wing death squads there. Before that, Gillespie was a CIA station chief in Viet Nam." I wrapped a strip of pancake around some sausage with my fork and popped it into my mouth. "In that case, there's another piece of information we need."

"Let me guess," Vallerie said. "You want to know who sits on Black Wave's board?"

I nodded. "You're quick and you're right. Forget reporting, you'd make a good intelligence officer."

"You think so?" she chuckled. "Are you looking for someone in particular on the Black Wave Board?"

"Uh huh," I said. "Rear Admiral Vincent Ritchie."

Vallerie snapped her fingers. "He's the—"

"CO of District Thirteen," I said.

After breakfast, I headed back to the *Noble Lady*. I practiced scales and the two minuets for about a half hour, before deciding it was time to poke a stick into the third hornet's nest. Besides, I wanted to test out my theory about the guys in the unmarked car.

I always berthed the *Noble Lady* straight ahead into my slip, which meant her bow faced the harbor's parking lot and her stern faced away. My inflatable dinghy hung from the arms of davits off the stern. I rolled up the plastic cover on the back of the boat and slowly lowered the dinghy into the water. Then I climbed over the stern and lowered myself into the dinghy. I pulled the starter cord and brought the outboard engine to life, hiding behind other boats as I slowly made my way out of the harbor.

Halfway across the bay to Fairhaven, I still hadn't seen the Coast Guard. When I got to Fairhaven, I tied the dinghy along a dock used by boaters with trailered boats and walked the several blocks up from the water to the back door of Janet's gallery. I rang the bell several times before a young man in a tie and short-sleeve blue shirt opened the door.

"We're not expecting any deliveries today," he said.

I pushed past him, and he stumbled backward. "Tell Janet, Charlie Noble's here to see her."

"Sir, may I suggest that you call for an appointment first."

"And may I suggest that you tell her I'm here. Hell, I'll do it myself."

I walked over to Janet's office, while the young man back-pedaled in front of me with his hands out, trying to push me away. I rapped on her door, and she answered.

"Hi—"

"Do you want me to call the police, Ms. Paulsen?" the young man said.

She grimaced and swept him away with a backhand flip. "It's okay, Kenneth. Mr. Noble's a friend."

"Oh." Kenneth turned around, glowering as he pushed past me.

"Protective, isn't he?"

"He's been that way since Thomas's death," Janet said. "He cares about me and I suppose I should be grateful."

I walked into Janet's office and she closed the door behind me. I stood, while she leaned against the front edge of her desk.

"How are you doing?" I asked.

"Better," she said. "I wasn't over the grief of our marriage ending, before being thrust into the grief of Thomas's death."

"I'm sorry," I said. "I know how hard sudden loss is. Do you have time for a walk?"

"Right now?"

"Yes."

"I suppose so," Janet said. "But I'm not dressed for walking." She pointed to her navy skirt.

"Along the paved part of the Fairhaven trail?" I asked.

She nodded. "I'll slip on some tennies."

We left through the back door.

A stiff southwest breeze, and bright, early-afternoon sun spread a glittering sheet of waves across the bay. Bicyclists and skateboarders passed us as we ambled along the trail.

I placed my hand on Janet's shoulder as we walked. "I need your help in making a telephone call," I said.

"To whom?"

"Richard Collingsworth."

"Richard? Why?"

"I need to rule him in or out of Thomas's death."

Janet grabbed my arm and held me back. "Richard? You're kidding?"

"No," I said. "Something he mentioned earlier's been bothering me ever since. How, like a dead poet, Thomas was even more popular after he disappeared. It made him mad."

We started walking again. "Richard was jealous of Thomas, but he wouldn't resort to something crazy like murder."

"Would you make the call?" I asked.

"Sure, I'll make it. What do you want me to say?"

"Tell Collingsworth that you have Thomas's data. Make up anything. Say he left it in a safe deposit box for you, which you could not open until after his death. Tell him you're not sure what to do. He'll probably ask you to deliver the data to him. Tell him you're not sure that you should. That you're thinking about turning it over to the police, but you called him first."

"You want me to drop the hint that for the right price I'd turn the data over to Richard?"

"That's right. Nothing overt. Don't make him an offer over the phone. If I'm right, he'll get back to us."

"You're setting up a sting."

"Uh huh."

"For when?"

"Tomorrow night."

Janet stopped. She swallowed hard. "Tomorrow night? You're kidding?"

"No. I'm not."

"This sounds risky."

"It could be," I said. "But I'm tired of chasing red herrings."

"At least you have a plan," she said.

"I'm working on it, and making that call is the first step."

We turned around and walked back to Janet's gallery. Once inside her office, she kicked off her shoes and threw herself onto the couch. She got Collingsworth in his office and played him like a pro. When she hung up, she laughed. "It's like sending up a trial balloon on the value of an artist's new work," she said. "You put the word out that you have this new piece, and see what response you get."

"Call me if Collingsworth gets back to you," I said.

◎ ◎ ◎

I ALSO DECIDED TO put Mr. Oller to the test. After I putted back in the dinghy to the *Noble Lady,* I pulled out my guitar, but instead of practicing scales and the Minuets, I launched right into the Prelude. Damn. It worked. When my fingers reached that tricky part, it was like they had a mind of their own and knew exactly what to do. But then I tried to play the passage again, and my fingers knotted right up. Close, but not there yet.

Vallerie called early that afternoon.

"You were wrong," she said.

"Okay, well, then—"

She cut in, laughing. "But you were also right."

"Now I'm also confused. I'll meet you at your office," I said.

I hung up.

Ten city blocks up from the marina, the 1920s-era Bellingham Herald building is one of a handful of historic landmarks that make up the city's meager skyline. Part of an antique printing press dominates the building's lobby, reminding me of a gigantic nutcracker with its oversized turn screw. I walked into the ground floor newsroom, an open pit of metal desks adorned with computer screens. Vallerie waved me over to her, grabbed a stack of papers, then ushered me into a conference room and shut the door. We sat at one end of a long, highly polished wooden table.

Vallerie read from her notes. "Ritchie doesn't sit on Black Wave's board," she said. "Apparently, military regs don't allow it."

"So, I was wrong," I said.

"Hold on." She waved her notes at me. But here's the thing…" When she lifted her head, she had a "gotcha" smile. "Ten years ago Black Wave issued private stock in order to raise operating capital. And guess who's the second largest stockholder after DiAmbrosio."

I leaned back in my chair. "Rear Admiral Vincent Ritchie."

"Right."

I smacked the table. "Write up everything that you have."

Vallerie waved her folder of notes, then grimaced. "Everything I have. I still don't have a story. Just a collection of suggestive facts. There's nothing to write up. My editor would laugh me out of his office."

I put my hand onto hers, and stared into her eyes. "Trust me, you'll have your story. But I need you to write up your notes and e-mail them to Captain George Townsend, MIFCPAC. He's my former CO. Tell him I requested that you do so."

I scribbled Townsend's e-mail address on the corner of one of Vallerie's sheets of paper.

"MIFCPAC?" she asked.

"The Coast Guard's intelligence coordination center for the Pacific. One other thing, tell Townsend he needs to monitor all communications traffic out of District Thirteen, beginning at 1700 hours tomorrow."

Vallerie took some notes, then raised her head. "And what are you going to do now?" she asked.

"Get you your story."

I got up to leave.

Janet called on my cell phone as I walked back from the Herald building toward the marina. "It's on," she said. "Richard called back to arrange a telephone meeting between me and someone, he said, might help me make up my mind. I'm supposed to receive a call at my office at seven tonight."

"Good. I'll be there at quarter to."

◎   ◎   ◎

LATER THAT EVENING, Janet sat behind her desk, fidgeting with the ends of her hair, while I sat on her couch. We waited for the call, and when the telephone rang she jumped. Then she hit the speakerphone button. The voice on the other end spoke in a low monotone, metallic growl created by an electronic disguising unit. I couldn't even distinguish whether it belonged to a woman or a man.

"I understand you have an item of value," the voice said.

"In the art world, value is always relative to the appraiser. Particularly for a rare item like this," Janet said.

I smiled, and flashed her the "okay" sign. A long pause followed, before the robotic voice continued.

"If, indeed, you actually had this item in your possession, it might be worth one hundred thousand dollars to the right party."

Janet laughed. "One hundred thousand dollars for an item critical to a project worth hundreds of millions of dollars? Perhaps I should shop for another buyer."

The caller breathed, which, distorted, sounded like wind howling through a deep canyon.

"One million dollars?" the metallic voice said.

"We're moving in the right direction," Janet said. "Try two and you might get my attention."

"That's a lot of money," the voice said.

"Nowhere near what an adverse judgment would cost."

"I'll tell you where to make the exchange."

I waved my hand and shook my head.

"No, I'll tell you," Janet said. She read from the paper I'd slipped in front of her. "The exchange will happen tomorrow night. I'll—"

"That's impossible. I can't get my hands on that kind of money on such short notice."

"I'm sure you'll manage. I'll call back before midnight tonight and leave two sets of numbers on the voice-mail of the ecology department's chairman. Both sets will be longitude and latitude coordinates. The first, where you can find the item. The second, where I expect to find my money. I'll place the item in a watertight container with a red and white crab pot buoy attached to it. And I'll expect to find the money in a watertight container attached to a red and white buoy as well."

The phone line clicked dead. Janet sighed and slumped back in her chair.

"What do I do now?" she asked.

"Grab your tennies. Don't go home. Meet me at Gate Six in an hour. And be ready to spend this evening and most of tomorrow on the water."

"Gate Six? I thought the *Noble Lady* was berthed at Gate Nine."

"She is," I said. "But I need you to meet me at Gate Six."

J anet walked up to the Gate Six ramp toting a small canvas
bag over her shoulder and wearing jeans and a woolen
sweater.

"You didn't go home, did you?"

She shook her head. "No. I stopped by a store and picked up
a few things. Where are we going?"

"I'll explain when we get to the boat."

"The *Noble Lady?*" she asked.

"No." I checked my watch and waved her along. "C'mon.
We don't have much time."

We walked past two rows of slips, then turned right, stopping several berths before the end.

Janet gasped. "A GB 36? This is what we're taking out? It's
just like the *Gaia Goddess.*"

"Almost," I said. "Except she's a Woodie." I patted the sides
of the boat. I climbed aboard and turned back. "Think you can
handle her?"

"Damn right I can." She squinted at the boat's name. "*Big
Ben?* People come up with god-awful boat names."

"It's Ben Conrad's boat."

"That Bellingham detective?"

"Uh huh."

"And he let you borrow it?"

I chuckled. "Only after he called the San Juan County Sheriff for a reference, and I promised to pay for any damage to the boat."

She looked the boat over, then pointed to the dinghy resting on the dock. "We need to attach it," she said.

I shook my head. "We won't need that dinghy."

"Why?"

"Trust me," I said.

Janet climbed aboard, then grabbed my arm. "The last time I trusted someone who asked me to step aboard a Grand Banks, he turned up dead."

"I'm not planning on following his lead," I said.

"Good," Janet said.

I pulled open the cabin door and stepped inside. Janet followed.

"Take the boat out into the middle of the bay." I took a slip of paper from my pocket. "Call Collingsworth's voice-mail from your cell phone and give him these coordinates. We'll leave the CD here." I pointed to the first set of numbers. "They're to leave the money, here." I pointed to the second.

"That seems easy enough. Then bring *Big Ben* back to port?"

"No. Stay out. Cruise around. But be back at the yellow flashing buoy out from Starr Rock by nine. Do you know which buoy I mean?"

"Small, low to the water. Easy to miss. Sure, I know it. But why?"

"I need time to join you."

"In the *Noble Lady?*"

"No. I'll meet you there in my dinghy."

"I don't—"

I held up my hand. "Trust me. I'll start the engine and then help you shove off."

"Wait. If you want me to take the boat out, then I'm the captain. Now give me the keys." She smiled with her hand out. "And get off my boat. Go do whatever you need to do, and I'll meet you at the yellow buoy. I can shove off on my own."

I ducked under the cabin door and stepped out, when Janet called to me.

"You do have Thomas's data, don't you?"

"No," I said.

She raised her eyebrows.

"But I know where to get it."

"Tell me you have a plan beyond meeting me at the yellow buoy?"

"You want me to lie?"

She sighed and shook her head, then reached over and yanked the cabin door closed.

I strolled back to Gate Nine, waving to my friends in the unmarked car as I passed them. Once aboard the *Noble Lady,* I checked the fridge. Then I walked back up to the parking lot and drove to a nearby supermarket. I returned with a load of groceries that filled a dock cart. Anyone could have easily guessed that I was about to head out. An hour after Janet left, I fired up Miss Perky and when she got warm I pushed the *Noble Lady* back and cruised from the harbor.

I'd barely made it past the green entrance buoy when a coast guard patrol boat zoomed from its dock. I cut my engine and drifted. Hard-nosed Chief Hanrahan commanded the patrol boat. He asked the same stupid questions and then informed me that he needed to board. He went through the normal check of life-vests, valves, and running lights. Then he asked me to pump out my bilge. Something I'd never been asked to do before. I hit the manual override switch and the pump whined. He hurried to the rear deck and shined a flashlight over the side of the boat.

"You won't find an oil slick," I said.

"Sir, I'll need to see the lowest spot on your boat," Hanrahan said.

"That'd be the engine room," I said.

I pulled back a floor panel in the galley, and the chief climbed down. He ran his fingers underneath the engine, withdrew them, and then thrust his hand at me.

"Oil," he said. "Could drip into the bilge."

Only a thin film covered his index finger.

"Bilge's lined with oil absorbent material," I said. "That small amount will never find its way out."

"Sir, coast guard regs state that if the boarding officer determines that the danger of an oil leak exists, that danger must be reported, and the offending vessel towed back to port."

I pointed to his finger. "You're kiddin? For that much oil?"

"Yes, Sir, for any amount. But we'll make an exception in this case. Instead of towing you back to port, we'll allow you to steam back under your own power."

"How generous of you, Chief."

He left me with a document that said I couldn't leave port again until another inspection had determined I'd corrected the violation. So I cruised the *Noble Lady* back to her berth with the coast guard patrol boat following. When I tied up, Chief Hanrahan and his crew sped away.

After the coast guard boat disappeared, I walked onto the rear deck of the *Noble Lady*, rolled up the cover, and lowered my dinghy into the water. Then I lowered a small icebox packed with groceries and a duffle full of my gear into the front of the dinghy before climbing in myself. I putted slowly out of the harbor, making sure to keep the hulls of large boats between prying eyes and me.

It took me a half hour to reach Janet. She stood on the back deck of *Big Ben,* waiting for me. I handed the icebox up to her, tied the dinghy to a cleat and let it follow behind us as we took off.

"Where to?" she asked.

"Fossil Bay."

"For what?"

"I'll tell you when we're underway."

And for the first time in two weeks, I cruised across the bay, up Hale Passage and over Rosario Strait to Sucia without the pleasure of a coast guard boarding. The biggest difference was that *Big Ben* moved more swiftly than the *Noble Lady* and Janet wouldn't let me take the wheel.

Along the way, I gave Janet a synopsis of what'd happened in Canada, on Waldron Island, and why I'd left Bucky and Matthew on Jerry and Wanda's tug.

We glided into Fossil Bay and tied up to the *Wanda K.* I hopped off and knocked on the forward door. There was no answer. I knocked again, then whispered, "Bucky, it's me. Charlie."

The door cracked and Bucky peeked out. She must have seen Janet at the helm of the GB because she hissed. "Like, what's she doing here?"

"It's a long story, but right now I need the CD with Thomas's data."

"For what?"

"It's another long story."

"I suppose you want me to trust you again?"

"If I'm right, we'll catch the people that murdered Thomas."

"How?"

"It's—"

"Like, another long story, eh?" she said.

"Uh huh."

Bucky disappeared from the crack of the door and Matthew returned a moment later, waving a plastic CD case.

"It's the only complete copy I know of," he said. "Thomas encrypted the CD, making it impossible for anyone else to make a normal copy. We hadn't finished decrypting it back on Waldron when all hell broke loose."

"So you do have an incomplete copy?" I asked.

"Yeah." Matthew nodded. "But it won't do you any good. Half the data sets are missing."

I motioned for it with my hand. "Give me that one instead."

Matthew left and returned with another CD, which he handed to me. I turned to Janet. "I can leave you here now," I said.

"Leave me on Sucia with her?" Janet's voice rose, she motioned toward the tug. "I don't think so." She fired up the GB's engine and poked me in the chest. "I'm the captain, remember? And I'm in this until the end. Now go out on deck and untie us. Where to next?"

"Satellite Cove at Stuart Island. Know it?"

"Know it? I could take us there blind."

I cast off our lines. Janet spun the boat around and headed out of Fossil Cove. Forty minutes later we were cruising down President's Channel along the southeast shore of Waldron Island.

"Were you serious about leaving me at Sucia?"

"It could get pretty rough tomorrow night."

"Yeah, but whoever arrives will be expecting to see me, not you," she said.

"That's what I'm afraid of," I said. "These people play for keeps."

"So do you have a plan all worked out to deal with them?" she asked.

"No."

Janet smiled. "All the more reason you need me, to give you time to figure out what you're going to do."

R ounding Point Disney, Janet spun the wheel right and we headed for the opening between the rocks at the entrance to Prevost Harbor. A crescent moon hung in the starry sky. I opened the cabin door and stepped out on deck. Dark waters gurgled beneath the boat's hull. Closer to Stuart Island, I stepped back inside and looked over Janet's shoulder as she navigated around the reefs just inside the harbor. She ordered me back on deck to handle the anchor, while she maneuvered into position. Janet reminded me of Sharon, with her comfort around boats.

After we anchored, I brought out a bottle of wine.

Janet sipped hers. "I feel alive out here."

I raised my glass. "I'll toast to that."

When it came time to turn in, we looked at each other and smiled. We hadn't talked about arrangements.

"Can we sleep together again?" she asked.

"Same ground rules as before?" I asked.

"Uh huh," she said.

"Works for me," I said.

So we crawled into bed. Janet snuggled her back into me and grabbed my arm so it came around her body, and my hand rested gently underneath her breast. Holding a guitar is sensual, the curves of the instrument remind me of a women's body. But falling asleep holding a woman is close to sublime, and it wasn't long before I drifted off.

◎　◎　◎

THE NEXT MORNING, after breakfast, we took the dinghy into shore, then walked the long way to the Turn Point Lighthouse. We didn't see orcas, but walking helped me blow off stress. I think it helped Janet too. When we got back, I turned on the VHF radio. The weather forecast called for a small craft warning with twenty- to twenty-five-knot winds from the northeast, which meant the sky would be crystal clear and the water choppy. I pulled out the CD with Atherton's data.

"You're sure someone will show up?" Janet asked.

I shook my head. "No."

"Damn. You are frustratingly and unreassuringly honest."

"What do we do after we lower the CD?" she asked.

"Wait." I said.

"Wait? That's it? That's your plan?"

"I figure it's something like fishing. Bait the line and see what bites. Different strategy to pull in a minnow than to pull in a shark."

"Frustratingly and unreassuringly honest—and yet confident. How do you pull all that off at the same time?"

I smiled. "Training," I said. "*Semper Paratus.*"

"*Semper Paratus?*"

"It's the Coast Guard motto: Always ready."

"As in, ready for whatever comes our way?"

"Let's hope so."

I stuck the CD into its sleeve and placed it in a waterproof box, which I put into the middle of a crab trap. At three in the afternoon we took off from Satellite Cove, navigating by GPS to the location Janet left on Collingsworth's voice-mail. The northeast wind created quite a chop, but I managed to lower the CD into one hundred ninety feet of water.

To kill time, we circumnavigated Stuart Island, especially since the other side of the island would give us protection from the northeast wind. We climbed up to the flybridge and Janet piloted the boat from there. A strong current ran against us as we rounded Turn Point, and I scanned for orcas.

Suddenly, what looked like a torpedo knifed through the water, disappearing under *Big Ben*'s hull. Then from the other side, another torpedo-like object came at us. Two black and white Dall's porpoises rode our bow wave for several minutes.

We threaded our way through a chain of reefs at the south end of Stuart and navigated twisting, turning Johns Pass back to the windward side of the island. I had hoped for the calm that often happens at sunset, but the breeze stiffened.

We took up a position about a half mile from the spot where the money was supposed to be left. I scanned the water with my night-vision binoculars. The crab trap with the money had not yet been dropped.

I flipped on *Big Ben's* radar and watched as a blank screen filled with the glowing green masses of Waldron Island on one side, Stuart Island on the other, and, straight ahead across Boundary Pass, Bedwell Harbor and the Canadian Gulf Islands. Other than a tanker moving at a brisk pace eastbound along the Pass, no other traffic plied the waters. I switched on the VHF radio. Janet made us both a cup of coffee.

Eight o'clock came and went, with only another tanker traveling westbound this time. By eight-thirty, I could feel my stomach beginning to tighten. I don't know if Janet sensed my unease, but she stepped behind me as I sat at the helm and massaged my shoulders until my muscles let go.

Then a blip appeared in the upper left corner of the radar screen, and my shoulder muscles tightened again. The small target left a trail of green across the screen, like a tiny comet hurtling through space. It came out of Bedwell Harbor, and I estimated it traveled at close to twenty knots. I tapped Janet on the shoulder, pointed to the radar screen, then handed her the binoculars.

"I think we're on," I said.

Through a side window, she scanned the darkness. "There," she said. "I see them. Are you ready?"

"*Semper Paratus,*" I said.

"There's one thing," Janet said. Her voice shook slightly. She talked while gazing through the glasses. "I want to help, but I don't want to die."

"I'll remember that," I said.

She chuckled nervously. "Frustratingly and—"

"Unreassuringly honest," I said.

Janet lowered the binoculars. "Uh huh."

She handed the binoculars back to me and she took over at the helm. The night-vision binoculars turned everything green but still allowed me to see the small fast boat lower a trap and a buoy into the water, then zoom over to the spot where I'd dropped the CD. I pointed forward and to the left.

"Head over toward the money," I said.

Janet spun the wheel and brought the engine revs up, while I watched phosphorescent green figures moving around the other boat, then leaning over its side to reel in the crab trap with Atherton's data.

"What's to prevent them from zooming over here after they have that CD, killing us, and then taking their money back?"

"If I'm right, they're about to discover that they only have half of what they came for."

"And if you're wrong?"

"Then, Houston, we've got a problem."

"Do you always joke?"

"When I'm nervous."

"That's good."

"What? That I joke?"

"No. That you admit you're nervous."

"Why?"

"It lets me know you're human, like me." Janet's laugh tapered off into a sigh. "But don't they need to be pretty sophisticated to figure out that we left them only half the data?"

"I'm counting on them having a chemist."

"A what?"

"I ran drug interdiction boats out of District Seven in Miami for two years. When a big cocaine deal goes down, the buyer usually bring a person law enforcement calls a 'chemist.' He shows up holding a test tube with a colored liquid. He extracts a sample of powder, inserts it into the tube, and shakes it. If the liquid turns colors, the deal goes down."

"And if it doesn't?"

"That's when the shooting starts."

"Frustratingly and unreassuringly honest," she said.

I reached above the instrument console and fiddled with the squelch knob on the VHF radio. Suddenly, static burst over the speakers, then a voice.

"Money Trap. Money Trap. This is CD One."

"Guess we're being hailed," I said.

I handed Janet the microphone.

"CD One, this is Money Trap. Switching to Six Eight."

"Six Eight, Roger."

Janet pressed a button on the VHF to switch channels.

"Money Trap, CD One. We pulled up only half of what we expected. Repeat, only half of what we expected is aboard."

"Copy, CD One. We'll be pulling our trap and counting crabs. When we have our count, we'll point you to another trap where you can get what you need."

"Negative, Money Trap. Negative. We are proceeding to your location now."

"Negative, CD One. Negative. We have yet to pull our trap."

No reply.

"CD One, do you copy?" Janet said.

Still no reply.

She hung up the microphone.

"Look." She pointed out the window toward a pair of red and green lights moving fast in our direction. "They're coming for us. What do I do now?"

"Stay calm. Point the boat directly at them so they won't see me out on deck."

"What are you going to do?" Janet's voice cracked.

"Hide upstairs under the flybridge covers."

"And leave me alone in the cabin with them?"

"Stay calm and follow whatever instructions they give you."

"I hope you've got a goddamn plan." She hissed.

I squeezed her shoulder. The boat bounced from side to side in the chop as I made my way, handhold to handhold, back out onto the rear deck and then up to the flybridge. I stretched across the bench in front of the upper helm, pulling a canvas cover over me like a blanket. A gust of wind swirled around the boat, sending a taut line somewhere above me vibrating with a shrill howl. The boat rolled and snapped back sharply in the rising seas. Then it shuddered as a large object thumped into the hull. An agitated voice called out.

"I'll secure the helm, you sweep and clean the boat. Get doc and his computer aboard."

Heavy footsteps moved along the decks. The cabin door squealed as it opened, then slammed close.

Janet yelled, "Get off my boat."

"Keep both hands on the wheel, lady," a voice said.

She shrieked. "Richard? Richard, what the hell are you doing with them? You bastard. You're their chemist. You traitor. You set up Thomas. You knew all along what had happened."

"He thought he was such an important man. That the world couldn't get along without him." Richard Collingsworth's voice was unmistakable. "Not only would he solve important scientific problems, but social and political problems as well."

"So you set him up to be murdered?"

"It wasn't supposed to—"

"Shut up and sit down," a man's voice said. "And you, lady, keep both hands on the wheel so I won't be tempted to use this gun."

Footsteps moved through the boat. Then the aft cabin door swung open and someone climbed up to the flybridge. A point of light swept over the canvas above me. And the footsteps came closer.

A circle of light steadied just above my head. Then when the end of the flashlight touched the canvas, I whipped both arms up, grasped the man's neck, and wrapped the canvas around him. I pulled him down and into the back of the flybridge bench. I rose up and crashed my elbow repeatedly into his back until his body slumped forward. Then I grabbed his head, slamming it twice into the seat. He sighed. I pushed his legs up, wrapped them in the canvas and dumped his body along the seat. That's when the cabin door opened and a gust of wind took it, slamming it into the side of the boat.

"Topside's clear?" the voice yelled.

The cabin lights flashed on. I tried to move to the opposite side of the flybridge, but the boat's pitching prevented me.

The man called out. "John?"

I heard him moving back along the side deck, saw his hand grip the railing. The tip of his pistol appeared first as he pulled himself up. And for a brief moment I looked into the eyes of the man with the SEAL insignia tattooed to his biceps.

He yelled. "What the hell?"

He took aim at me with his pistol. I started to dive on top of the man I'd just subdued, when the boat swerved sharply. Janet had lined us up broadside with a big wave, which shook the Grand Banks from one side to another violently, nearly submerging the handrails. I ran over to the man, now holding on with one hand, and kicked his gun from the other. It flew into the water.

The boat turned again, this time heading into the waves. Janet popped out of the cabin, running forward, then scrambling over the foredeck and around to the side deck on the other side. When I went to kick the man's other hand off the rails, he grabbed my ankle and yanked me down, pulling me toward him. I jammed my heel into his hand until he let go. But by the time I'd sprung to my feet, he'd also climbed onto the flybridge and stood before me.

I yelled to Janet. "Jump into their boat and take off."

Then I crouched, and the man in front of me dropped down, sweeping his foot at my legs. I backed off, but a wave took the boat, throwing both of us to opposite sides of the flybridge. I sprang up, trying to steady myself. I heard outboard engines fire up and saw Janet zooming away. The man sprang up too, and lunged at me. He caught hold of my leg and raised it up to throw me overboard. But another wave crashed into the boat, tossing me away from him.

Metal creaked as I tried to stand, and the Grand Bank's boom came flying out of the darkness at me. I ducked, but too late. The swinging metal arm caught me in the gut and hurled me over the side of the boat.

The cold water hit me like a fist, and I struggled to keep my head above water. My hands seemed to grow numb instantly, and I groped to find the tab to inflate my vest. I tugged once, but nothing happened. I could barely feel the tab in my hand. I yanked it again with all my strength and the vest ballooned around my head and neck.

The Grand Banks, lit like a miniature cruise ship, turned around and headed back toward me. Wind and current swept me out toward Boundary Pass. I tried to wiggle my toes, but I couldn't feel them. I patted my pockets, looking for something to signal Janet with, but I couldn't find or feel anything. The man at the helm of the Grand Banks began to circle, starting wide, then narrowing, like a shark honing in on its prey.

I looked around, but I didn't see the lights of the small boat Janet was in. I curled into a fetal position, trying to conserve what warmth I had left, trying also to keep my head above the water. The Grand Bank's circle grew tighter as it disappeared behind my back.

Suddenly, a brilliant shaft of light stabbed the darkness. Twisting my head felt like moving a mountain, and then what I saw sank my spirit. The man at the helm of the Grand Banks had found the vessel's searchlight, and he swept the water as he circled. He was now only two hundred yards away and closing fast. When the searchlight beam found me, the water exploded with a flash of green. The engine of the Grand Banks revved higher as it made a beeline toward me. I closed my eyes in the blinding light, opening them when the boat was not more than fifty yards away.

I tried to swim out of the boat's path, but I could barely move a muscle. Then something splashed in the water in front of me, and a voice yelled, "Grab the ring." I looked up and saw Janet.

The life-ring was only ten yards away, but the Grand Banks was almost upon me. I reached down deep and found a last reserve of strength, uncurled from my fetal position and fought with everything I had toward the life-ring. I hooked my arm through it. Janet gunned the engines, pulling me out of the way just as the Grand Banks swerved toward me.

Janet reeled me in before the Grand Banks could turn and make another pass. I lay in the cockpit of the aluminum boat, while she zoomed us into the darkness at twice the speed of the Grand Banks. And then she cut the engines, dragged me into the small cabin, and flipped on a light.

"Some plan," she said.

I smiled weakly. "Making it up as I go."

"I'm running with lights off. He won't find us. We're behind Sandy Point on Waldron Island now. That should give us leeward protection."

She removed my life-vest and started unbuttoning my shirt.

"How'd you know I fell overboard?"

"I didn't," she answered. "But when I saw the Grand Banks circling, I knew it was looking for something that'd gone overboard. I figured you might not look for him, but he sure as hell would look for you. So I ran without lights, staying just out of his way until he found you."

"Good plan," I said

"Someone had to have one. Now, the plan is to get you out of those wet clothes."

"We should go back after him." I tried to stand, but my legs wouldn't allow it.

Janet gently pushed me down on the bench. She patted the aluminum wall of the boat. "We do almost thirty knots. He does ten, max. He's not going anywhere that we can't get to quickly. And we need to make sure you don't go hypothermic. So lie down and let's get you out of those clothes."

Pulling off my undershirt proved frustrating for Janet, and I wasn't much help. So she slipped her hand beneath its collar and ripped it in two. I tried to undo the zipper of my pants but my fingers refused to function, so Janet undid it. She went to my feet, pulled off my shoes and socks, then tugged off my pants. She started to reach for the band of my boxers, but I grabbed her hand.

"C'mon, Commander. You know the hypothermia drill. Everything off."

She stripped off her clothes off, until she was down to her panties and bra. She unhooked each bra strap spun the bra around and undid the clasp. In the dim light, her breasts bounced softly against her chest. She pointed to my underwear.

"Everything," she said.

Then she reached overhead and flicked off the light. I heard her step out of her panties, felt her hand grab my soaking wet boxers and pull them off. She used her sweater to dry me.

"Move over," she said.

She lay down next to me on the small bench, draping her clothes around us and pulling her body into mine. Janet's body felt every bit as warm and comforting as a fire. Ten minutes later, I rolled over onto my other side and Janet buried her breasts and her body into my back, wrapping her arms around me. It wasn't long before my body responded to hers.

She whispered, "In aboriginal societies far north, a woman will let a returning hunter slip his cold hands and feet under her warm breasts, whether the man is her husband or not."

After another ten minutes, Janet stood up. "I'll turn on the cabin heater when we start the engines. I saw a stash of camouflage pants and jackets in the v-berth. They'll have to do."

She slipped back into her clothes. When I stood up and stretched, blood did indeed flow throughout my body.

"Thanks," I said.

"Anytime," she said. "Well...maybe next time in a warm, romantic setting."

She laughed softly, then handed me the clothes. I stepped into the camouflage gear while Janet fired up both engines. I joined her at the helm, switching the radar on.

"The Grand Banks was heading east," she said.

We sped away from the protection of Waldron Island, and when we hit open water the waves threw us from side to side.

"They won't make ten knots in this," I said.

"And we won't make thirty either," she said. She pushed us close to fifteen knots, and we slapped through the waves.

Twenty minutes later, I pointed to the radar screen. "There it is, heading across the Strait."

Janet nudged the engines higher and we skipped across the waves, the entire boat sometimes taking flight, then landing with a jolt. We made steady progress on the Grand Banks, to a point that radar showed us only a mile away, near Patos Island. Suddenly another fleck of light appeared on the radar screen, streaking across from Canada toward us.

"Slow down and pull in close to the shore of Patos," I said.

"Why? We've almost caught up with him."

I touched Janet's arm. "There's another boat heading over from Canada toward us. Maybe he called for help. We won't show up on radar if we're close to shore, and with this much chop, anyone who did see us would think it was a radar ghost."

With waves crashing on the shore of Patos, Janet ventured just outside the breakers, though we got the swell and the chop from the backwash. While she kept us off the rocks, I watched the radar screen. The green target from Canada merged with the

Grand Bank's target. Then five minutes later, that green target separated and streaked across the screen, back from where it had come.

"He's going back to Canada, and the Grand Banks is still moving, headed toward...I eyed the top of the screen. Damn." I slammed my fist down on the console.

Janet jumped. "What?"

"I'm willing to bet the men are off the Grand Banks and it's on autopilot, headed toward Cherry Point with a load of explosives aboard."

"You're kidding."

"Wanna bet?"

"No," Janet said. "Got a plan?"

"Yes."

alfway across the Strait of Georgia, the Grand Banks moved toward Cherry Point at about six knots. Janet had us up to fifteen as we careened through steep, choppy seas. I estimated we'd reach the Grand Banks in about twenty minutes at this speed, and that meant we'd be too late. So I tapped Janet on the shoulder and hiked my thumb. She brought us up to twenty-two knots, and we bucked into seas coming at us from our forward port quarter. If we kept this up, we'd reach the GB just in time.

Ten minutes later, the VHF radio speaker hissed. "Small boats crossing the Strait of Georgia, heading toward Cherry Point. Small boats crossing the Strait of Georgia, heading toward Cherry Point. This is the United States Coast Guard patrol vessel *Twenty-Three.*"

I plucked the microphone from its holder. "Twenty-Three, this is one of the small boats headed across the Strait of Georgia for Cherry Point."

"You are requested to break off your course immediately. I repeat, break off your course immediately. The Coast Guard is under standing orders to fire upon any vessel traveling at high-speed within a half-mile radius of Cherry Point."

I scanned the radar screen and pointed. "There. The CG's all the way down Hale Passage. They'll never get here in time."

"Twenty-Three, this is Coast Guard Commander Charles Noble, retired, in pursuit of a Grand Banks 36 bearing down on Cherry Point under autopilot, with possible explosives aboard."

Another voice broke in. "Commander Noble, this is Group Seattle. Sir, requesting that you break off pursuit. Our active duty unit will handle this."

"Group Seattle, Noble. Your active duty unit will not arrive on scene in time. Proceeding with interception."

"Negative. Negative. Break off pursuit. A Maritime Safety and Security Team has been scrambled from Seattle, and an Air Marine team from Blaine is en route."

"Group Seattle, I don't think you copied me. They will not arrive in time. I'm the closest to that GB and I'm going in after it."

"Commander Noble, Twenty-Three requesting once again, Sir, that you break off pursuit and follow Group Seattle's orders."

"Negative, Twenty-Three. By the time any of you get here, that GB will be at the refinery's docks. And it looks like a tanker is in there."

A woman's voice came on next. "Break. This is United States Coast Guard patrol boat *Eighteen*. Lieutenant Katherine Sullivan in command. That's affirmative, Commander Noble. The tanker *Susitna* is in the process of refueling. We'd appreciate any help you can give us. We estimate thirty minutes until we're on scene."

Channel Sixteen went ballistic. "All coast guard vessels in the vicinity of Cherry Point, switch and answer Security One. Repeat, switch and answer Security One."

"What's that?" Janet pointed to the VHF.

"A special coast guard frequency. Katherine's about to get her ass chewed out for that transmission."

A moment later, Katherine was back on the air. "Commander Noble, Eighteen here. Lieutenant Sullivan still in command."

Janet struck the air with her fist. "You go, girl."

"Coast Guard Eighteen. Coast Guard Eighteen. This is United States Coast Guard Group Seattle. Ma'am, you are ordered to switch to Security One. Repeat, ordered to switch and answer on Security One."

"Damn. She's not going to play ball with Seattle," I said. "She's taking a huge risk."

Janet had us almost upon the Grand Banks.

"Commander Noble, Sullivan, here. Sir, when we intercepted the last boat, we cut the hydraulic lines to the rudder, then steered it with our high-speed patrol boat."

"Roger that, Lieutenant. I don't have an ETA until impact, but I suspect I won't have time for that. Was the autopilot wired to the explosives?"

"Don't know, sir. We never got a report on the first boat."

"Coast Guard Eighteen. This is Twenty-Three on Channel Sixteen. Chief Hanrahan in command. Ma'am, Group Seattle now requests that you break off all radio contact and return to the barn."

"Hanrahan, tell Group Seattle that Eighteen is proceeding to Cherry Point, with an ETA of…twenty-one minutes."

"Damn. She's got balls," Janet said.

"How close can you get me to that boat?" I asked.

"As close as I got to you with my clothes off."

"You're on. I'm going out on deck."

"Commander," Janet mimicked Kate's voice. Then her tone dropped low. "Please be careful."

I turned to Janet. "When I get aboard, I want you to back off. Understand?"

"What if you need a push?"

"I'll radio you if I do."

I jammed my arms into a life-vest and walked along the narrow side deck, holding onto a rail on the roof of the boat, while we bucked in the seas. The bright orange lights of the refinery dominated the view like a stadium lit for a game. Creaks and groans emanated from the dock as the lumbering steel giant waiting for oil tugged on her mooring lines in the wind.

On the first pass at the Grand Banks, Janet brought us in too close. Our speed and the force of the wind threw us into *Big Ben's* hull. I gripped the handrails tightly as we bounced away. Then Janet sped ahead of the Grand Banks and positioned us so we drifted with the wind into its path. The bow of the Grand Banks grazed us, and when the stern came around, I lunged for a handrail, catching a wall of water in my face but holding on long enough for my feet to find the swim platform. I gave Janet a thumbs-up and hopped over the railing, running along the side deck and throwing open the cabin door.

Richard Collingsworth lay on the floor, a pool of blood around his head. I stooped down to check his pulse, which was thready but still there. It looked like he'd been clobbered pretty hard on the back of his head.

I hit the lights, sucking in a breath at the sight of a mound of putty-like material on the counter above the instrument panel. Red and black wires ran from it to the back of a handheld GPS. I looked ahead. The refinery was coming on fast. I picked up the VHF.

"Eighteen, this is Noble, now aboard the *Big Ben*. Lieutenant, I have one person with a serious injury, and plastic explosives wired to a GPS. Any chance of patching me through to the MSST team?"

"Negative, Sir, no one's responding to my calls."

I quickly checked around the boat—in the stove, behind doors, under cushions, in lockers—but I didn't see any other mounds of plastic or any wires that looked out of place. I also popped a hatch and checked the guts of the autopilot. Nothing there.

The radio cackled with Janet's voice. "Charlie, whatever you're going to do, you need to do it soon."

I didn't bother to respond. The depth sounder read twenty-five feet and dropping fast. Ahead I could see the huge pylons of the dock, and the large white numerals along the hull of the tanker marking how far down in the water she sat. My finger hovered over the "Off" button on the autopilot control unit.

I closed my eyes and punched it. And when I opened my eyes, I smiled. The depth sounder was now at five feet, and I was well past the tanker, in close to shore. I spun the wheel hard right, taking a wake over the side of the boat and heading back out to open water.

I got on the VHF radio. "This is Noble still in command of *Big Ben*."

"Way to go, Sir," Kate said.

"Standing by to give you a lift home," Janet said

Ten minutes later the sea off Cherry Point came alive, as though a waterborne laser show had begun. Both patrol boats screamed up to me, blue lights beating the night. A rescue helicopter circled overhead, shining a monstrous searchlight down on the scene.

The radio duel continued.

"Commander Noble, Twenty-Three, Chief Hanrahan. Sir, you are being placed under arrest for violating a restricted security zone and disobeying direct orders from the United States Coast Guard."

"Chief, Lieutenant Sullivan. Stand down. Commander Noble will be boarding our patrol boat."

I looked out the window, listening to the chatter on the VHF. Three men stood on the deck of the *Twenty-Three,* with automatic rifles pointed at the *Eighteen*.

"Eighteen, this is Twenty-Three. Ma'am. I'm sorry, but my orders are to disarm you and your crew and to assume command of both patrol boats. I need for you all to step out of the cabin with your hands raised."

Suddenly, one of the men on the *Twenty-Three* fired a shot above the *Eighteen.*

"Ma'am. I will not ask you again to disarm."

"Break. Chief Hanrahan." The new voice surprised me. "This is Captain George Townsend of MIFCPAC being patched through by Group Seattle. Order your men to stand down now and return to the cabin of their boat."

"Twenty-Three." The operator sounded exhausted and exasperated. "This is United States Coast Guard Group Seattle, requesting that you now relinquish on-scene control to Lieutenant Sullivan."

"Roger that." Frustration soaked Hanrahan's voice. "Ma'am, what are your orders?"

"Assist us in transporting Commander Noble to the Eighteen."

Twenty-Three threw me a line and rafted to the Grand Banks, then *Eighteen* rafted to them. I jumped down from *Big Ben,* walking across the back deck of the first patrol boat to reach Kate Sullivan's. She extended a hand and helped me aboard. Afterward, she dropped her hand and saluted me.

"Well done, Sir."

I n a city where most panoramic views occur outdoors, I sat at a window table inside Nimbus, a restaurant in the penthouse of the Bellingham Towers with a panoramic view of the bay, the islands, and the mountains. I nursed a cold glass of Guinness while waiting for Vallerie McKee. I took in the sights out the window and mulled over the events of the last few days.

After I got done with the Coast Guard on the water, Janet and I drove the aluminum boat we took from the Black Wave guys back to Station Bellingham. But we stopped first at Sucia for Bucky and Matthew. They'd had such a good time exploring the island with Jerry and Wanda's girls that they decided to stay for a while. Maybe I'd take the *Noble Lady* over in a few days to fetch them.

The Canadian Coast Guard picked up the Black Wave guys from Port Browning. Richard Collingsworth was medevacked to a Seattle hospital in critical condition, but apparently he was going to pull through. I'd spent most of the following morning at Station Bellingham, filing a report, being debriefed by the district intelligence officer.

I saw Ben Conrad when he stopped by the coast guard station to take possession of *Big Ben,* glad to have it back in one piece. He told me the police chief chewed out the district's congresswoman about DHS snatching a body from under his jurisdiction. Apparently the congresswoman then chewed out someone in DHS, who called the chief to apologize and to tell him that the gunman who shot at Janet and me was a former Army Special Forces sergeant.

Conrad didn't know where ex-Special Forces types looked for work, so I clued him in to Black Wave. It still left unanswered the question of who killed the gunman before he killed me. But I know my obsession with unanswered questions. So I decided just to let this one go. I raised a glass to the picture window. Sharon would be proud of me.

I sensed when Vallerie walked in. Perhaps it was because heads rose from dinner plates and turned in her direction. She wore a vibrant, low-cut, lavender dress. An amber pendant set in silver rested on her bare chest. Matching earrings dangled from her ears. She'd rolled her hair up. Elegant. That described Vallerie. She strolled into Nimbus like a model walking a runaway. I stood up to greet her. She hugged me and then we sat, the subtle sweetness of her perfume lingering in the air. She ordered a Kir Royale.

"It's my celebration drink," she said.

"And the occasion is...?"

"Friendship. And the publication of a great investigative series that's about to be picked up by the international press."

"It sounds like you scored your first time up."

She smiled. "I did, thanks to you. You know, I interviewed George Townsend, your former CO, late this afternoon for a follow-up story that will run tomorrow."

"You did? What did George have to say?"

"That you were the best intelligence officer he ever had under his command. That Ritchie railroaded your original threat assessment report on Puget Sound and the Inside Passage."

"Too bad he didn't have the guts to stand up to Ritchie before."

"But Ritchie's out of the picture now," Vallerie said.

"I doubt he'll be tied to Black Wave, other than sitting on the board. He'll probably get a promotion."

Vallerie frowned. "A promotion?"

"To Washington, or maybe he'll be asked to retire early."

"Townsend said that he called you earlier today and offered you reinstatement in the Coast Guard at your previous rank. It sounded like he really wanted you back. But he said you turned him down, and settled for an honorable discharge instead."

I sipped my Guinness and looked to the sun, now sinking behind the islands. "The world's changed," I said. "And the Coast Guard had to change too. It's not the same service that I joined twenty years ago. It's better that I left now, rather than spend my time pushing up against men like Vin Ritchie. Besides, I know there are of a lot of fine young men and women like Katherine Sullivan in coast guard uniforms."

"Townsend also told me that when he heard you were involved in this investigation he 'chapped you.'"

I stared at Vallerie, then I raised my glass to the open window again and stared out. "In that case, George, I owe you one."

"'Chapped?' What's that mean?" Vallerie asked. "He wouldn't tell me, but he said you'd know."

I sat my glass down and pointed at Vallerie. "Only if this is off the record and doesn't appear in any of your stories."

She put down her glass and held up her hands. "Off the record, I promise. Besides, I don't have a recorder on me. You can search me if you want." She smiled mischievously.

"Townsend has his own vocabulary. He loves to give words new cryptic meanings. 'Chapped' means that at times in these last few days, I've had a chaperone I didn't know about, courtesy of Coast Guard Intelligence."

"'Chapped,'" Vallerie said, nodding. "Of course. So that's who killed the gunman on the trail before he could kill you?"

I shrugged my shoulders. "I don't know. One thing about a chaperone is that you never ask and you're never told what they had to do for you."

"Like a guardian angel," Vallerie said. "Boy, I can think of times in my life when I wish I'd had one." She sighed, then she took a sip of Kir Royale. "I'm leaving the *Herald*," she said with subdued excitement.

"Soon?"

"In two weeks. I had feelers out even before I accepted the job here. Today, a television station in Portland offered me an on-air job. I gave my notice before I came over to meet you."

"It's what you wanted," I said.

She smiled weakly. "It is, and this investigative piece on Cherry Point clinched my new job. But I also enjoyed working with you, however briefly, and I looked forward to getting to know you better. Portland's not that far away. Any chance that we might see each other on occasion?"

I smiled. "I never say never."

"Thanks," Vallerie said.

I raised my glass of Guinness. "A toast to each of us," I said. "May we find new horizons in our lives, and relish the adventures they bring."

We clinked glasses.

"And the pipeline?" I asked.

"This afternoon a judge issued a stay on pipeline construction, pending a review of Thomas Atherton's environmental impact statement. DiAmbrosio and some other high-ranking PDI officials were arrested and charged with a host of crimes, including conspiracy to commit murder. Collingsworth was charged in the conspiracy as well. The full story will run in tomorrow's paper."

"With your byline." I said.

She grinned. "But of course."

I took another sip of Guinness. "I don't think of myself as an environmentalist," I said. "I'm a boater first. I love the sea, and I love the Inside Passage. But the thought of someday cruising over dead waters, unable to fish for salmon or see a pod of orcas, frightens me. I'm glad that Atherton's data is being taken seriously. And if that data says the pipeline shouldn't be built because of the Cherry Point herring, well then it shouldn't, and we should all thank those little fish for rescuing us from making a big mistake."

Over dinner, Vallerie talked about how exciting it was to be asked to report the news on camera. I talked about my plans to circumnavigate the globe. After dinner, I saw her to her car. Before she got behind the wheel, she kissed me on the cheek.

"I'm alone in a huge house overlooking the bay," she said.

"It must be lovely on a night like tonight," I said.

"It is," she said.

She slipped a card with her cell phone number into my pocket and drove off. It was only eight-thirty, so I walked back to the marina. Glimmering stars graced the night sky, and a quarter moon rose over Mount Baker. I pulled out my cell phone as I walked, and checked messages. Janet had left one. She said she'd found the perfect piece of artwork for my boat. She also said that helping apprehend the men involved in her ex-husband's death lessened her grief. She looked forward to getting on with her life, and asked if I wanted to go out with her later tonight to hear some jazz at a local club.

When I got to the *Noble Lady,* I found a long, wrapped package and a card lying on the rear deck cushions. I stepped into the galley, set the package on the table, and slowly peeled back the scotch tape. Then I unfolded the wrapping paper and opened the box. A huge smile spread over my face as I pulled out a bottle of Red Mountain Reserve 2000. The card read simply, *Please don't drink this alone. Kate.* That made me smile even more. At the bottom of the card, she'd printed her number.

I set the wine bottle down and got my guitar out, propped some music on a stand. Then I began the Bach Prelude. When I got to the measure that had given me so much trouble, my fingers glided through it, and on through the remainder of the piece. But I only managed ten minutes of playing before putting the guitar aside and picking up my cell phone to make a call.

And that night I did not drink the wine alone.

If you enjoyed

Red Herring

By Clyde W. Ford

you won't want to miss Charlie Noble in . . .

Precious Cargo

Coming soon from Mystic Voyager Books

Register online at:

www.mysticvoyagerbooks.com

for advance notification of the availability of this book.

S*arabande* swayed gently at anchor in Eagle Harbor, while Marvin Baynes clutched his coffee cup, savoring daybreak from the pilothouse bench. A pale blue sky backlit the crisp, white dome of Mount Baker. Muted cries of seagulls broke the early morning quiet. The coffee's aroma seduced Marvin, relaxed him, the warmth of the cup a buffer against the springtime chill in the air. He smiled and sank into the leather seat. Today was the first day of a season of early mornings at anchor; the first day of the fortieth year that he and Angela had embarked on a cruise up the Inside Passage to Alaska.

Forty years. One wife. Five boats. He sipped coffee, raising his cup forward, toward the berth where Angela slept. Then he sipped some more, raising his cup this time in honor of the boats, which marked the passage of their lives together. *Prelude,* the twenty-six-foot wooden sailboat he took Angela on for their first date; *Allemande,* a thirty-foot ketch they got the first summer of their marriage; *Minuet,* the fast thirty-three-foot fin-keel sailboat they raced for years; *Cantata,* the steel sailboat they bought, thinking they'd make a circumnavigation. Marvin winced, clutching the coffee cup even tighter, recalling the years spent on *Cantata* with their daughter. After Amy's death, he and Angela found it difficult to sail *Cantata,* so they purchased *Sarabande,* their last boat, an older motorsailer that chugged along at seven knots, with an inside helm where they could escape harsh Northwest weather; a perfect boat for two retired concert musicians, two aging sailors.

"Time to weigh anchor?" Angela's voice rose from below.

"Almost," Marvin said.

The boat creaked and rocked as Angela ascended the spiral pilothouse steps. The khaki pants and dark gray woolen sweater she wore matched Marvin's. Angela carried her floppy, wide-brimmed hat in one hand. Marvin reached for Angela's other hand, and gently pulled her down to sit with him.

They held hands in silence. Through thinning skin, his pulse throbbed against hers. He tapped his feet to the rhythm of waves lapping softly against the hull. From the tree-lined shore, a raven's clucking recalled the striking of a wooden block. And the raucous cries of seagulls mimicked blaring trumpets.

Marvin let go of Angela's hand and stepped behind *Sarabande's* wheel. Then, like a conductor waving a baton to cue an orchestra, he turned the key. A high-pitched buzzer sang out, then *Sarabande's* diesel sprang to life with a pulsing bass tone, and throbbing tenor overtones.

Angela stuffed her hat down onto her head. She slid the pilothouse door back, then stepped out onto the deck, walking slowly toward the bow. When she got there, she turned back, and Marvin flashed her a thumbs-up. Then she stepped on the large, black rubber footswitch. The anchor winch motor whined. The main engine groaned under the load. Metal clinked and scraped against metal as the winch pulled the anchor chain in. *Sarabande* glided forward as the chain rose. Then with a clunk, the chain stopped moving. The winch motor whined louder. Marvin stuck his head out of the pilothouse window. Angela cupped her hands and called to him.

"Guess we set the anchor really well."

"It's a mud bottom," Marvin said. "I'll drive over the anchor and see if I can break it loose."

He eased the gearshift and the throttle forward. *Sarabande* moved ahead. "Try it now," Marvin called out.

Angela stepped on the footswitch, and the chain jerked up a few feet before stopping again. The chain pulled tight, and the boat began to swing around in a circle.

"Maybe we've snagged an old logging cable," she said.

"Damn," Marvin said. "Some way to start our cruise. Look, I'll try rocking the boat back and forth."

He threw the gearshift forward, powered the boat ahead until the anchor chain tautened, then reversed gears and moved backward. Between each forward and reverse movement, Marvin waved to Angela and she tried the winch, but it only moved the chain slightly. Angela shook her head.

"Stop," Marvin said. "We'll burn out the winch motor this way."

He sighed, then let the boat idle in neutral. He slid back the pilothouse door and stepped out, grabbing a red and white crab pot buoy.

"We'll have to unhook the chain from the boat and attach a buoy to it so we can retrieve it later. We'll throw the chain overboard. Then we'll go back to port and hire a diver to come out and see what we've snagged."

"That's too bad," Angela said. "It means we won't get going to Alaska for several days."

"We'll lose three hundred feet of chain and an anchor if we don't come back for it," Marvin said. "Then we'll have to buy a new anchor and new chain."

"Okay," Angela said. "Give me the buoy. I'll tie it on, while you unhook the chain."

Marvin walked back toward the pilothouse. He'd just reached the door, when he heard the winch motor whir and Angela cry out. When he turned back, he saw her reeling in anchor chain.

"The motor's working," Angela said. "A little." She held her thumb to her index finger. "It pulls in about a foot of chain and then stops. It might take time, but let's see if I can pull the anchor up this way before you unhook it."

Marvin nodded. "Maybe we broke free. I'll go back inside and stand by the controls."

The engine rumbled beneath Marvin as he watched Angela step on the switch, then wait. Step, then wait. The chain moved slowly, link after link winding up and over the bow roller, before dropping into the anchor well.

Angela moved slowly too, bent over the railing, directing spray from a nozzle to wash down the muddy chain. A twinge of pain stabbed Marvin each time he saw her stiffen and rub her hip. Perhaps the problem wasn't the anchor but the winch motor, old and losing strength like the two of them.

Suddenly, Angela screamed. She staggered backwards from the bow, then crumpled to the deck. Marvin rushed from the pilothouse. "Not now," he whispered, shaking his head. "No, please. Not now. One more trip north together. Please, just one more trip."

Marvin knelt beside Angela, picked up her hand. She breathed in short, sharp puffs, the steam released into the cold morning air reminding him of orcas breathing. A tortured look enveloped her face. Her eyes registered fear. She opened her mouth but no words came at first. Her arm flopped out, finger pointed toward the bow.

"There," she said, her voice hoarse, raspy. "Marvin, it's Amy...she's there."

Marvin knew he needed to get Angela medical attention. He also needed to finishing pulling in the anchor so they didn't drift into the rocks. He walked to the bow, looking over and down at the muddy anchor emerging from the dark green waters. A clump of seaweed snaked around the shank. He gasped. Beneath the seaweed, the sharp point of the anchor fluke stuck into the pallid flesh of a young woman's lifeless body.

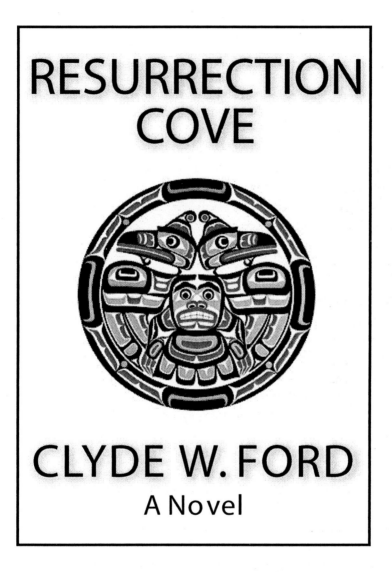

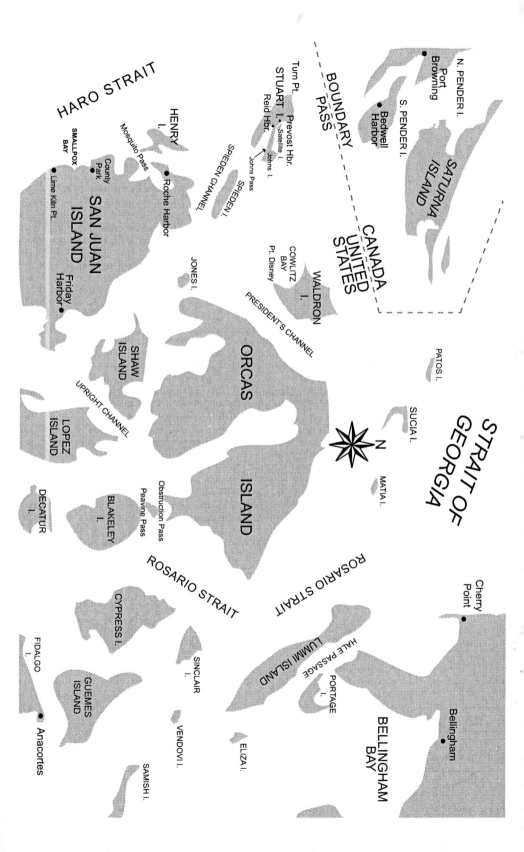

Printed in the United States
47609LVS00006B/71